CINDY DORMINY

In a Pickle

Red Adept Publishing
Unlocking New Worlds

In a Pickle
Red Adept Publishing, LLC
104 Bugenfield Court
Garner, NC 27529
http://RedAdeptPublishing.com/

Cover Art by Streetlight Graphics

For Daisy Mae

CHAPTER ONE

Regina

My back muscles clench in pain from having moved Mr. Douglas up in the bed all by myself. I know better than to do that, but no one else was around to help me, and he seriously needed to be turned. So the choice was either to let him get a decubitus ulcer on his booty or pull a muscle. I lean over the nurses' station to stretch out my back in hopes that I can make it through my shift without being hunched over like an old lady. If Mel were on duty, she wouldn't have let the staffing get so low. But our new doc, Dr. Gilbert from Tifton, runs a tight and efficient shift.

Like an angel from heaven, Mitch saunters in and grins. "Hello, Nurse Purple Locks. Need a big strong man to help you out?" His EMT tool belt swishes with every step.

"Yes, but I guess I'll have to settle for you."

He clutches his chest with his hands. "Ouch."

Mitch and I go way back, so he knows I'm only kidding. His friendship has never wavered, not even when his brother left me.

I glance around to make sure Doc Gilbert isn't nearby to hear our conversation. "Thanks for coming in. I thought I was going to have to duplicate myself to keep up."

"No problem. I don't mind helping out."

I keep hoping the hospital will hire him on in the ER, but until he passes the paramedic exam, he'll be riding in the rescue box. He's a great help, but everyone here knows he has ulterior motives for lurking around the ER.

He scans the room. "Is Doc Mel working today?"

Case in point.

"Sorry to disappoint, but she's off."

His hopeful face deflates. I wish he and Mel would put us all out of our misery and get together, but I don't think it's ever going to happen.

Rolling my shoulders in the hope of getting the kinks out, I ask, "You didn't bring in another Googlechondria patient, did you? The last one was certain she had the Zika virus."

Mitch chuckles as he hands me the paperwork. "I can't promise I didn't, but at least no incontinence this time."

I stretch my arms overhead. "Thank goodness for small favors."

After he glances over his shoulder, he says in a hushed tone, "Word on the street is you're still with that Ken doll."

If I've heard it once, I've heard it a thousand times how he resembles Barbie's boyfriend. The comments are annoying, and it's not his fault he's perfect in every way—perfect body, perfect face, perfect career. It would be nice if his name weren't really Ken. That only makes matters worse.

I tighten my ponytail and jut my chin high. "I am still seeing him, and we're doing fabulous, thank you very much." If by "fabulous" I mean Ken pencils me into his busy schedule, then we're überfab.

He snorts.

"In fact, he's coming into town this weekend." *Take that, Mr. Perpetual Bachelor.*

Mitch leans against the nurses' station as he reviews a patient chart. "Don't you think you're moving kind of fast with this guy?"

I tilt my head to the side. "Should I really be taking dating advice from you?"

He rolls his eyes. "Not funny. I'm trying. Besides... are you sure you're completely over—"

"Absolutely," I say with my chin jutted as high as it can go. "That ship has sailed. Clint took the oars and shoved the boat far out into the ocean. Can't you be happy for me? I know Clint's your brother, but I'm not the one who abandoned every single person in this town. Remember?"

His shoulders sag as he hands me back the patient chart. "Okay. I just want to make sure you're happy."

"I'm super happy." My voice screeches an octave higher than necessary. "Except for my back. It's killing me."

Mitch pats my shoulder and points to a chair. "You rest your feet and back. Steve and I will take care of the patient's intake paperwork. Okay?"

"Thanks."

Mitch waves over his ambulance partner, and they saunter to bay number four. Dr. Gilbert may have my hide for delegating intake paperwork to EMTs, but if it were a real emergency, that would be different.

I close my eyes and take a deep breath, when someone clears their throat. I whimper as I open my eyes to see Mel standing there.

"Howdy, girl. Need some help?"

"Hallelujah!"

Mel flips her long braid over her shoulder. "I heard you were drowning, so it was the least I could do."

I give Mel a big hug. Ever since Andie moved to town, Mel has really softened toward me, and we've become really good friends as well as coworkers. She never plays the doctor card, and she appreciates every staff member at the hospital.

"You're a lifesaver."

Mel giggles but stiffens when Mitch enters the nurses' station.

His smile broadens when he lays eyes on her. "Hey, Doc."

"Hi." Mel buries her head in a chart as Mitch glances over my shoulder and nods.

"I think you have a visitor."

I swing around to see my awesome and extremely amazing boyfriend, Ken. He wears his standard-issue Armani suit with a steel-gray tie that matches his eyes while carrying a bouquet of balloons and a dozen red roses. *Swoon.*

"Surprise."

I bounce into his arms. "Oh my gosh. I didn't think you would be here yet."

He squeezes me around the waist as he spins us in a circle.

"I wanted to surprise you." He plants me back on my feet and hands me the roses then straightens his tie as the balloons float up to the ceiling. "Regina, as you know, we've been together for a while now."

If two months of hooking up every few weekends constitutes a while, then yes, we have.

"And I want to take it to the next level."

Oh no. I slide the purple streak of hair behind my ear. I don't know if I'm ready for the "next level." That might mean more than the occasional meetup to have fun.

He pulls out a black velvet box, and my heart plummets into my stomach. Right before his knee hits the floor that probably has a nasty strain of MRSA on it, he cringes and stands upright again. I guess hospital funk on his pant leg wouldn't be a good thing.

"Gin Gin, will you marry me?"

"Aww," Mel says from behind me.

My jaw drops as I stand there like a bumbling fool, not answering him. *What is wrong with me?* He's perfect. The answer should be a no-brainer. While I regain the ability to breathe, I dare a glance at Mitch. If I didn't know better, I would think his head did a slow, subtle shake, as if to tell me not to accept. If he can give me one reason to say no, then I can give him fifty million in stock options why I should say yes.

I snap my attention back to Ken.

His eyes grow wide, waiting for my response.

"Of course, I'll..." I swallow hard and finish my sentence. "Marry you."

He pulls me toward him and gives me a deep kiss in front of Mel and Mitch. Mel claps and bounces, but Mitch crosses his arms over his chest and lets out a caveman grunt.

Ken slides a huge diamond ring on my hand, and the stone is so big I'll have to exercise my arm in order to hold up my hand.

"It's beautiful."

Ken clears his throat. "It's a Verragio Couture with white and rose gold, and it's four carats." He shrugs as if it's no big deal, which it probably isn't.

"Four carats?" Mitch asks, taking my hand to check it out. "Jeez Louise. I bet that cost more than I make in a year."

Ken beams. "Like my father always says, if you've got it, flaunt it."

Mitch snorts, and Mel swats him on the back. "Oh, hush. Lands, it's beautiful."

"Thanks," Ken says, rocking back on his heels. "My father picked it out."

Daddy issues?

Mitch chuckles, and Mel nudges him in the ribs.

He clears his throat. "I'm sure Regina's father will be thrilled. When do you expect to tell the reverend?"

Ken's eyes dart to me. "Uh... your father is a preacher?"

Mitch snickers, and I give him the death stare. "Yes, honey. I told you that. At least, I think I did."

Did I? I usually keep my father's occupation a secret until I feel the need to whip it out. It has a tendency to send guys running.

Mel takes another gander at my ring. "This is, wow, yeah." She clears her throat before she adds, "I'm sure your father is going to love this." The sarcastic way she drags "love" out speaks volumes.

My spine stiffens, and I take a deep breath. "He will love you, Ken. And you'll love him."

I give Ken a kiss while I check out my ring again. It's everything I've ever wanted. Ken won't leave me hanging, like another certain person did, but Dad will flip out when he finds out I got engaged after dating someone for only two months. Plus, the fact that he hasn't met Ken yet isn't going to be a gold star in my favor. He's complained for years that I should get over Clint, so here I am, finally getting over him. I've been over him for a long time, and now, I have Ken. Things are finally looking up for me. I hope and pray my father doesn't ask me if I love Ken, because the last thing I want to do is to lie to my father again.

CHAPTER TWO

Clint

Another day, another shiner. I will never learn. Last night's fight was a doozy. I'm not sure why I let Leo Fernandez tick me off so much I had to sling him across the bar, but I did, and now I'm waking up in the pokey... again. I would never sleep with his girlfriend, or anyone else's girlfriend, ever. Besides, she's totally not my type. I walked away from my type a long time ago.

The door clanks shut, and I jerk my attention to see Phillip, my agent. His scowl says it all. I groan as I sit up, my head pulsating with pain. Even without a mirror, I'm pretty sure my right eye is three shades of purple. It's going to be awesome on the cover of *Baseball Weekly*, and no matter how well I play next season, I'm going to be the number-one hothead.

Phillip's got his angry face on as he paces in front of me. "You did it again."

"Yep." No use denying it. I am what I am.

He stops and stares down at me. "I should leave you here for a month so you can see how it's going to be if you don't get your act together."

I stand, stretching my stiff back. "Relax. It's not that bad." Even I don't believe my words.

"You are something else. This is the fourth time you've pulled this stunt this season. Philly, Washington, Los Angeles, and now in Atlanta. The fans are not going to like this, and Parkerson is livid. Your contract is up for renewal, and you are a liability."

My heart sinks into my ulcer-filled stomach. I'm a liability. Somehow, deep down, I guess I knew that, but still, I always thought I was a typical pro baller. I clear my throat. "What's that supposed to mean?"

He crosses his arms over his chest. "It means you are ending this season on a low note, both on and off the field."

I sneer at him. "It's not my fault Kruger can't catch my throws to first base."

Phillip chuckles. "It's never your fault. It's also not your fault you're batting two hundred and your field percentage is barely point nine."

"Now, you know that's only part of the story."

"It's enough. You're a hothead, and if you don't get your head in the game, you're going to be shipped back to that Podunk town you're from. What's the name? Smallville?"

Under my breath, I mutter, "Smithville."

"Same thing. Come on. I'm taking you home so you can get cleaned up. Time to grovel."

I shake my head. "I don't grovel. I've worked hard to go from the minors to the majors within one year. I earned my position."

"It's more than that, and you know it. Parkerson has been battling bad press for a while, and he's made it a point to put together a franchise built on family values. It's a sport where fathers take their sons to see their favorite player. You are supposed to be a role model, not the poster boy for how not to be."

He's never going to believe I can change, and next year, I will be better off and on the field. He only sees things as percentages and ratios. I take a deep breath and say, "Next year will be better. I promise."

Phillip swings around so fast I bump into him. He stares up at me. "There may not be a next year. I hope you're good at changing oil or flipping burgers, because that's where you're headed."

My chest clenches as bile rises in my throat. I can't do that. I screamed out of Smithville for a reason, and that was to get as far away from nowhere as possible. My parents made sure we kids had the lousiest reputations available. Mitch and Silas may have had the guts to stick around with all the rumors, but I took my chances and got out of Dodge as soon as there was an opening, leaving everyone in my dust. There's no going back there. Besides, Regina would have me burned at the stake before sunset of the first day and for good reason.

"Okay, Philly. What do you suggest?"

He scrubs his face and stares at the ceiling. "Don't call me that. I took a big chance when I signed as your agent. I have a lot riding on this too. You're going to get cleaned up, and we're going to Parkerson's house for lunch. You better have something nice to wear."

I've never been summoned to the owner's house before. If the rumors are true, it's the kiss of death.

"If I don't, I'll find something."

"Good. Because if he isn't in a good mood, you can kiss your professional baseball career goodbye. Do you understand me?"

Knowing better, I salute him anyway.

"You're pushing it. By the way, I called your brother."

Son of a... "Why?"

"Because he's family, and I had an obligation to let someone know you got arrested again. He said for you to call him when you get a chance."

"Great." I couldn't muster excitement if I wanted to. "By the way, which brother?"

"I don't know. I think the one without kids. It was kind of quiet on the phone, so I can only assume."

He must mean Mitch. I might get a slightly less severe tongue-lashing from him than from Silas, Mr. Family Man. But one never knows. Mitch may be as settled as Silas now.

"I'll call him when I get home."

"Maybe he can knock some sense into that thick skull of yours."

I sling an arm around Phillip as we walk out of the cell. "Calm down. You're going to burst a blood vessel. It always sounds worse than it is. I have it all under control."

Not really, but I have to make him think so. He's the only one left in my corner. If I lose him, I'm done.

He pushes my arm off his shoulder and grunts. "I've heard that before. I'm serious. This is it. If you can't convince Parkerson to extend your contract, we're done."

He wouldn't cut me loose. Surely, he wouldn't. I hope not.

I HAVEN'T DRESSED THIS good since my photo op when I signed my contract five years ago. My double-breasted suit makes my shoulders appear even wider than they really are, and it hides the hint of a beer gut I've started to grow. *Note to self: increase cardio during off-season.* Since we didn't make it to the playoffs, I have almost five months to get back in shape, both physically and mentally. It's more than enough time.

As Phillip and I wait for Mr. Parkerson to appear, I chomp another antacid while I take a look-see around his home office. Pictures of former players on his team adorn the walls. Tons of family photos litter every horizontal space. Phillip wasn't kidding when he said Parkerson was a family guy. I lean down to get a good view of one of his three kids, and oh, crap. I think I fooled around with his oldest daughter one time a few years ago. I sure hope she's not home today. From the wedding photo on the armoire, she's found someone much better for her, thank goodness.

A deep throat clearing jolts me to attention. Mr. Parkerson stands in the doorway. Phillip pumps the owner's hand so much I think it's going to fall off.

"How are you, Larry?"

"Been better."

I hold out my hand for him to shake while I slide a roll of Tums into my pocket with the other. "Hello, Mr. Parkerson. Nice to see you."

He ignores my outstretched hand and walks around his desk to sit in his leather chair. He motions for us to sit in the chairs in front of his desk.

Phillip takes a document out of his briefcase. "So as you know, Clint's contract will be up for renewal soon, and now is as good a time as ever to begin that discussion. Don't you think?"

Parkerson nods. "I've met with my budget analyst, and we have come to the conclusion that Clint's return on investment is lacking."

I blink like a buffoon. He talks like I'm a product on an assembly line instead of one man out there with eight other players doing our best to beat teams stacked against us day after day.

Instead of keeping my mouth shut, I say, "I would have to disagree."

Phillip groans. "Please, let me do the talking."

"No, it's my butt on the line. I need to say something." I face Parkerson and say, "I know this year hasn't been the best—"

"That's for sure. We didn't even make it to the playoffs, but your face seemed to make the press quite often, now didn't it?"

On instinct, I grimace. "True, but I've got a plan."

Parkerson shakes his head. "This organization is bleeding money, and I need to trim the fat somewhere. Some very talented blood is coming up in the colleges this year that are more promising than what you've been able to provide. Plus, they don't have reputations for being more aggressive off the field than on."

I close my eyes to figure out how to make him understand I really do want a second chance. After a deep breath, I say, "I may have let my pro career go to my head just a little."

Parkerson snorts. "More than a little. I'm used to you boys who come from nothing, and all of a sudden, you have millions in your bank account and girls throwing themselves at your feet." He taps the wedding photo for emphasis, and I want to crawl under his desk. "But I want a more wholesome image for my franchise. I want it to be a family sport again. You're not helping with your bar fights and black eyes, not to mention skirt chasing."

I focus on my bruised right hand, wishing I could go back in time and fix everything that's happened in the last five years, but I can't. The best I can do is grovel. "Sir, I know I can be a better person."

He stares at me for an eternity, and I wish I knew what he was thinking. He taps a pen on his desk as he clenches his jaw. "When's the last time you went home?"

"Home, as in where I grew up?"

He nods.

"Uh... I don't remember." Actually, I do remember. It was the same day I signed my contract. I said goodbye to Mitch and Silas, packed a duffle bag with a few belongings, and hightailed it out of Smithville faster than I could say "greased lightning." I didn't even say goodbye to Regina. I did my talking in the form of the papers I served her.

Parkerson snorts. "That's what I thought. I want you to improve your image during the off-season, starting with the people you grew up with."

What the...?

"I can do that right here on a much bigger scale. I can volunteer at the food bank or coach kids at the Y."

"Shut up," Phillip says through gritted teeth.

"You need to start on a small scale and work your way up. I want you to remember what it's like to be normal."

"But—"

"I know you think you're destined to be a troublemaker because of your family situation, but you can do better."

I close my eyes to try to block out his words about my family. Homelife sucked. When Mom left town with her latest crackhead boyfriend, Dad went on a downward spiral landing him in the state penitentiary. After all that, I never wanted to call Smithville home. And then I got a tongue-lashing from Silas when he saw me on the news after my first pro game, claiming I was from Atlanta and not Smithville. I'm pretty sure I would get the cold shoulder from all thirteen thousand residents if I showed up now.

"I'm not my father. I'll show you. I'll work hard during the off-season, and I will be a better man and ball player next spring. I promise."

Phillip agrees, and I hope his encouragement will convince Parkerson.

After too many silent moments, Parkerson sighs. "Let me think about this. In the meantime, if I see your face on the news for anything other than talking about ball, you will wish you never met me. Do I make myself clear?"

"Crystal."

CHAPTER THREE

Regina

Andie pours a glass of sweet tea for Mel and me as we sit at the counter of In a Jam. She shades her eyes with her hand. "I'm going to need my sunglasses in order to stare at that thing. It's so big and sparkly."

"Ha ha. It is pretty, isn't it?" I wave my left hand in front of Mel's face.

She shoves it away. "Yes, it is. I didn't know you two were that serious already."

I didn't either. I do my best to hide my shaking hands by guzzling some of my tea. "Sometimes it doesn't take long." I point to Andie. "She didn't know Gunnar very long, and they're engaged already."

Mel sneers. "That's different, and you know it."

I plant my hands on my hips. "Why can't you be happy for me?"

Mel's shoulders slump. "I am happy for you. If this is what you want, then I am thrilled."

"It is," I reply, my voice shrieking through the small café. "He's all I ever wanted."

Andie wipes the counter with a bar towel. "So why hasn't he met your folks?"

I stare at the ceiling and let out a huge sigh. "Because I thought we were just having fun. I never imagined he would propose. He lives in Atlanta, and I'm here, and we see each other from time to time. It's been very casual. I don't, I mean... I didn't want to be tied down."

Mel's eyes grow big, and she faces Andie. Mel's mouth drops open. "Then why did you say yes?"

I stand to pace the café, thanking the Lord that Mrs. Cavanaugh isn't working today to overhear this conversation. She wouldn't spare a moment to give me her two cents. As I nibble on a fingernail, I try to figure out how to answer. Quite truthfully, I don't really know the answer myself, or maybe I don't want to admit the answer.

"Have you noticed him? He's drop-dead gorgeous. He's successful. He dotes on me. Duh."

Andie does a one-shoulder shrug. "But do you... love him?"

"Marriage is a business arrangement, nothing more."

Mel gasps and yanks me back down onto my barstool. "Are you kidding me? An arrangement? Didn't your preacher daddy teach you anything about the sanctity of marriage? You know, 'What God has joined together, let no man separate'?"

I roll my eyes. No one can out-quote me when it comes to the Bible. "It also says, 'Two are better than one.' Maybe I make him a better person."

"How?"

I blink at Mel's question. While I brush crumbs from the counter into my hand, I try to figure out how to answer. "We complement each other. And to answer your question, Andie, yes, I'm pretty sure I love him." Bile rises in my throat as I say the *L* word. I vowed never to love another man. Love disappoints. Love isn't forever.

"Pretty sure." Mel raises an eyebrow. "Okay. As long as you're pretty sure. All I know is that I would never get engaged unless I was one hundred percent head over heels in love with the guy."

"If you're happy, I'm happy," Andie says, painting on a smile. "I'm here to help in any way I can."

Mel rubs her temples. "Sweetie, I want you to be happy too, but you've been down this road before, so be careful."

Andie's mouth drops open. "You were engaged before?"

Mel motions for me to answer.

I clear my throat. "Actually, I was married."

Andie sucks in all the café's air. "Shut the front door."

"It was a long time ago, and it ended before we could make it to the one-year mark." I glare at Mel for making me spill the beans.

Andie grins. "Who was it? Was it Stanley?"

Mel spits out her tea as she giggles. Stanley only has eyes for Jolene, thank goodness. He's not the sharpest tool in the shed.

"No. He doesn't live here anymore."

Andie holds her hands out as she glances from me to Mel as if she hopes to obtain more details.

I groan. "Fine. It was Clint, my high school boyfriend."

Mel holds up her index finger. "She's leaving the good part out. He's a professional baseball player now, and he also happens to be Mitch's brother."

Andie slings the bar towel over her shoulder. "Drama, drama, drama in a small town."

"It caused quite a ruckus. Everyone thought she was pregnant."

"Don't remind me." People in this town love to gossip, even if there's no truth to it. Clint and I had our reasons for getting married so young and in such a hurry, but a bun in the oven was not one of them.

"People do love a good story. When's the date?"

My chest tightens. Being joined to a man for the rest of my life causes me to hyperventilate, but I can do this. He'll be a good provider, and this marriage will be everything I want it to be. "I don't know. He keeps pushing for a date in the near future, which is not like him. He's a huge planner. Everything has to be organized down to the tiniest detail. It's almost like he'd rather just go to the courthouse and get it over with. It's all very odd."

"What?" Mel screeches. "You're not...?"

"Shh. Don't even think that. You know the walls have ears." I scan the café, hoping the Jackson sisters aren't sitting at a booth. If they heard that, they wouldn't even consider getting the facts before they published that in their *Biddy's Blog*. "I am not... you know what. And please don't say anything until I can talk to my parents. They need to meet him first."

Andie chuckles. "Boy, I'd love to be a fly on the wall when that happens. Is your dad going to make him do the welcome song at church, like he did me?"

I throw back my head and laugh. Daddy always makes a new person in the congregation stand in the middle while the church members sing a welcome song around them. It's incredibly embarrassing, which may be why we never have many guests attend church. "You know Daddy. He can't stop tradition. Please don't say anything. We're meeting with Mom and Dad tonight. I hope Daddy locks up his guns before he sees my ring."

Mel grimaces. "How have you kept Ken a secret, and in this town of all places? Nothing goes unnoticed."

I shrug. "I'm good, I guess."

But the truth is, I don't want to answer a thousand more questions like Mel just peppered me with. This time, the marriage will be perfect, especially when I take love out of the picture.

KEN'S WHITE KNUCKLES and ghastly complexion say it all. He's as nervous as I am. I kept our relationship a secret from my family and this town for a reason. Everyone here is too meddlesome. The rumor mill would have a field day with him, just like they did when Andie rolled into town. If I wanted to run Ken off, that would be the best way to do it.

"My parents are going to love you. Don't worry." I'm not sure if I'm trying to convince myself or him.

"I'm sure they will. It's still a little nerve-racking."

I take a sip of my latte, and when he hits a bump in the road, a drop of my drink lands on the leather seat next to me.

His brow scrunches. "Love, clean that up. I don't want my car to get sticky."

With a wide grin on my face, I say, "Of course." I point to the next street. "Turn left here."

"But the GPS says to go to the next street."

He passes my parents' street and continues because the sexy voice on his GPS knows this town better than someone who was born and raised here. When the voice says, "Recalculating," I want to throw him a smirk, but I don't. Ken whips around in the Erickson's yard, making their pit bull go into full-on defense mode. The dog nips at Ken's tires until we're back on the street, heading in the right direction.

When Ken swings onto my parents' street, he cuts his eyes toward me. "I guess I should listen to you, huh?"

I give him a kiss on the cheek. "Yes, I always know best. Okay, here's the rundown. Daddy is the pastor at the church. He's hardcore, but a sweetie deep down—way deep down. Mother is the librarian at the high school. To earn points with her, you might want to throw out some quotes from classic novels."

He mulls over my words. "Good to know."

"And then there's Robert. He's my brother. He's the football coach at the high school."

"Hmm. I don't like football."

I snicker. "You better learn to like it. How have you lived in Atlanta for three years and not learned that football is everything down here?"

He shrugs as I point to my parents' home, a simple Cape Cod style on a small yard within walking distance to the church. "I guess I'm too focused on running the family business."

I poke him in the side. "You've got to live a little. The high school season is just around the corner, so we'll have to go to some of the games. I'll even get you a purple-and-yellow jersey, not to mention a foam finger. You have to have one of those."

Ken cringes. "That's not going to happen."

I take a deep breath and do my best to put on a happy face, but if this meet and greet goes even a tiny bit well, I'll be relieved. "No time like the present." As we walk up the sidewalk, I take his hand in mine. "It's all good. You'll see."

Mom greets us at the front door, her flowing blond-gray hair sweeping across her shoulders.

"Mom, this is Ken Ashcroft."

He takes her hand in his and kisses the back of it. "Pleasure to meet you, ma'am."

Her eyebrows rise, and in a giggly voice, she replies, "Nice to meet you too."

I hustle Ken inside the house, and Mom mouths, "OMG," behind his back.

Heat rushes up my neck. At least Mom isn't turned off at first glance. Dad might be a different story.

Ken stops to gaze at my high school graduation photo hanging on the wall, but I grab his hand to move him toward the living room. Dad sits in his easy chair, reading his Bible, and I'm pretty sure I hear Ken gulp. When Dad's eyes flick up to us, he closes his Bible a little louder than necessary. He stands and sizes up Ken. There's nothing to hate about him. Ken is successful, kind, and very good-looking, not that Daddy would care about any of those qualities, but they matter to me.

"Daddy, this is Ken, Ken Ashcroft. We've been seeing each other for a while now, and I thought it was time for him to meet my family."

Dad swings a stiff arm out for Ken to shake his hand. Ken takes it, and they stand there shaking, almost like it's a test of wills. Dad's jaw clenches. He hasn't liked any of my boyfriends since the fiasco with Clint, so I shouldn't expect anything to change. I was hoping Robert would stop by to help be a buffer, but it doesn't seem like that's going to happen, so I have to go it alone.

I usher Ken toward the sofa, where we sit next to each other. Mom perches on the ottoman, wringing her hands. When Robert's not here, she has to play referee, and I never envy her position. "So, Ken. Tell me what you do."

"I'm the chief financial officer of my family's toy company."

"Oh. There's always a market for toys. Regina loved her dolls when she was little."

Oh dear. Here we go with the Regina stories.

"She had so many of those Barbie dolls, and the little sister—I think she was Skipper—and Barbie's boyfriend. What was his name?"

"Ken," Dad says in a dry-as-toast tone.

Mom's eyes shoot up. "Did anyone ever tell you, you look an awful lot like that doll—"

"Mom, that's not why we're here." I face Ken and, through gritted teeth, say, "Isn't there something you'd like to say?"

He clears his throat. "Yes." He takes a deep breath then wraps an arm around my shoulders. "Regina and I are engaged."

Crap. That's not what he was supposed to say.

Dad steels his eyes at Ken. "What did you say?"

Ken smiles at me. "We're engaged."

Mom chews on her lip then forces a flat-lipped smile onto her face. "That's lovely, but don't you have something you should ask first?"

Ken takes in each of our expressions, then when his eyes land on me, I whisper, "You're supposed to ask if you can marry me."

He snorts. "Really?"

I nod.

Dad slides his Bible onto the table and leans forward. "Yes. Really. It may be the twenty-first century, but it's still proper to ask the father for permission."

Ken chuckles then glances at me. "Is he serious?"

"Yes. I guess I didn't make it crystal clear, but yes." I wave a hand toward my father. "So ask."

Ken acts like he's just stepped into the *Twilight Zone*. He shakes his head then says, "Okay. Reverend Price, would you give me permission to marry your daughter?"

Daddy doesn't answer. He places his readers on and picks up his Bible to flip to a passage, and without glancing at Ken, he asks, "Do you love my daughter?"

"Uh... yeah. Sure. Of course."

Dad's eyes shoot up over his reading glasses. "Yeah, sure? That's it?"

Ken, obviously realizing his mistake, stands and paces. "I mean, of course I love her. We're good together." He throws his shoulders back and winks at me, like he's got it all under control.

"Mr. Ashcroft, do you know what Ephesians five, verse twenty-five says husbands are to do?"

"Should I?" Poor Ken sinks back down on the couch.

I whisper, "Love your wife like Christ loved the church."

Dad dips his head with an approving smile. "That's right, sweetheart. And until you come back in here with that kind of love bursting from every pore of your body, you can't have my permission."

My jaw drops. "Dad."

"I'm sorry. Get married if you want. You're an independent woman. You can do whatever your heart desires, but I can't give you my blessing without knowing one hundred percent that this is the *only* man for you."

His emphasis on the word *only* makes tears pool in my eyes. He never pulled the I-told-you-so card when things went belly-up with Clint, but I knew he felt it. Now, I'm paying the price for my hasty decision years ago. "Daddy, he is, but to be respectful to you, we won't set a date just yet." I turn my attention to Ken, who's gone from pale to almost gray. "That's fine with you, right?"

"Uh... not really. I wanted to get married by Labor Day. The fall and holiday seasons are very busy for our business. You know how it is. Plus, there's..." He lets out a deep breath then adds, "never mind."

I couldn't speak if I wanted to. For him to decide on a date without consulting me first is more than unnerving. The bride is supposed to be in the driver's seat on these decisions. Something's off for him to insist the wedding date be so soon, but maybe it's just because of business. Business before pleasure is practically tattooed on his forehead. I was really hoping to drag this engagement out for one or two years, or longer.

Mom stands up and says, "I'm sure we can work something out. For now, let's have some lunch and talk about the weather or football. Everybody likes to talk about football, right?"

This is a disaster.

CHAPTER FOUR

Clint

Normally, I would delete all emails that even seem remotely like fangirling, but this one makes me chuckle. The subject line reads "Smithville's Fall Festival: Calling all former Pickle Kings and Queens." This ought to be interesting. I wipe the crumbs of my bagel from my chin with the back of my hand as I open the email. I throw my head back in laughter as I see the country-style invitation.

Out loud, I read the email. "'As you're a former Pickle King, the Smithville Fall Festival committee would like to invite you back for a special fiftieth-anniversary celebration. This year, each past Pickle King and Queen couple will experience what life was like during their reign.'" A bubble of giggles springs out of my throat, and I try to hide it behind my hand. "'And the more activities each couple completes together, the greater their chance of winning the grand prize.'" I stop laughing. From what I remember about my hometown, the reward could be a ride in a hay truck or an award-winning pig from Old Man Gilbert's farm. "'The couple will split fifty thousand dollars...'" I choke on my coffee. *Who in Smithville has that kind of money?* "'And another fifty thousand will be donated to a local business in need of renovation. Come join the festivities and remember what life was like in the best little town in Georgia.'"

"Oh, I have to know more." I pull out my phone and call my brother, Mitch.

On the second ring, he picks up and says, "Let me guess, you got the email."

I cackle. "Yes, I did. What's happening in Smithville?"

He puts me on FaceTime as he lets out a yawn. "Ever since Andie showed up, things have been different. It wouldn't surprise me if she's behind the money."

My brow scrunches together. "Who's Andie?"

"Long story short, she's Mary Grace's granddaughter. She inherited her grandmother's lottery winnings, and she's revitalizing the town. Plus, she's engaged to Gunnar."

I drop my phone. While I find it on the floor, I clear my throat. "Gunnar Wills is engaged?"

"Yep."

"I thought we were the last of the he-man woman haters club."

"Sorry, bro. It appears it's just you and me now."

"That sucks. You gonna do the contest?"

Mitch lets out a deep sigh. "That would mean having to hang out with Laura Beth for a week. She's seven months pregnant with her third kid. I don't want that to rub off on me."

"Ha. I'm not doing it. That's for sure."

Mitch slants his head to the side. "Why not? A little Smithville time might be good for you. Nice shiner, by the way."

"Shut up."

"Want to tell your favorite brother all about it? Your agent didn't go into much detail."

I let out a groan. "Let's just say my baseball days are numbered."

Mitch's grin fades. "Oh. Sorry about that."

"I'm a liability. I need to change my image."

Mitch props his phone on the kitchen counter as he proceeds to make a pot of coffee. "What better way to change your image than to come back and get reintroduced to small-town living? It might get you out of a pickle. Ha ha. See what I did there?"

"Stick to the medical stuff. Dude, if I can't play baseball, what am I supposed to do?"

"If you think I have one bit of sympathy for you, you couldn't be more wrong. You had a full scholarship to UGA, and you left your junior year to play pro ball. One fricking year. Do you know how much I would have killed for to go to college for free?"

It's hard to complain to Mitch, seeing as he's the smart one in the family and didn't have a chance to attend college because our parents were too busy selling crack to provide for us kids. And I wasn't much better. I made enough to send him to school, but instead, I wasted it all on myself. As he's the frugal brother, it wouldn't surprise me if he has more in his bank account than I do. "I know."

His eyebrows scrunch together. "There's something else you need to know."

"Mel finally gave you the time of day?"

He grumbles as he pulls out the milk for his coffee. "It's Regina."

My heart stops. He knows better than to bring her up, but if she's in trouble, that changes things. "What about her?"

"She's getting married."

My lungs forget how to work. My legs wobble, and I have to prop myself up against the wall to avoid face-planting on the floor. "Who's the lucky guy?"

Mitch chuckles. "Some bigwig in Atlanta. I swear, he looks like a life-size doll."

"She can't get married." My head is about to explode with this new information.

He slurps down his coffee and sighs. "Dude, do you expect her to be a spinster with ten cats forever?"

I scratch the back of my head. "No, but... she just can't."

He gulps down his coffee and scratches his jaw. "She can and she is. Rumor has it the wedding is in about a month."

"No!"

Mitch backs away from the phone. "You okay, bro?"

I'm not okay. I am nowhere near okay. Sure, I'm the one who left Regina without a backward glance, and I always expected she would find someone who gave her the respect she needed, but I guess a part of me hoped she wouldn't. "I, uh... I have to go."

"Does that mean you're going to fulfill your duties as your graduating class's Pickle King?" Mitch's eyebrows waggle, and if we were in the same room together, I would have given him a matching black eye.

But come to think of it, the Fall Festival is the perfect excuse to come to Smithville. Regina won't ever think it's for any other reason than that. No one will suspect that I'm close to being penniless and within days of losing my baseball career. I can kill two birds with one baseball. I'll show Parkerson that I am a wholesome, small-town boy with family values. I'll show Smithville I still care about the town, and I'll show Regina I'm not the jerk she thinks I am. The last is going to be the hardest, because I am a jerk, but when she finds out what I did, or rather what I didn't do, I may never be able to play ball again.

I've put this off for five years, and now, too much is riding on it for me to delay any longer. Regina may hate me, but I can't let her marry that guy. She can't marry anyone, because she's still married to me.

CHAPTER FIVE

Regina

After our little meet and greet with my folks, Ken went radio silent for four days. He finally called on Wednesday, saying he was stuck in Pittsburgh with a big company event, but he sounded weird, like he was frustrated. I think he would have invited me had I not had to work a double shift at the hospital. At least, that's what I am telling myself.

As Ken and I sit in the back booth at In a Jam, we stare at each other, not knowing what to say. It's never been this awkward, but he's never had to meet my parents before, so I'm going to assume that's the source of tension. Andie brings us two piping-hot cups of coffee as Mrs. Cavanaugh conspicuously sweeps the same spot in front of our booth over and over. If it weren't her, it would be the Jackson sisters hovering. In fact, I'm shocked I didn't make the headlines of their blog, but it won't be long before our news is spread all over the county.

Mrs. Cavanaugh stares down at me. "So are you going to introduce him before you're pregnant with your third child?"

Ken spits out his coffee, and Andie plants her hands on her hips. "Mrs. C., where are your manners?" She focuses on Ken and holds out a hand. "Don't mind her. I'm Andie, and I used to be the outsider. Trust me, they'll warm up to you."

He grins at Andie, and he doesn't even try to hide the not-so-subtle head-to-toe gander he gives her. "Boston, right?"

"Good job, but Smithville is my home now."

He acts like he just smelled a rotten egg. "So you moved here to work in a café?"

Andie glances over at me and giggles. "Something like that. You two have a nice afternoon." She snaps her fingers. "Oh, Regina, you should check your email."

"Why?"

Andie shrugs.

Mrs. Cavanaugh huffs. "It's about the Pickle Festival."

Ken snickers. "The what?"

The bell over the front door rings, and Gunnar walks in, his police uniform muddy. He walks straight up to Andie and plants a huge kiss on her lips. Ken pouts, but when he catches me staring, he focuses on his coffee cup.

"Hey, Gunnar. I want you to meet my fiancé, Ken. Ken, this is Gunnar Wills. He's Andie's fiancé and Mel's cousin. You remember her from the hospital, right?"

"Oh, yes." He stands and shakes Gunnar's hand.

The two guys size each other up, and if they don't back down, I think they will do an arm wrestling match on the counter. I'm not sure why Gunnar feels the need to get territorial on my behalf, but it's kind of sweet. Plus, Gunnar can take Ken down with one hand tied behind him.

Keeping his eyes on Ken, Gunnar asks me, "So did you read the email yet?"

Why is everyone asking me about my email?

I take out my phone and pull up my email account. "If it so important, I'll do it right now."

As I pace through the coffee shop, I notice the email in question, and I want to hide underneath the booth. "Oh my gosh."

Gunnar chuckles. "Yeah... I thought that's what you would say."

I sink back down in my seat and paraphrase the message. "Apparently, for this year's Pickle Festival—"

Ken's eyes bug out. "There's one every year?"

Andie shrugs. "Yes. But this year, they're doing something special. We're celebrating fifty years of the festival."

"Fifty years, huh?"

I scan the email and forget how to breathe. "Apparently, all the kings and queens of past years will compete for a grand prize of fifty thousand dollars with an additional fifty thousand going toward a building project of the pair's choosing." I stare at Andie and sneer. "I wonder where the money's coming from."

She wipes down a table nearby as she hums Ray Charles's "Georgia on My Mind." "I have no idea what you're talking about."

"Of course you do."

Ken glares from me to Andie. "I'm not following."

I point to Andie. "She inherited her grandmother's lottery winnings."

"Ahh." His brow scrunches. "And you still want to live here?"

The café gets completely silent as we all gape at him like he committed an unforgivable sin. Mrs. Cavanaugh sweeps Ken's foot with the broom, sending food crumbs all over his wing tips.

He shakes out his foot. "Okay, so what's the big deal?"

I motion to myself. "I was Pickle Queen my senior year of high school."

Ken moans. "Please tell me you're kidding."

Harsh. I was quite proud of the title at the time. It was a big deal. I got to ride on a float in a parade, plus it gave me some scholarship money. "Nope. Gunnar was Pickle King the year before."

Gunnar does a silly princess wave, making me and Andie laugh.

Andie gives him a playful shove. "He can't compete because of a conflict of interest. Plus, that would mean he would have to spend way too much time with Willow."

Gunnar shivers. "Not happening."

"I'm confused," I say.

Andie lists her head. "Did you not read the rest of the email? The couples have to work together all week leading up to the festival, doing activities that were popular the year they reigned. So to get the money, you have to compete as a couple. I'm not supposed to say anything else about it just yet."

Gunnar chimes in, "Which means I am not doing it. I'm not giving my ex any reason to believe we're getting back together. Not. Happening."

"Simple. I won't be doing it either. My king moved away a long time ago." *Thank God.*

Andie pouts. "You don't think he'll come back for it? I know all royalty still alive got the email. Even the older people have email now. I know it's kind of short notice with the competition starting in two days, but most people still live locally, and he doesn't live *that* far away, right?"

"Pfft. He probably doesn't check his own email. His agent probably does that for him."

Ken scrunches his eyebrows together. "I'm confused. Who is this person?"

The bells over the entrance chime, and all eyes go to the tall guy standing in the doorway.

"Hey, y'all. Long time no see."

I could pick out that voice in a crowd. His twang used to make me weak in the knees. Now, it just grates on my last nerve. Every day for the past five years, I hoped he would get beaned in the head with a baseball. And when he started showing up in the tabloids with a new skank every week, I had to stop watching baseball and going to the convenience store. It just rubbed salt into my wound, and it was then that I decided no man would ever hurt me like that again. My heart scabbed over, and if I couldn't have a happily ever after, I would have as much fun as he was having.

While Gunnar and Clint do the bro hug, I stare at Ken, who appears more out of place than he did at my parents' house.

Ken clears his throat. "I'm sorry. Who are you?"

Clint's eyebrows rise, like he can't believe someone doesn't know who he is.

Jerk.

He scowls when his gaze lands on my engagement ring. He recovers and holds out a hand for Ken to shake. "I'm sorry. Where are my manners? I'm Clint. Regina's king."

I want to crawl under the table and disappear.

CHAPTER SIX

Clint

While Gunnar introduces me to his fiancée, Andie, I do my best to analyze the situation in front of me. Regina is as lovely as ever. Her blond hair falls just below her shoulders and frames her face like always, and I'm digging the purple streak next to her right ear, but where there used to be adoration, those pretty blue eyes shoot daggers my way. I deserve it and more. Her usual ivory skin has red blotches rising up her neck, and she clenches her fists.

This is not a good start to our reunion.

Her dude in a suit has a curious expression on his face, then he points to me. "Do I know you from somewhere?"

Regina groans and rests her head in her hand.

"You should," Gunnar says. "He's a legend around here. He broke Adam Dutch's batting record."

That was last year. This year, I could be outbatted by a T-ball player.

As if a light bulb turns on in his brain, the suit dude jumps up and grabs my hand. He pumps it up and down. "Oh, man. Now I remember. I was at that game." He turns to Regina. "Father took me to that game last year to celebrate making me CFO of the company."

My stomach churns, making me wish I had popped another antacid before I walked in here. He's a sharp dresser, a high-ranking businessman, and he's nabbed Regina. There's so much to hate about this guy. It would have been easier if he had blown me off.

"Can I get your autograph? How about a selfie with you?"

Regina pounds on the table with her fist. "Ken, stop."

I rack my brain, trying to recall something Mitch mentioned about Regina's boyfriend, and when I remember the doll-like resemblance, a chuckle bursts past my throat. I clear it to tamp down a laugh as I take his phone and we pose for a photo. He *does* look like Barbie's boyfriend. I wonder if he's anatomically the same as the doll too.

Regina glances up at me, and with a painted-on smile, she says, "Hello, Clint. Fancy seeing you after all this time. What's it been? Four years? Five? I can't remember exactly. It's all faded into the past."

Burn. "I've been wanting to come back home for a while."

She snorts. "I bet you have. Home? Home is where your heart is, and it sure isn't here, so skedaddle." She shoos me with her hands.

Her reaction is to be expected, but I'm not going to let that deter me. "It's not always about you, darlin'."

Regina jumps up from the table, and Gunnar steps in between us. "Now, Regina, assault is a crime. You know that."

Her face beet red, she jerks out of Gunnar's grasp. She stabs me in the chest with her index finger. "Just stay out of my way. I think you know how to do that just fine."

Ken squeezes her shoulders. "Now, I don't understand anything in this town, but how about we just take a breather and settle down?" Peering over at me, he adds, "I'd love to meet you for dinner to discuss some business ideas I have."

Regina gasps. "Ken, you don't want to make a business deal with him. Trust me, he always goes back on his word."

Andie removes the coffee cups from their table. I would, too, if for no other reason than to eliminate any breakable objects within throwing range. "Clint, I'm guessing you heard about the Pickle Festival."

Regina pokes me in the chest again, this time making sure I get a good view of the rock on her hand. "That's why you're here. You think I'm going to compete for the title with you, don't you? Mr. Big Shot, it isn't going to happen."

"Why not?"

She inches even closer, so close I can smell her peach shampoo. "If I had to spend any time with you, I would have to start taking blood pressure medication and go to anger management sessions." Regina grabs Ken by the hand. "Come on, Ken. We need to leave. We can talk about our wedding some other place."

Right before she opens the door, I throw out, "Fifty thousand dollars would go a long way for a wedding, especially for a preacher's daughter. I'm sure your parents would welcome the extra money on a wedding that's sure to be the event of the season."

Ken leans down and stage whispers, "He's right. Traditionally, it's the bride who pays for the wedding."

Her jaw drops. "You're not going to help pay for our wedding?"

He shrugs. "I hadn't planned on it." He stiffens his spine and mansplains to us, "You see, in my social circle, the bride pays for the wedding and the reception. The groom pays for the rehearsal dinner." He grins before he adds, "We can work out an arrangement about who pays for what on the honeymoon."

Oh, snap. What a class act.

She points to the door. "Clint. Outside. Right now."

I give her a patronizing salute. "Yes, ma'am." To Andie, I say, "It was a pleasure meeting you. I've heard nothing but nice things about you."

Andie giggles. "Even though you aren't a Red Sox, if you need a place to stay, my apartment above the shop is available." She points to the ceiling.

Regina groans.

"I might take you up on that."

Gunnar leans in toward me and says, "Word to the wise: the bed frame is a bit weak."

I cock my head to the side.

Andie pops him on the shoulder. "Gunnar, you have to stop saying things like that."

Regina clears her throat. "Hello? If you guys are through fanboying this... this sorry excuse for a baseball player, I need to talk to him alone."

I stifle a chuckle.

Ken flicks a business card into my hand. "Call me later."

While I stuff it in my pocket, I say, "Nice to meet you... Ken."

Ken blushes. I've never understood men getting all flustered about meeting me. That's odd on so many levels. "We'll get together soon. I'm not leaving for a while."

Regina tugs on my arm and drags me toward the door. "Let's go. I'm assuming that horrid overpriced, gas-guzzling SUV out there is yours."

I wink at her, and she gives me the evil eye. "You are correct, ma'am, and if you're a good girl, I'll even let you drive my G-Wagon."

She jerks open the shop door and stomps outside. "Not in a million years."

Ken follows us to the door. "Gin Gin, I need to leave anyway. See you soon?"

Gin Gin? Oh man, this keeps getting better.

Regina latches onto his arm. "No, don't leave. This will only take a second."

He kisses her cheek, and I want to pounce on him. "Sorry, but I have an early meeting in the morning. We'll touch base later."

Touch base? I bet he also thinks outside the box, is out of pocket a lot, and incorporates onboarding for his new employees.

She watches him leave, her mouth gaping. After I salute Gunnar, I follow Regina outside. In front of my ride, she taps her toe as she crosses her arms. I click the key fob to unlock it, and as she attempts to get inside. I stand there drinking in the sight of her. Leaving her was the dumbest thing I ever did, but I had my reasons. If she hates me now, she's going to be ready to put me six feet under when she finds out everything else.

"Let me help you," I say as I put my hands on her waist to assist her in getting into the tall SUV.

She smacks my hands away. "I don't need your help."

I hold up my hands and back away. "As you wish, darlin'."

After several grunts and failed attempts, she finally succeeds in getting into my SUV. Regina slams the door and adjusts the seatbelt, then stares out the windshield as I jog around to get in the driver's seat.

"Stop calling me 'darlin'.'" She drags it out real Southern-like. "And don't ever quote my favorite movie. Do you understand?"

Without even thinking about it, I said, "as you wish," the famous line from *The Princess Bride*. She forced me to go see it with her at the dollar theater. It was about the only place I could afford to take her. I think I enjoyed it as much as she did. We used to quote that movie on a daily basis. Now, it's off limits.

"Yes. Yes, I do. Where to, miss?"

"Just drive, and stop with the polite crap. It's not appealing."

I chuckle as I pull out on to Main Street. "I am polite."

She snorts. "Yeah, on camera, you are so syrupy sweet it's nauseating."

"Ah, I see you've been keeping up with my career."

She rolls her eyes. "As if I care. Mitch bores me with YouTube clips of you. He worships the ground you walk on for some reason."

Even though I ran out of Smithville like a scalded dog, I never lost contact with Silas and Mitch. They're my only family, and I know they're proud of me, even if they both wish I'd finished college first. But that sum of money was hard to walk away from, especially since we hardly had a pot to pee in growing up.

"You're close to your brother too. Or at least, I hope you still are. Robert's a good guy."

She leans her head back on the headrest. "Please tell me Robert hasn't been stroking your ego too. If he has, I'm going to disown him."

I clutch the steering wheel, my knuckles white from the force. "He's one of the few real friends I have."

"Pa-leeze. You have lots of friends."

I have lots of acquaintances—too many—but not friends. It didn't take me long to figure out they were my "friends" as long as I was paying. Once I realized how shallow most of them were, I started to retreat. Too bad it was after most of the money had been spent.

"Fewer than you might imagine."

Regina chuckles. "I don't imagine anything when it comes to you. How dare you come back to town after all this time? And right when I'm about—" Her head snaps around. "You are trying to keep me from getting married, aren't you?"

I pull into the Piggly Wiggly parking lot for lack of any other place to go in this small town. I take a deep breath before I say what I have to say. "Yes, but—"

"I knew it. You're pure evil." She unbuckles her seatbelt and opens the door. "I'm going to call Ken. I'm sure he hasn't made it out of town yet. He'll pick me up."

I grab her arm to keep her from leaving. Her soft skin sends a goosey feeling up my spine. "Don't leave. I have to tell you something."

Regina curses under her breath before she slams the door. "Make it fast."

I know I should just spit it out, but I need to ease into the mistake I made. I didn't do it for spite, but right now, she wouldn't believe me, so I go with what she already knows. "You know, Ken might not like it if he found out you've walked down the aisle before."

Her jaw drops. "You wouldn't."

I raise an eyebrow. "Try me."

Her chest rises and falls as she stares at me. "You have a lot of nerve to bring that up after all this time. It's old news anyway."

"But your fiancé has a right to know."

She removes her phone from her pocket, and her fingers fly across the screen. "You're more horrible than I remembered, which is saying a lot."

With a swipe of her finger to her eye, she stares out of my SUV. "Gah. Ken turned his phone off. I'm calling my brother. Please don't say anything. Of course I need to tell Ken, but I will in my own time."

I drum my fingers on the steering wheel as the Jackson sisters waddle into the Piggly Wiggly. One of them takes a picture of us with her cell phone. Things sure have changed since I left. "What's it worth to you?" *Jerk.*

"It's worth a lot. Ken wants to marry me. Don't mess this up."

I throw my hands up in defense. "Hey, I'm here for the Pickle Festival."

"Liar."

As much as she needs to tell Ken she's been married before, I need to tell her we are *still* married, so I understand her reasoning for doing it at the right time.

After a deep sigh, I add, "Okay, here's the real deal. I need to improve my image, or I'm going to get canned."

She throws her head back with a hearty cackle. "'Bout time, you whore of Babylon."

"I'm serious. The manager wants me to have a more wholesome image. What better way than to assimilate back into the community that made me who I am?"

"You got the 'ass' part right. You're talking about the community you ignored for the past five years."

I nod. "Come on, Regina. Help me out. You do this silly contest with me, you help me seem like a decent person, and I'll help you win the money for your wedding."

She chews on her bottom lip, and at that time, her brother Robert drives up in his old beat-up truck he's had since tenth grade. He gets out and walks to my side of the car.

"Please help me out," I say.

"Nope."

I let out a breath and exit my SUV to greet Robert. We do the bro hug, knuckle bump.

"Dude, you look good."

He pats my back. "It's all this clean living. You're not so bad yourself." He peeks over to see Regina in my SUV. "She texted that she needed me to pick her up. You two at each other's throats again?"

I stare at the parking lot. "I was hoping I could get her to do me a favor, but..."

"I'll do it," Regina says from behind us.

I spin around to face her to make sure she's being serious. "Really?"

She nods like a bobblehead. "We have a deal, right?"

I hold out my hand for her to shake. After a moment of hesitation, she takes my hand in hers. Mine swallows hers whole, and a flood of memories comes washing over my brain. I forgot what holding her hand could do to me. I blink to clear my brain and nod. "We have a deal."

She yanks her hand away like I burned her then storms over to Robert's truck.

"See ya later," Robert says as he laughs.

One step forward, but she's going to have my hide when she learns I left out an important fact.

CHAPTER SEVEN

Regina

I pray that Robert doesn't ask any questions. All I want is for him to drop me off at my apartment and drive away. It's not too much to ask, especially since he's the kind of brother that never meddles in my business. It didn't matter that Clint Sorrow broke my heart. Robert never intervened. He would've if I'd asked, but making a big stink of the situation would've made it even worse.

"Is it a strange coincidence, or is it fate that Sorrow's back in town right when you get a wedding proposal?"

So much for my prayers being lifted up for silence. "Neither. Can you just drive, please?"

Robert chuckles. The crinkles around his eyes accentuate his crystal-blue irises. "Regina Price is in a love triangle."

His singsongy voice grates on my nerves.

"I am not." I flaunt my engagement ring in his face. "I'm engaged to one man. Clint is nothing but a pain in my backside. He's back for the stupid Pickle Festival, and he's going to help me win fifty thousand dollars."

He whistles. "What's he going to do? Pose nude for next year's Smithville Bank and Trust calendar?"

"He wouldn't make a dime off that."

Robert cracks up as he turns down the street toward my apartment building. "I'm a guy as straight as they come, and even I can see he's a hot slice of pizza. You can't tell me just seeing him doesn't make you all jiggly inside."

I cringe and cover my mouth to keep from throwing up. "You're disgusting, and I'm going to tell Maddie Rose you have the hots for a professional baseball player."

He waggles his eyebrows as he throws his truck in park. "She knows better. Besides, this isn't about me. This is about you and this little quandary you're in."

I jump out of his truck to end the conversation, but he decides to follow me to my door. He makes himself at home while I head to the kitchen. It doesn't seem like I'm going to get rid of him anytime soon, so I might as well be hospitable. I pull two beers from my refrigerator and walk into the living room.

"Yes," he says, holding out his hand.

Before I give it to him, I say, "This conversation falls under the Price Code of Ethics."

Robert groans as he stands. He holds up his hand, and with no emotion in his voice, he says, "P is for private, R is for respectful, I is for involved, C is for confidential, and E is for empathetic. Price forever. Happy now?" He holds out his hand for his beer.

After a second of hesitation, I hand it over. I plop down on the couch next to him and take a swig from my beer. "This doesn't leave this room."

"I just recited the Price Code. What more do you want?"

"Okay." I take a deep breath as I pick at the label on the bottle. "It's just really embarrassing."

He props his feet on my coffee table and takes a long pull from his bottle. "Is it as embarrassing as when you went to New Orleans and—"

"Stop talking." I blow out a breath. "Everyone thought I was pregnant because we got married while we were still in college."

"That part I know."

"He promised he would graduate from college, but then he got drafted to the majors... he said he couldn't pass it up. So he just up and left me."

Robert stares at the ceiling and groans. "Sis, you're still not telling me anything I don't already know." He places his empty beer bottle on the coffee table and clenches his teeth. "Are you saying you two are still...?"

"No! Heavens no. When he left me to play major-league ball after he promised he wouldn't until after he graduated, I was devastated."

"I remember. You almost flunked out of nursing school because of that idiot."

Thinking back, I don't know how I managed to finish my clinical rotations and pass the nursing boards on the first attempt all while I was in the deepest, darkest place I had ever been. Someone must have been praying for me, because it took all I had to get out of bed every day. "When he left... I was happy for him. You know the terrible home life he had. I couldn't blame him for taking the money and running, but then it didn't take long for the money to consume him. The first picture I saw of him with some model wrapped around his neck, I literally threw up I was so upset. After a yelling match on the phone, we decided to file for an uncontested divorce. I didn't want any of his money, and he didn't want me."

"Wow."

"Yeah. I let people think I was the bad guy because he needed his image to be clean. As long as I knew the truth, it was okay." I take a deep breath and continue. "But here's the kicker. The real reason we got married was because his scholarship only covered tuition. I found out he was sleeping in the hallway of his teammate's dormitory. Someone ratted him out, and he had nowhere else to go. I knew Dad would have a fit if we rented an apartment together, and married housing was pretty cheap, so..."

"Sis, why didn't you say anything? I mean, everyone who had a clue would have understood."

I shrug. "I figured the fewer people who knew that part, the better. You know how Smithville is. One person tells someone and makes sure they don't tell anyone. That person tells someone but says, 'Don't tell anyone,' and before you know it, my secret winds up in the *Biddy's Blog*. Clint had had enough of the rumor mill his entire life. He didn't need any more humiliation."

A tear trickles down my cheek, and I swipe it away before my brother notices. Even though I'm as mad as a wet hen at Clint, I still carry a great deal of compassion for him and his horrible upbringing.

"So why now? Why is he here now?"

"Other than to mess with me, it's the Pickle Festival. Apparently, he's in jeopardy of losing his contract or something if he doesn't clean up his image. He thinks being seen in the town he grew up in, doing simple town stuff, is going to make him more wholesome."

"And what do you get?"

"He's agreed to give me the money. I need it for the wedding. Ken made it explicitly clear that we have to have a fancy wedding, but it has to be traditional, meaning the bride pays."

"What a dick. Has Dad met him?"

I nod. "That was... uncomfortable, to say the least."

Robert laughs as he removes his feet from my coffee table. "Let me guess. He whipped out the 'love is patient, love is kind' scripture."

I nudge Robert's shoulder with mine and grin. "It was the one about loving your wife like Christ loved the church. Apparently, Ken didn't have the *look* that Daddy was expecting of my fiancé."

He cringes. "I will hold judgment until I meet the guy, but does he have the '*look*'?" He uses quotation marks, and I swat his hands away from my face.

"I don't know. All I know is that he pays me a lot of attention." I take the beer bottles to my kitchen.

Robert rises from the couch and follows, in search of food no doubt. "I'm glad you finally landed on someone for more than a week."

I gasp. "It hasn't been that bad, has it?"

He gives me the *look* that tells me I'm an idiot. "I'm happy for you as long as you're happy."

"I am. Very. I just have to get through the Pickle Festival without any hiccups."

Robert chomps down on an apple as he heads for the door. "You should be fine, then. He gets what he wants. You get what you want. I only have one question."

I raise an eyebrow, waiting.

"Do you want the same things as you did yesterday?"

"Of course. I don't trust Clint as far as I can throw him. He's only out for himself, as always."

He salutes me and opens the door. "My work here is done."

He leaves, and I slide down the door to sit on the floor. I hate it when Robert's words make me think too hard. He has Dad's gift of saying the exact words that someone needs to hear. I'm just too mad to hear them right now.

My phone buzzes in my pocket, and when I check the screen, I don't recognize the number. I almost ignore it, but like a dummy, I answer. "Hello?"

"Just making sure you got home okay."

I can't keep my groan from turning into a growl. "Clint, how did you get my number?"

"Mitch gave it to me. Let's FaceTime."

"First off, I'd rather not. Second, when I see Mitch at work tomorrow, I'm going to give him a piece of my mind."

My phone beeps for me to switch to FaceTime. He's just not going to let it go, so I swipe until I see his ugly mug. I scan the apartment with my phone. "See? I made it home. Bye."

"Wait. Don't be that way."

I give him my pissy face. "You don't get to tell me what 'way' to be. You waltz in here and expect everyone to just welcome you with open arms, including me. Buster, it's not happening."

His face falls as he chews on his lip. "I don't want to fight. I'm sorry. I didn't mean to start anything or bring back bad memories. I... didn't know what else to do." He swallows hard, making his Adam's apple bob.

His sad puppy dog eyes used to get the best of me, but not anymore.

"Let's just go to the festival meeting and find out what we need to do to win. By the end of next week, I'll have the money, and you'll have a clean reputation, and we won't have to see each other ever again."

Clint smirks. "I'm not sure which one is going to be harder, winning the money or polishing my rep."

I roll my eyes. "Oh, please, we're going to win that competition. If it's the last thing I do, I am going to have the money to say 'I do.'"

He dips his head low. "Yeah. A promise is a promise."

I clear my throat and my head, because his voice has been known to make my entire spine like jelly. "Yep. Easy peasy."

He stares a hole through me, and even though it's only over the phone, I feel him reaching into my soul. "I'm very sorry for hurting you."

"Whatever. I'll see you tomorrow."

"Bye, Regina."

After I hang up the phone, I whisper, "Bye, Clint."

CHAPTER EIGHT

Clint

Marlo showers me with kisses, and Silas backslaps me to death. I may never throw a baseball again. The twins don't care that I've never seen them. All they want is for me to carry them around on my shoulders. Family life suits my big brother. He even has a dad belly growing. If my parents could see him now, they would realize their terrible mistakes didn't trickle down to the next generation. Silas rocks responsibility, and with the growing baby bump, Marlo seems to enjoy her little family too.

"Hey, bro. Good to see you."

He gives me a big hug. "Good to see you too."

"So where are you going to stay? You know you're welcome to stay here." Marlo takes Carson off my shoulders and tickles his tummy, making him erupt in an enormous rumble of giggles.

I scratch the back of my neck as I hoist Caleb over to Silas. "That's sweet, but I better get a hotel room. I'm used to being alone."

Silas chuckles. "Hotel? Yeah, Sorrows don't stay in hotels."

The door opens, and Mitch stumbles in, sweat stains under his armpits and white powder all over his shirt and pants.

"What happened to you? Did you fall into a vat of flour?" I kick his steel-toed boot with my shoe, and white particles fly through the air.

He slumps down into a chair and flips me the bird. "You see, little brother, not everyone in this room has four point five million in their bank accounts."

No one in this room has that anymore.

Mitch rotates his neck. "This is called drywall dust. Some of us need more than one job to get ahead in life."

If he needed money, he should have asked. I would've helped him.

Caleb wiggles out of his daddy's arms and runs toward Mitch. "Unc Mitz."

Mitch tosses him in the air before he snuggles into a big hug. "Howdy, buddy. I see you met your Uncle Clint." In Caleb's ear, he whispers, "I'm still your favorite, right?"

Caleb bobs his head up and down then holds his arms out for his mother to take him.

Marlo asks, "What's your plan now that you're back?"

I shake my head. "Just trying to spruce up my image."

Marlo wraps an arm around me and squeezes my middle. "Are you going to do the Pickle Fest competition?"

Heat rushes up my neck, and Mitch covers his grin with his hand.

"Seems that way. I'm in town, so I might as well. By the way, Mitch, you're in trouble for giving Reggie's phone number to me."

Marlo kisses his cheek. "Aw, Mitchy was being a sweetie."

Mitch rolls his eyes. "He practically had to beat it out of me. 'I gotta have her number. We need to talk.' Blah blah blah. That doesn't sound like a man only here to spruce up his image."

Silas pinches my cheek. "Aw, little brother's in love..."

Caleb and Carson cover their ears and run off.

"Y'all aren't making this any easier."

They all follow me into the living room. Marlo sits in Silas's lap while he rubs little circles on her bulging belly.

Marlo yawns. "It's okay. I know your little secret."

I reach over to punch Mitch in the arm, but Marlo blocks me. "Now, now. We love you, and we know all about what happened."

"It's my fault. I forgot to file the divorce papers."

At the same time, everyone in the room yells, "What?"

If I could sink into the couch cushions, I would. There goes my big mouth again.

Marlo slaps her hands over her mouth and mumbles, "I was talking about your contract."

Oops. "Yeah. That's what I meant too."

Marlo wags her finger in front of me. "Nope. You spill the beans. What in tarnation are you talking about?"

I stare at Mitch for help out of my situation.

He holds up his hands to defend himself. "You did this to yourself. I didn't rat you out." He pinches his finger and thumb together and runs them across his mouth. "My lips were sealed."

Marlo gasps and swats Mitch on the arm. "You knew about this? Since when?"

He shrugs. "I guess since the beginning."

"And you never said anything?"

"In this town? No way."

Thanks, brother.

Marlo and Silas stare at me, waiting for me to answer, so I tell them the entire horrible story.

Marlo's complexion becomes a bit green. "I wish I could have a drink right now."

Mitch goes to the kitchen. "I'll have one for you."

Silas stretches his arms over his head. "I'm impressed you've been able to keep it a secret. What's done is done. It's all in the past. If you two don't want anyone to know, it's none of our business, right?" He points to each person in the room.

I stand to pace. "Here's the deal." I smack my fist into the palm of my other hand. "She didn't know so..."

"Holy..." Mitch yells from the kitchen.

"Yeah."

Silas doubles over in laughter, and Marlo delivers half-hearted smacks to his arm. He chuckles and covers his face with his hands. "Bro, only you would forget to file divorce papers. What does that mean?"

"I don't know, other than she can't get married to someone else in a month."

Marlo slumps back on the couch. "What did Regina say when you told her today? I bet she pitched a fit. I know her temper. I'm surprised Gunnar didn't get called for a domestic assault."

I lean my head up against the wall, too afraid and embarrassed to face my family.

"No way," Silas says, breaking the silence.

"Yep."

"Are you kidding me?" Marlo's voice reaches eardrum-piercing levels.

Mitch starts another round of laughter as he saunters back into the living room with a beer in one hand and a peach in the other.

I'm glad someone thinks it's funny. I punch him on the arm. "I'm so happy to be the entertainment tonight. But when you told me she was getting married, I had to stop her. This stupid contest was the best way, plus it makes my agent and owner happy. I'll spend time with her and ease the little snafu into a conversation. It's not like I lied to her about it. I just forgot to file. We'll start the paperwork over. She'll just have to postpone the wedding for ninety days, and boom, we're done."

Silas lifts an eyebrow. "You're in denial. You didn't file because you didn't want to."

"Nope. I got busy and didn't think about it again until Mitch brought her pretty little face back into my memory."

"Oh, blame me. So maybe ten years from now, you might have run into her and her Ken doll of a husband with their three kids, and it would suddenly hit you that she's committed bigamy?"

I snap my fingers. "You're right about him resembling a Ken doll. It's kind of creepy."

Mitch leans over to Silas and holds his hand out. "Pay up, buddy. Told you so."

Silas groans and pulls out a five-dollar bill from his wallet. "Dang it."

I rub my temples in an attempt to get my throbbing headache to subside. "You guys are driving me crazy."

"That's our job," Marlo says, kissing my cheek. "The offer still stands. You're welcome here as long as you like."

I wave her off. "That's sweet, but I think Andie mentioned an apartment above her shop. I might stop by there to see if it's still available."

"It is." Mitch leans in and whispers, "Watch out for that bed. Gunnar says it's seen better days."

I raise an eyebrow at getting the bed warning for the second time. "I'll see you guys tomorrow. Love you all."

ANDIE OPENS THE DOOR to the upstairs apartment and motions me in. The small studio is stuffed full of old furniture and knickknacks and has the unique smell of a hot attic combined with a touch of home.

"It's not much, but I loved living here." She points to the bay window. "You can see all the bustling activity of Main Street from that window. Plus, Mrs. Cavanaugh always makes more food than we can ever sell, so you won't go hungry." She leans in and adds, "Although, you might have to fight Stanley for the leftovers."

It appears as though Andie has befriended the loveable doofus of Smithville.

"Ah. How is Stan the Man?"

She beams as she says, "He passed his GED. I'm very proud of him."

By the way she bounces on her heels, I'm assuming that was a big feat, and if I don't figure out what to do with my owner, I might have to ask Stanley for a job.

"Good for him. He's a good guy." I walk around the apartment, taking it in. It's small and cramped, but it's very homey. "I won't be here long. A week, maybe two at the most."

"Stay as long as you like. My treat."

I wave her off. "I have money."

Andie plants her hands on her hips. "You may be a big-shot baseball player, but I can out-dollar you every day of the week and twice on Sunday."

I throw my head back and laugh. "How very Southern of you."

Her mouth cracks into a huge grin. "I've been practicing. Anyway, I have more money than Carter's got pills, so stay here as long as you want."

There is so much to like about this little transplant in Smithville. I see why Gunnar snagged her. And I've never seen him so happy. Mitch kept me informed about all the Willow drama and the almost wedding. I didn't think Gunnar would ever take a chance on another person, but I'm glad he did. Andie is perfect for him in every way.

I stare out the bay window that overlooks Main Street. Several people meander down the sidewalk. One couple actually stops and smells the flowers in the planter box at the store across the way. It's been ages since I've relaxed enough to take in little things like that. A teenager jogs by, and my hand finds my softening abs, reminding me I need to get some cardio in this week.

"I really appreciate you letting me stay here."

Andie steps up beside me. "Regina has become a good friend of mine in the short time I've lived here."

Without glancing at her, I reply, "I'm glad. She's a good egg."

"Yeah. We run most mornings at six o'clock. You know, in case you want to join us tomorrow. And just as a gentle reminder, the contest starts in two days. It's going to be so much fun." She claps her hands.

"Can't wait," I say in a deadpan voice.

I swivel to face her, and she winks.

"I'll leave you to get settled in."

"Thanks, Andie. Oh, I have one question."

She smiles as she waits.

"Is that the bed with the faulty...?"

Her face pales as she pivots on a dime. "You'll have to figure that out for yourself."

Maybe I will.

CHAPTER NINE

Regina

After the surprise visit from Clint yesterday, I need a good long jog in the worst way. As I pull my leg behind me to stretch out my quads, someone trots down the stairs from the upstairs apartment.

"I didn't know you were already—"

The rest of my sentence dries up in my mouth. What I thought was Andie coming out of the shop is Clint, dressed in shorts, a tank top, and his Atlanta Braves baseball cap pulled down low over his eyes.

"I thought you were... what are you doing here?"

He stretches his arms over his head, making his tank top rise to expose his abs with a trail of hair running from his navel and disappearing beneath the waistband of his shorts. I blink to come back to reality.

When his eyes meet mine, they twinkle with delight. "Andie said I could stay here while I'm in town."

"Oh, she did, huh? Good to know. I'll make sure I stay clear of the place from now on."

"Don't be that way." His large hand bears down on my shoulder as he towers over me while he stretches out a quad. "You were always the perfect height for this."

I squirm away from him just as Andie drives up in her convertible.

She rushes toward the shop and says to Clint, "Hey. I see you took me up on the offer to go jogging with us."

My head snaps around so fast I'm going to need a chiropractor. "What? You invited him?"

Andie bounces to us and pokes Clint in the stomach. "Can't let him become a little doughboy, now can we?"

I jut my chin high. "Running is our girl time." I glance over at Clint. "If you haven't noticed, you're not a girl."

Clint chuckles.

Andie concurs. "Oh, I noticed. Come on. Be nice. Besides, I can fill you in on some classified information about the contest. You guys are going to do it, right?"

"Yep," Clint says before I can reply.

The last thing I want to do is spend time with him, but since he agreed to give me all the money, I have no choice. He begs with his eyes as if I'm thinking about going back on my word.

Through gritted teeth, I say, "Yes, we're going to 'do it.'"

Clint snorts, landing him a smack to his abdomen, and I notice it's a little softer than usual.

Andie bites her lip then waves at Mel as she drives up. Mel's usually perfectly braided hair is a rat's nest. "What happened to you?"

"Doctor Dougl-ass got called away for an urgent meeting with Norma Bentry." She rolls her eyes. "There's nothing normal about her. Anyway, he never showed back up, and I couldn't leave the ER unattended, so I'm just now getting off work."

Andie messes up Mel's hair more and motions with her head. "Come on, sleepyhead. Let's go before it gets too humid."

Clint walks beside me on the sidewalk as we make our way to the high school track. Occasionally, his arm brushes mine. In my ear, he whispers, "Do you think Mel will ever give my brother a chance?"

I shrug. "I doubt it, but unlike you, Mitch knows what he wants and doesn't get distracted."

"Ouch, Regina Noelle Price. Just cut to the chase next time."

"That's me." I scoot past him to catch up to Andie. "Is there any way I can bribe the judges to just giving me the money without having to work with that Neanderthal?"

She giggles. "Those are the rules, and no matter how much you try to butter me up, you have to do whatever the festival committee decides. Come on. It's free money, plus there's extra cash to donate for a building makeover in town."

From behind me, Mel says, "Andie has a point."

"Ha. You're just saying that because you don't have to work next to him." I jut my thumb behind me toward Clint. "And your conflict of interest will keep Gunnar from working side by side with Willow."

She does a full-body shiver. "Thank goodness I'm on the committee. I'd have to hose her off him daily."

"So tell me what the committee has up its sleeve."

"Well..." She grins and picks up the pace as we reach the high school football field. With their long legs, Mel and Clint take off ahead of us. *Braggarts.* "The committee researched each year's pop culture, and there's a different list for each couple depending on the year they won their crowns. It all starts bright and early Friday morning, so don't be late, or points will be deducted."

"Wait, tomorrow? I have to work. I can't spend time doing this."

Andie points to Mel. "It's all been taken care of."

I'll repay her the un-favor one day. "So what's up for me, I mean, us?"

"Hmm, just be thinking of your favorite movie, favorite clothes, stuff like that from the year you were crowned."

"Great..."

When the two long-legged people get half a lap ahead of us, Andie directs her attention to me. "Okay, spill. Gunnar is so tight-lipped. Give me all the details."

Ugh. I'm not sure where to begin. "The abridged version is Clint was my boyfriend in high school, and we got married when we were in college."

"And..."

I sigh and stop running, walking to let Mel and Clint pass us by. "And he broke my heart."

She stares off in the distance, and it's as if she's been there. We may have grown up in different states, but I think heartache is a universal feeling.

I put my hands around my mouth and yell, "Hey, Clint!"

He runs backward. *Show off.* "Yes, Reginald?"

He's lucky he's not close enough for me to smack. "What was your favorite movie our senior year?"

Clint shrugs. "I don't know. What I do remember is that you made me watch that horrible *Twilight* movie over and over and over."

Mel tugs on his tank top to get him to keep running, and off they go again.

In a singsongy voice, Andie says, "You might want to remember that."

We fist-bump as we take off jogging again. When Mel and Clint come up behind us, they slow down to jog with us. They're both soaked in sweat, and the way Clint's tank top sticks to his body is hot in more ways than one. He lifts the hem up to wipe his sweaty brow, and I trip over my feet and tumble to the ground, sending my body one way and my water bottle, along with my pride, another.

"Oh my gosh," Mel says, stopping to hover over me.

I hold my right ankle. *Dang, that hurt.*

Clint kneels down and touches my leg. I flinch, and he snaps his hand back. "I'll let the professional handle this."

"Are you okay?" Andie asks, retrieving my water bottle.

"Yeah. I think my shoestring came loose and I stepped on it."

While Mel checks my ankle, I cut my eyes toward Clint.

The smirk on his face obviously shows that he doesn't buy my lame excuse. "Yeah, her shoestring was loose. It must be because of her tiny feet, and the laces are too long."

"Exactly. Can you help me up?"

He takes my hand and helps me back to my feet, but my ankle gets wobbly. As I lose my balance, his arms go around my waist.

"Whoa, hold on there. I've got ya."

Mel steps forward, but Andie throws out an arm to stop her from advancing. "Clint, why don't you help her back to the shop while Mel and I finish our run?"

I can't believe Andie's bailing on me, but when Mel agrees, I'm seriously miffed with my best girl buddies. As they take off to finish their run, I pry myself away from his grip. "I've got this. You go finish your jog."

I start to hobble away, when a large arm slips around my waist.

"Don't be weird. Come on. I promise I won't tell Ken doll."

If I didn't need Clint right now to keep me from hobbling down Third Street back to In a Jam, I would stomp on his foot and make it so he couldn't ever run around the bases again. "Ken doesn't need to be bothered with stupid stuff like this. He's used to my weak ankles."

Clint snorts. "Let's get you home."

We don't talk for the longest time, but when we get back to the shop, I push away from him. "I think I'm okay now."

He jerks his thumb over his shoulder. "You want some coffee?"

"Nope. I need to ice my ankle. See you later."

"Why did you ask me about our favorite movie?"

I really should let him know about what Andie said, but I think I'll keep that to myself. "No reason. Just going down memory lane."

His eyes drift to the ground. "I've been doing that a lot lately."

That wasn't what I needed to hear.

His phone rings, and I'm grateful for the interruption. Clint groans as he scans the screen. "I better take this."

I salute him as I hobble back to my car. While I fidget with my seat belt, I watch Clint pace back and forth in front of In a Jam. He runs a hand through his hair, his telltale sign that he's frustrated. He can't be more disgruntled than I am.

It doesn't matter. Within a week, he'll be back to swinging a bat and chasing women, and I'll have fifty thousand dollars and a wedding to plan.

CHAPTER TEN
Clint

My agent won't let me get two words in edgewise as I pace back and forth in front of In a Jam. He rambles on and on about contracts and litigations, but all I hear is the whooshing sound of my career as it speeds past me, leaving me in the dust.

"Phil, I said I have a plan."

He laughs through the phone. "To play some pickle in a festival?"

"I didn't say anything about playing a pickle." *Oh God.* If I have to dress up as a pickle, I'll never live it down. "It's a competition. I'm helping out... a friend. She needs the money, and I need to remember who I am."

After a long, agonizing pause, Phil says, "Parkerson will be making a decision about you by the end of next week. You should come back to Atlanta and work in some soup kitchens or sling a hammer on a Habitat for Humanity house like you suggested."

Gunnar saunters across the street, coming from Big Ash Gym. I should go over there and beat the crap out of a punching bag. "Parkerson wants me here. I need to go." I hang up the phone and switch on the charm.

"Hi, Gunnar."

"Morning. Want to join me for coffee?"

"Sure."

He leads the way inside the shop, and when we enter, the aroma of fresh-baked biscuits wafts around the room. Mrs. Cavanaugh, who's as old as the building, shuffles around behind the counter.

"Morning, Officer," she says, then her eyes land on me, and her smile slides off her face. "Look what the cat dragged in. I heard there was a new tenant in my shop."

I scrunch up my brow. "Your shop?"

Gunnar agrees. "Yeah, Andie sold it to her for a dollar."

"You found a gem in Andie, didn't you?" I ask Gunnar.

Mrs. Cavanaugh huffs as she pours two cups of coffee. "She found him."

As Gunnar sips his coffee, he murmurs, "She's right, as usual."

"Are you happy?" *God, I sound like Marlo, asking about feelings and stuff like that.*

He takes another swig of his black coffee and grins. "Yep. I've changed into a big sap, but I think I like the new me." He waggles his eyebrows. "What about you?"

Loaded question. When I left this town, vowing never to look back, I was happy, or at least I thought I was. The money made me happy. I had a nice apartment, women throwing themselves at me, and a batting average that no one could beat. Then, the worst thing that could happen to a pro player happened to me. I got cocky. I loved the attention, the money, the ability to wake up at noon and party till dawn. But one day, I woke up behind bars, without anybody to bail me out.

"You've heard the saying 'bad press is better than no press'?"

He shrugs.

"It's not true. Nope. Not at all. You know what's worse than that? In sports, someone younger and faster and shinier is always ready to swoop in to take your place."

Mrs. Cavanaugh slides a plate of hot biscuits toward us, and Gunnar and I scarf them down. "Little fish in a big pond, huh?"

With a full mouth, I say, "You can say that again."

Gunnar yanks the last biscuit away from me and pops the entire thing in his mouth. "Is that why you're back here after all this time? I mean, of all people, I get it. Big-city life isn't for everyone."

Mrs. Cavanaugh harrumphs again. I'm not sure what's up with her.

"I liked that lifestyle, maybe a little too much, but I need to clean up my act, and what better way than to come back to the clean-living hometown we all love?" I don't even believe that whopper of a lie.

Mrs. Cavanaugh cackles as she pulls another pan of biscuits out of the oven.

The bell over the door chimes, and in walks Liza Jane. She and her husband, Jake, own the local hardware store and have been together since middle school. Her big grin consumes her face. "I heard the big bad boy of Smithville was back, but I had to see for myself."

She grabs me around the neck, and I swing her in a circle. Her chin-length hair swishes with every turn.

"LJ, how's it going?"

Liza Jane kisses me on the cheek then pulls back to gaze at me. "Aw, he gave me a nickname. What will all those girls in Hot-lanta think? Or better yet, what will one little blonde with a purple stripe in Smithville think?"

Mrs. Cavanaugh refills my coffee cup. "Yeah, how about that little blonde? Something tells me there's more to this story than just you wanting to appear like a squeaky-clean small-town boy, and don't give me that crap about coming home for a contest." She taps her finger to her chin. "Perhaps this has something to do with her engagement."

Liza and Gunnar swing their heads around to focus on me. Heat rises up my neck. If they knew the truth, the three of them would skin me alive.

"Maybe a little."

Liza leans her head to the side. "And why would you care, especially since you were the one who left? You should be happy she hasn't turned everyone in this state against you. She's finally moved on and found someone, and now you show up. That's quite the coincidence, if you ask me."

She's never been one to hold back. Like the time we got caught toilet papering Willow's yard when we were in middle school. We all wanted to scram like cockroaches, but she stood there arguing with the police, saying it was her constitutional right because Willow was a bitch. Good thing the policeman was her uncle twice removed, or we would have all been arrested.

I shrug. "It's complicated."

Mrs. Cavanaugh hands Liza a to-go cup of coffee. "Oh, it's complicated all right. Like this isn't her first rodeo. She's been down the aisle once before, remember?"

My sip of coffee goes down the wrong pipe, and Gunnar pops me on the back. "You need me to get a nurse to resuscitate you?"

After a couple more stifled coughs, I wave him off. "I'm good. Regina hasn't told Ken about our past yet."

Liza rolls her eyes. "He's going to find out if he spends any time in this town."

"Of course she has to tell him, but I have to respect her wishes and let her spill the beans in her own time."

"I'm sorry," Mrs. Cavanaugh butts in. "Did you start respecting her before or after you divorced her so you could screw every girl in the city?"

I grit my teeth. "I did not screw every woman in the city. I left to fulfill my dream, and together, we decided we shouldn't have gotten married." At least that's the lie we concocted so my rising-star status wouldn't be tarnished. I'm sure she regrets being so cordial about the whole thing.

"Oh," Liza says, sipping her coffee.

"Yep. Ancient history. Signed and sealed a long time ago."

With an evil twinkle in her eyes, Liza asks, "So if I go to the courthouse, I can search for the exact date the divorce was final. Is that right?"

Blood drains from my face, and the grip on my coffee cup is so tight I could break it. "Don't do that."

Liza rushes to the door to lock it and pull down the shade. "Hells bells, Clint. I was only kidding." Liza's slack jaw tells me that was a truth bomb she didn't see coming.

Gunnar covers his ears. "I'm going to pretend I didn't hear that."

"Oh, Lord have mercy." Mrs. Cavanaugh walks away, picking up a broom. "You take the cake on stupid acts."

"Guys, I forgot to file. I... got busy and didn't think any more about it until Mitch told me she was getting married."

Liza gasps. "She doesn't know?" She smacks me on the back of my head. "What are you thinking?"

"I tried to tell her."

Gunnar's eyebrows rise, and it's obvious he's not going to come to my rescue.

Liza snorts. "Apparently not hard enough. She's been texting me pictures of wedding dresses. That doesn't sound like a girl who knows she's still married to someone."

"Shh." I glance around, hoping no one else is in the shop. "I'm going to fix this."

"Boy, you sure got yourself in a pickle." Gunnar snorts at his pathetic excuse for a joke.

"Not funny." I run a hand through my hair. "What am I going to do?"

Liza says, "Tell her, you idiot. Unless..."

"What?"

With a broad grin, she replies, "Unless you 'forgot' on purpose."

I blink at her like an idiot. Of course it was an accident. I would never trick her into staying married. I loved her, and it killed me that our short marriage came to an end, even though it was the right thing to do. I did leave her, after all. Life got messy and busy, and it just slipped my mind. *I think.*

"Of course I forgot, and not on purpose—at least I don't think so."

Gunnar and Liza have a private, hushed conversation, and when I clear my throat, they jump. "Oh, sorry. Gunnar was just saying that maybe we could help you... you know, fix this little oops-you've-been-married-for-years-and-didn't-realize-it problem. I could help Regina warm up to you again, or if you want, Gunnar could probably grease some wheels to get you a quickie divorce."

Mrs. Cavanaugh grunts. "I'm not getting involved." She rotates her back to us to start another batch of biscuits.

"Absolutely not."

Gunnar's shoulders slump. "You're no fun."

Liza covers her mouth and speaks to him. "I'll wear him down. Just wait and see."

I stand and slap a ten-dollar bill on the counter. "This has been super fun for me, but I need some peace and quiet before tomorrow, when I start the competition."

Liza claps and bounces up and down. "This is going to be the best week ever. I wish I were a fly on the wall watching all the things you have to do together." She gasps. "I bet the Jacksons will be there at every opportunity."

The Jacksons. Nothing gets past them.

"Great."

Nothing like those two meddling blue hairs to bring down the mood. I'm shocked they haven't already been trailing me around town, or maybe they have, and I haven't noticed. They're stealthier than the paparazzi.

As I climb the stairs to my temporary apartment, I mull over Liza's words. Maybe I did forget on purpose. Perhaps it was a subconscious act. While I wish that were true, the reality of the situation is that I just plain forgot. I got wrapped up in my exciting life, and I didn't think any more about the divorce documents until recently, but that doesn't mean I wasn't thinking of Regina. She never left my mind. She was the first thing I thought about every morning and the last thing on my brain before I went to sleep. No matter if we were married, divorced, or broken up, she was and still is my girl. I couldn't get her out of my head even if I wanted to, and I'll be damned if some successful city slicker is going to take her away from me.

Tomorrow will be the beginning of winning my girl back. I know what I want but have no clue how to do it.

CHAPTER ELEVEN
Regina

Friday got here way too quickly. I was hoping Thursday would linger forever, because I would rather take a rectal temperature than spend any time with Clint. The only thing helping me put one foot in front of the other this morning is chanting "fifty thousand dollars." Dad made it clear he wouldn't be any part of a quick engagement, so I'm on my own. Ken's not helping either. Plus, he's putting pressure on me to have the perfect wedding but not willing to put his hand in his thick wallet to pay for anything. I still don't know why we have to get married so soon or why it has to be so hoity-toity. What he doesn't know is that he's setting me up to be in a foul mood for the next few days during this stupid competition.

And Ken had the nerve to fanboy Clint when they met. That's the last thing I need. When I get the courage to tell him I used to be married to Clint, he's going to choke about that little bromance.

I open the door to In a Jam, and today, the place is hopping. Every booth is full of females, ranging from teenage girls who should be in school to housewives and women older than my grandmother. Andie rushes around the counter. Her ponytail hangs to the side, and a splatter of batter cakes her cheek. She runs through the shop with a coffee pot, refilling each cup. I've never seen it so busy.

Galloping steps come from the upstairs apartment. A hush comes over the room as Clint appears in the café wearing a tight green T-shirt and low-slung jeans. One of the soccer moms sighs so loudly I think Liza Jane all the way down the street in the hardware store heard it. The teens jerk their heads around to stare. They whisper to one another and nod then giggle as the older females fawn over Clint, asking for autographs and selfies. One by one, he poses and smiles with them, and by the big smile on his face, he's eating up all the attention. When he sees me standing there, his eyes light up. Like wading through Jell-O, he walks through the small shop. He jumps when one hand gets too close to his crotch. By the smirk on Sarah Jackson's face, I'm sure she was the culprit.

Ick.

"Regina, I am *so* happy to see you."

I move in a circle, taking in all the females wanting a piece of him. "You should be used to all this attention." I gasp. "OMG. Can I have your autograph?"

He scrunches his brow and mumbles, "Not funny. Can we get out of here?" Clint grabs my arm and ushers me from the shop. Outside, he leans against the wall and groans. "I think I need a shower."

"What can I say? You're a famous, big-shot baseball player. These women would kill to get out of this town and live the high life with you."

After a shiver, he points to his G-Wagon. "Let's go. We have a competition to win."

"Are you serious? We're going two blocks. I think your legs can handle the short walk. This is how we do it in small-town America."

I start walking down the street when one of the soccer moms comes out of the store and starts up a conversation with him.

"Can I get a picture with you?"

Eye roll.

"Maybe later. I have to go. Regina, wait up." He jogs to catch up with me as I make my way toward the courthouse.

"So what do you think we'll have to do to win the money?"

"Not sure." I walk backward while I face him.

"Thanks for doing this. I really need the boost in my reputation."

"What can I say? I'm a sucker for helping a poor soul in need, and as long as I get the money, I'll do my best to make sure we win." We high-five as I add, "We're going to kick it. Just try to keep your adoring fans away."

"Got it."

"And no pictures of me with you better show up on social media."

With a thin-lipped smile, he replies, "Yes, ma'am."

I open the door to the courthouse, and all eyes stare at us. Mrs. Finklestein, the head of the Pickle Festival, grins as if she's won the lottery. "Well, Lord have mercy. I heard we were going to have a celebrity joining us this week. The most famous Pickle King ever, Mister Clint Sorrow of the Marietta Wildcats."

Every female in the building gushes over him, and I can't keep the groan inside anymore. Clint throws them a bashful wave as he grabs my hand and pulls me down to sit on the back row.

Mrs. Finklestein claps her hands. "Great. We can get started now. Five couples have registered for the competition. Here are the rules. For three days, you will receive a list of items to take photos of in a digital scavenger hunt. The hunt days consist of today, Monday, and Tuesday. I've given you the weekend off. The team with the most points at the end of the three days wins the prize of fifty thousand dollars and gets to choose a small business that will receive the same amount for renovations. On Monday, you will report at eight o'clock sharp to turn in your Friday entries. Every minute you're late, we will deduct ten points from your daily total. Friday's pictures are to be taken on Friday only. We'll know if you cheat. We have eyes everywhere."

Groans erupt throughout the room.

"You'll get your next list on Monday morning and hand in your results Tuesday. Then Tuesday's list will be submitted on Wednesday.

The results will be tabulated and the winners announced the following Saturday at the Pickle Festival."

The door bursts open, and a haggard-appearing Andie stumbles in. "Am I late?"

Mrs. Finklestein welcomes her with open arms. "Not at all. Everyone, if you haven't met Andie Carson, she's the reason we're able to do such an interesting contest."

Andie passes out a sheet of paper to each of the five couples. "Here is day one's list. Each item is worth twenty-five points. Unless otherwise stated, both of you have to be in each photo to get credit. Every list has some items that are the same but a little bit different, all challenging and worth the same amount of points."

Before I realize what's happening, all the people in the other four groups surround Clint and start taking photos. I stare at my sheet, and the first item on our list is to take a picture with a celebrity. *Ugh.* I pull out my phone and take a selfie with Clint in the background smiling for the other cameras. I guess we can all check that one off our list.

"Y'all will notice the football game tonight is on all the lists. Each couple gets double the points if they dress in clothes that were popular the year they won the crown."

Leo and Becca high-five. Their list is the easiest since they were king and queen just last year.

Carmen sneers at Nate. "What are we going to do? Ours is nineteen ninety-seven. So boring. The Taylors have the eighties, and the Lanes have it even easier with the seventies."

Nate covers his mouth and whispers to his partner. Carmen's eyes grow wide. "Yes. Perfect."

"Okay, y'all. Head out. Bring your phones and your checklists back tomorrow. And remember, every minute you're late, you lose ten points. Scoot."

The couples scramble out of the courthouse, and Clint takes my hand in his. "We should have driven my G-Wagon to get a jump on them."

"Nonsense. We're right next to the park." I scan the paper and see four items we can get in one place. "Follow me."

We rush toward the entrance of the courthouse to run down to the park. I point to the parking lot and say, "This time of day, it's empty."

Clint grabs me and takes a selfie of us with the vacant lot.

"Take one more of just us."

He snaps two more. "What was that for?"

I smirk. "A picture with a wild animal."

He seems confused, then he grins and points to himself. "Ah. I'm a wildcat."

"Yep. How good are you at jumping off the swings?" I motion with my head to the playground equipment that's begging to be used.

"The best."

He jumps on one of the swings and pumps to get going. He flies off the swing and into the sand pit. "Did you get it?"

"Sorry. All I got was your hand. Do it again."

He stands and dusts himself off. While he pumps his legs again, he says, "Don't blink. One, two, three."

Clint flies toward me, and on purpose, I watch him face-plant into the sand pit again. "Oops. Didn't get it."

He stares up from the ground. "You did that on purpose, didn't you?"

"Maybe. I used to love to watch you slide into second base. You've definitely perfected your technique."

He towers over me and shakes the sand out of his hair. "Last chance, Regina."

Trying to stifle a giggle, I say, "Okay, I promise to get it this time."

While he gets on the squeaky swing, the Taylors show up. Clint flies through the air, and I capture him midair. "Got it."

I point to the monkey bars. "Let's do it."

"Your turn this time."

Reading the list, I say, "I think we have to do this one together."

Clint starts on one side, and I begin the climb on the other. When we get to the middle, he says with the expression of a ten-year-old, "I can hang longer than you can."

I wiggle through the bars, holding my phone in my mouth. When I hang upside down, he mimics me. I take the phone out of my mouth and hold it between us. "Say cheese."

"Cheeseburger!"

"Got it."

He swings his legs through his arms and jumps off the monkey bars then holds his hands out for me. "I'll catch you."

He takes my flailing hands, and when his big arms have a good hold on me, I slide my legs off the bars, landing in his grip, nose to nose.

I say, "Thanks."

Right before he lets me go, he rubs his nose against mine, giving me an Eskimo kiss, like when we were little. I wriggle free and pull the sheet out of my pocket.

With him hovering over my shoulder, he asks, "What should we do next?"

I scan our items. "We could go to a store and pose with a mannequin. Ooh. Andie has a convertible. Let's go back to the shop."

I take off running, but his long legs catch up to me in five seconds flat.

"Told ya we should have driven today."

"Oh, hush. You need the exercise." From my phone, I pull up the picture of us hanging upside down on the monkey bars. His shirt came untucked, and part of his abdomen was exposed. "It seems like you got a little spare tire starting."

He snatches my phone from me and stops running to examine the picture. "I do not. I completely see part of my amazing six-pack peeking through."

I roll my eyes and grab for my phone. "You are so full of yourself."

Clint chuckles. "You love it. Admit it."

"In your dreams."

He stares off and takes a deep sigh. "Every night."

That sounded better in my brain than it did coming out of my mouth. The next few days are going to be excruciating. Thank goodness the hospital was nice enough to let me off to participate. Ken's supposed to come back into town tonight. Even though he's not into football, I should invite him to the game. He'll be a good buffer between me and Clint. If nothing else, it will tamp down that fluttery feeling in my stomach.

This is going to get awkward real fast.

CHAPTER TWELVE

Clint

The list reads like a fifth-grade birthday party game. I feel like an idiot as Regina stuffs four pickles in my mouth while sitting on the curb next to the Piggly Wiggly. The briny drool seeps out of the corner of my mouth as she tries to stuff pickles into hers. She leans over as she giggles, snorting juice all over the place. If I didn't know better, I would think she's kind of enjoying herself.

In a garbled voice, she says, "You look so funny."

A drop of pickle juice tickles my throat.

Her eyes get really big. "Don't you cough. I'm not done." She shoves one more pickle in her mouth, making her appear like she has a wide clown face, then ties my hands behind my back.

"Hurry." I hope she understood me.

Regina pulls out her phone and snaps three photos. The pickles in her mouth drop to the ground, but mine are wedged. I whine to draw attention to my face.

She holds a hand to her ear. "Sorry. I can't hear you."

My eyes bug out in an attempt to beg her to help me.

"Oh, all right." With one hand on my scruffy chin, she pries open my mouth to retract a pickle. Once one is gone, the others fall out. "I'm a nurse, not a dental assistant."

"Thanks. Now the hands?"

As she unties me, she says, "If your adoring fans could see you now."

I wipe the pickle juice off my chin with the hem of my T-shirt. "I think if I never eat another pickle in my life, it will be too soon."

"Shh. You're a Pickle King. You're supposed to love pickles."

"Naw. Just the queen."

Her smile fades as she wipes her mouth with the back of her hand. She pulls out the crumpled-up scavenger hunt list and clears her throat. "Okay, that one is checked off for today. I'm glad I got off work. Otherwise, we'd never get this stuff done."

"What's next?" I'm hoping she'll say mud wrestling, but I shouldn't hold my breath.

"The football game is tonight, but I'm supposed to have dinner with Ken and my parents too."

I clench my fists to keep the emotion from showing on my face. "Can't you do both? Eat, then while they talk wedding stuff, you can haul butt to the game?"

Regina lists her head. "Maybe I want to talk wedding stuff. I didn't have that..." She peers around as if to see who could be listening. "Last time."

I bow my head and hide the feelings I'm sure are etched across my face. "Yeah. You deserve better this go-round. I'm sure it will be perfect."

When Regina gives me a shy grin, I'm so green with jealousy about how some rich turd has her now.

I point to the list. "Let's see if Andie will let us use her convertible for a picture. Besides, I'm getting hungry for something other than pickles."

"You mean you're not up for getting your picture taken reading on a park bench in your underwear?"

Adorable. "Maybe after lunch."

She picks the pickles up off the ground and tosses them, along with the jar, into the dumpster. "As odd as it sounds after having my face stuffed with pickles, I'm a little hungry too."

"Now, about the underwear shot. We'd have to do it together." I could kiss Andie for putting that on our list.

Her face falls. "I didn't think of that."

"We have to do it. If the Lanes or the Taylors have that on their list, I'm sure they would never do it. It's a way to get ahead in the game."

She taps her finger on her chin. "You do have a point." She stands, wipes her hands on the back of her shorts, and takes off toward Main Street. "But I don't think you could handle all this," she says, popping her booty.

You got that right.

Regina waves an arm over her body, and my eyes follow. "I may not be a teenager anymore, but some things get better with age."

Yes, they do.

Thoughts of Regina in her underwear fog my brain, and my foot catches on the curb, sending me sailing across the concrete. I hit the ground with a thud and roll over, protecting my throwing arm.

She does an about-face and runs back to my crumpled body. "Oh my goodness. Are you okay?"

Regina kneels next to me as I lie on my back, legs spread out, staring up at the sun.

"If I can't play ball again, I'm going to blame it on the vision of you in your underwear."

She groans. "Are you still fifteen?" She holds out a hand for me to take. "You've probably seen so many females in their underwear—and less—I will seem like nothing more than a hick in a hideous bathing suit."

Regina pulls me up to a sitting position, and I squint to see her without the sun burning my eyes. I roll my shoulder to make sure I didn't break anything. All I need is to give my owner another excuse to bail on me. He would never believe it was because I tripped over the curb thinking about a gorgeous girl. "Regina, you're so wrong about one thing. I'm sure you'll be a hick in a *beautiful* bathing suit."

She pummels me with baby punches as I fall onto my back. I cover my face with my hands to protect myself.

"You're going to get it, mister."

"I'm kidding."

A police siren *whoops*, and both of us freeze.

Over the bullhorn, someone says, "No parking without a car."

Gunnar.

Regina springs off me like her clothes are on fire. "Gunnar, you scared the crap out of me."

Gunnar exits the police car with the cheesiest grin on his face. "You might want to take this display of affection inside before the local grapevine sees you."

She plants her hands on her hips. "He fell, and I was trying to help him up, but he was teasing me as usual, so he was getting a whooping from me."

Gunnar lowers his sunglasses so I can see his eyes. "Do I need to arrest her for domestic violence?"

Regina gasps. "You wouldn't."

I hold my hand out for her to help me stand. She tugs me upright then snatches her hand away from me.

Gunnar quirks an eyebrow. "I'll tell you what. I don't think there are many items on the list that pertain to the inside of a jail cell, so I'll let this little incident slide... this time."

Using her painted-on Pickle Queen smile, she says, "Well, aren't you the gentleman?"

Gunnar snickers as he adjusts his sunglasses. "You two have fun. Word on the street is the Taylors have already marked everything off their list for today except for the football game."

"We get double points for—"

Regina throws up a hand. "Yeah, yeah. I know. I'll see if I still have my Juicy Couture tracksuit, the one with 'Juicy' written on the butt."

My mouth waters just thinking of her baby-pink velour warm-up suit she used to have. The pants were super low cut, and the jacket was snug. They showed off her tight little booty mighty fine. I only hope she still has it.

Regina motions to me. "Come on. We're burning daylight, and I'm hungry."

Gunnar steps out of the way. "Don't mess with Regina when her blood sugar begins to drop. You've never seen anyone get so hangry as her."

She grabs my arm and drags me down the street. "Don't listen to him. He gets to ride around in a car all day. I have to work on my feet for twelve hours straight. It's a miracle if I get to go to the bathroom, let alone eat."

I nod. "Yeah, my—"

Regina rolls her eyes. "What? Your... job? You throw a baseball around for a living, a very good, insane living. Our *careers* are not even in the same ballpark, pun intended."

"You want to switch places?"

She snorts. "Oh, please. The first time Mr. Farnsworth peed on you, you would hightail it out of there."

I cringe, hoping I am able to get that visual out of my mind within the next thirty years. "Why do you do it?"

Regina crosses her arms over her stomach as she walks. She's silent for a while, then she lets out a sigh. "I love helping people, and I feel like I'm making a difference in my community."

"But will Ken like it here?"

She shrugs. "I'm not sure. We haven't talked about where we're going to live."

I stop her from walking. "You're supposed to be getting married soon, and you don't even know if he's moving here or you're moving there?"

She cringes. "I'm not moving to Atlanta. I couldn't handle the crowds."

"What about kids?"

Regina blinks. "What about them?"

"Are you two on the same page about that?"

She shakes her head and laughs. "It's really not your concern."

As she takes off toward In a Jam, I hustle to catch up. "It's not my concern, but—what about religion or how you stand on the environment or money management?"

Regina covers her ears with her hands. "I don't want to discuss this with you. None of it is your business."

Pulling one hand away from her face, I ask in a calm tone that even surprises me, "Have you discussed it with him?"

Her face changes to a bright red, and she chews on her bottom lip. "Let's just get something to eat so we can focus on the rest of the list. You stay out of my messed-up life, and I won't ask about yours."

Without thinking about it, I rub my hand down her arm, and she shivers. "I'm sorry. I didn't mean to upset you. This is supposed to be fun. No more deep conversations. I promise. You're a grown woman, and he's lucky to have found you." All that pickle juice is about to spew from my stomach.

She gulps as she takes a step backward, breaking contact. "Let's go. Remember, I get hangry."

"Can't have that, now, can we?"

"If you want to survive this contest with your balls intact, you'll always keep me well fed."

"Yes, ma'am." I would really like to keep the family jewels where they are. I might need them later on.

As we walk down Main Street toward In a Jam, a thousand memories flash through my brain. Countless times we strolled down this street arm in arm. The thought of her doing that very thing with someone else nauseates me, but I deserve it. If she only knew that she's not completely severed from me, she would make good on that ball-extraction procedure.

CHAPTER THIRTEEN

Regina

After convincing Clint to stop at the China Town restaurant for some takeout, we sit in his G-Wagon and scarf the food down. I'm surprised he lets anyone eat in this fancy monster of a vehicle. I incline the seat a little and prop my feet on the dash as I inhale my kung pao chicken. Clint slurps his lo mein, and it's cute watching him chase the noodles into his mouth.

"Can I ask you a question?" I ask, breaking the silence.

"Sure," he says, swirling more noodles onto his fork.

"Why do you have such a huge vehicle? I bet this thing gets ten gallons to the mile."

He rolls his eyes at my joke. "Ha. Close." He shrugs as he stares out the side window, watching Jacob French sputter down the street in his beat-up ol' truck. "I guess I never had anything nice growing up. You know better than anyone how bad it was."

"Yeah." If it weren't for my mother, the Sorrow boys probably would have starved to death. It was my mother's mission in life to make sure they had at least one warm meal every day. Even if my father tried to remain anonymous, I know he was behind all the extra cash that mysteriously showed up in their bank account. I guess that's what comes with having a pastor for a father. He really does practice what he preaches, most of the time.

"But you and your brothers have done pretty well for yourselves, don't you think?"

He agrees. "I should have done better when I had—I mean when I got all the money. I spent a lot of it on stupid stuff."

"Like a G-Wagon that probably cost more than my annual salary?"

Clint grins. "Probably double. But you have to admit, it is a sick ride."

"I bet it's a lot of fun to drive it." *Hint, hint.*

"Nope. Not happening."

I roll my eyes. "Buzzkill." I lean my head back on the headrest and soak in the leather aroma. "It even smells expensive."

"Maybe your man will buy you one."

My who? Oh... "He has expensive taste, too, but he's also very practical. He's offered to buy me a Chrysler Town and Country."

Clint chokes on his noodles.

I pat him on the back and say, "Good thing you have a nurse nearby, huh?"

He clears his throat and squeezes his eyes shut before he shakes his head. When he glances back at me, he asks, "A minivan?"

"Can you see me driving a mom van? I don't want a mom car even when I'm a mom."

I wish I hadn't said that. He might start in again about the kid situation. I honestly don't know what Ken wants. We never talk about stuff like that. I didn't even think we were at the engagement phase yet, but I wasn't about to let a successful man pass me by just so I could have fun playing the field. At some point, I need to settle down, so now is as good a time as any.

Clint rubs his tummy. "This is so good. If I eat one more bite, I may pop."

"Worth it though, right?" I wink at him.

He lets out a yawn. "Yeah, but now I want a nap."

"Oh no you don't. We have to get some more photos, or we're going to be in last place." I open the door and jump out. "Come on, Wildcat. Let's go."

"Pushy, pushy," he mumbles.

"I heard that." I rush into In a Jam and run up to the counter, where Mrs. Cavanaugh is busy making scones while Andie washes a pan in the sink.

Andie glances up and asks, "Where's the fire?"

"Andie, I need to—"

She groans. "I know. The car's in the alley behind the shop."

"Yes." I grab Clint's hand, and we scurry around to the back.

He whistles when he sees her sports car. "I've been drooling over that slick ride ever since I first saw it. I'd rather have that any day of the week."

"I know, but for now, we only get to sit in it. Maybe you can buy me one someday." I gasp. "I mean, you can buy *you* one someday." Heat rushes up my neck as I slink down into the buttery-soft leather driver's seat.

Clint pulls the passenger seat all the way back and folds his long legs into the small space. "I take it back. I am never buying one. In fact, I may never be able to extricate myself from this one."

"Big word for a baseball player."

He clutches his chest with his hands. "Harsh, Regina. Just take the picture so we can go scare some shoppers at Belk."

I pull out my phone as he leans in close, our heads almost touching, and I take the photo. When I show it to him, he nods in approval.

"Let's go."

For me, it's an easy slide, but I have to hold both of his hands to help him squeeze his big body out of the car. His foot splashes into a puddle.

"Hey," he says, pointing at the water. "Our reflection in something other than a mirror."

"Good job, Sorrow."

I stand in front of him as I take the photo of the puddle. It's blurry, but it's easy to distinguish our faces. I show it to him, and he gives me a thumbs-up.

"What do you want to do next? The underwear photo or...?" He points to a road sign. "I think I've found our next item."

I scan the list and giggle. "Oh yeah. Funniest road sign."

He rushes across the street and stands next to the No Shoulder Riding Allowed sign. "Climb up on my shoulders."

Clint leans down, and I jump on his back. With his hands on my butt, I shimmy my way until I have a leg on each side of his head. He holds my knees close to his ears with one hand, and I give him my phone.

"Don't drop the phone, or me, please."

"Have a little faith."

I hold my hands out, and he snaps the photo. "Definitely a keeper."

Like when I was a cheerleader, I place my hands in his and bounce until I fly over his head and land on my feet like a cat.

"Oh, she sticks the landing."

"Ta-da. Now, let's go scare some shoppers." I'm actually shocked I didn't face-plant onto the pavement. It's been a while since I tried a stunt like that, but Clint has brought out my playful side. I forgot where I hid it.

He hands my phone back, and I scan through the photos from the day. Any stranger checking them out would think we were a happy couple. The silly faces, the arms wrapped around each other, it's all starting to get to me. All those old feelings are starting to flood my heart again, and I'm not sure how I feel about it. I'm supposed to be angry at Clint, but every moment I hang out with him, doing silly small-town activities, reminds me of why I fell for him when we were younger. I'm starting to think this contest isn't such a good idea after all.

"What if we drop out of the contest?" I ask. I know I need the money, but all this closeness to Clint may not be worth it.

Clint stops and stares at me like I have a cyclops eye on my forehead. "Why?"

I shrug. "I don't know. I'm sure you have better things to do with yourself, and... I don't know."

"Is spending time with me giving you indigestion?"

It's hard not to smile, considering I've caught him scarfing down antacids like they're Skittles on more than one occasion. Even after only a few hours with him, it feels comfortable to be around him again. And I hate him for that.

"It dredges up a whole bunch of feelings I'd buried."

"Good or bad?" He crosses his fingers like a teenager. "Please say good."

I bump him with my shoulder. "Both. But my father taught me to forgive and forget. It's the forgetting that's so hard."

"I know. I feel the same way about my mother leaving us."

Sliding my arm through his, I lean my head on his shoulder. "I can't pretend to know what that felt like."

"But you were there through it all. Then, later on, I did the exact same thing to you."

I bite the inside of my lip to keep from crying. In all this time, I never put those two acts together like that, but his leaving me was so much like his mother leaving him. Except I had to listen to every single male in town talk about how stoked they were for Clint, how he made Smithville so proud. I had to pretend *I* divorced *him* because that's what I promised I would do. *Ugh.*

"It's in the past. We're adults now. Let's move forward."

Barely above a whisper, he says, "Yeah. Regina, I really need to do this contest. If I can't change my image, I don't know what I'll do. It's all I know."

Gah. The way his voice cracks just about does me in. I can't let him down. No matter how much he hurt me, I can't purposely walk away at this point.

"Race you to Belk," I say as I take off without waiting for his answer. I know with his long legs, he'll catch up to me in three seconds flat, but the head start doesn't hurt.

"I'm coming to get you."

I squeal as his big arms pick me up right as we get to the Belk parking lot. He dumps me into a shopping cart and pushes me to the front door, my feet dangling over the side.

"Isn't this another item on the list?" he asks.

"Yep, but you have to get in here too."

He mulls over the problem then smiles. "I got this." He jumps up and pushes his butt into the child seat, his legs dangling off the ground. "Hurry, take the picture before I turn us over."

After I click the photo, he launches out of the seat, landing with his feet on the ground. And with the swiftness of a professional baseball player, he scoops me up and plants my feet on the ground right next to his. "One more down."

He has to stop touching me. I'm starting to like it.

"I have an idea for the next pic, if you're game." His eyes twinkle, and that scares the crap out of me.

"Will it get me one step closer to fifty thousand dollars and be good for your image?"

"Yes, ma'am."

"Lead the way, Mr. Baseball."

I have a bad feeling about this.

CHAPTER FOURTEEN

Clint

The teenage worker's jaw drops to the floor when she sees us scurrying into Belk.

With my winning smile, I say, "Excuse me..." I notice her name tag. "Trinity. We're doing this photo scavenger hunt, and we need to—"

"Of course," she squeals. "This has been happening all day. I never dreamed you, of all people, would be part of this. How exciting. Can I take a picture? My brother will be jealous squared."

I mouth to Regina, "Help me."

She throws up her hands as if to say I am on my own.

"Here is the window display. It's a back-to-school scene." She pushes the curtain aside so we can see the setup. It seems pretty simple—two mannequins in school attire holding books and a backpack. It seems okay to me, but it's not quite what I have in mind.

"Trinity, here's the deal. We're trying to check off two items with one photo." I steal a glance toward Regina, and she scowls. "We'd like to change this display to be an underwear scene."

Trinity quivers as she scans my body, and I feel a bit creeped out by the attention from someone so young. I never mind signing autographs for fans, but I always get a little skeeved out when they touch me and especially when they get handsy. On the outside, I'm all smiles, but on the inside, my stomach goes in knots.

Regina cackles. "Are you kidding me?"

"What? It's on the list. We get points for the pose, and we get points for reading in public in our underwear." I point to the display. "Trinity, would you consider this public?"

She nods so much I think she's going to give herself a concussion. "Uh-huh. We have some very nice underwear you can model." Trinity fans her face. "Can I take the pictures?"

"I'm not doing this." Regina crosses her arms over her chest and wags her head. "No way."

I take Regina by the hand and lead her away from Trinity so we can talk in private. "Regina, it won't take more than a few seconds. Come on. Live a little."

"This is all great for you. You have this hot body and are used to being seen on camera in the locker room with nothing on. I saw you on ESPN being interviewed wearing nothing but a towel." She clasps a hand over her mouth. "Did I just say that out loud?"

Busted.

"I didn't hear anything. Come on, please." I lead her to the women's section and whisper in her ear, "It was Sports South, but that's not important."

She grits her teeth as I pick out a sexy set of bra and panties.

"This will look amazing on your hot little body."

She swats at my arm. "I can't believe I'm going to do this."

Trinity pushes a fuming Regina toward a dressing room, and while groans and curses that would make a sailor blush come from the stall, I mosey over to the men's section with Trinity right on my heels.

"This would be fantastic on you. It's our best seller."

She hands me a ball-crushing pair of Calvin Klein micro bikini briefs. *Not happening.* "I'm sure they are, but I'm a boxer kind of guy." I pick up a pair of plain plaid boxers and a white tank top and head to the dressing room with Trinity on my heels.

"If you need anything, please don't hesitate to call for me."

"Thanks, but I think I can manage."

Across the store, I hear Regina's voice. "I cannot believe I'm doing this."

I chuckle as I peel out of my clothes and put on my very conservative underwear for the photo. When I step out of the dressing room, Trinity whimpers a bit. Regina plants her hands on her slim, uncovered hips, making my mouth water. *Holy foul balls.* She's still as curvy and gorgeous as ever, maybe even more so.

She gapes down at her exposed body. "I have to wear this—this—barely there piece of thread, while you get to wear nothing less than a pair of shorts and a tank top? Not fair." She stomps her foot like a petulant child, and it's adorable.

With one hand, I grab her arm, and with the other, I pick up a sale catalog and head to the window. "You can do it. Trinity, will you take our picture?"

Trinity's face is going to break from the wide grin. I grab a chair from the display and sit on it. "Regina, plant yourself on my lap, and we'll read the sales catalog."

Regina shakes her head with massive force. "I'm not sitting on your... lap, wearing nothing but this."

In a stage whisper, I say, "You've done worse, so come on. The longer you wait, the colder I get and the more shrink—never mind. Sit."

"Ugh. You're impossible."

She slams her butt onto my lap, and the contact of her warm body is something I didn't quite think through. Having her creamy, soft skin on my lap wakes up a dormant part of me. *This can't be happening. Bad idea, bad idea.* My body starts to react to the feel of her on my lap, and it doesn't go unnoticed.

"Oh my Lord, Clint. Really?"

"It has a mind of its own."

"Let's just get this over with."

I wrap my arms around her and hold up the catalog to pretend we're reading. A knock on the glass jolts me back to reality. Ten people, including the Jackson sisters, sit and stare at our little scene.

Under her breath, Regina whispers, "You're going to pay for this."

"Trinity, take the picture, please."

"I don't know how to use your phone."

Regina groans. "Oh, for crying out loud. You're a teenager. Can't you figure it out?"

"Got it. Smile."

We smile for her, and a round of applause erupts outside the window. Regina stands up and covers her breasts with her arms. "Are we done now?"

My smile fades as I stare out over the growing crowd. "Uh, yeah, but..." I point out the window.

When Regina sees her fiancé standing there, arms crossed, scowl on his plastic face, she screams and runs back to the dressing room. I wave to everyone at the window with one hand and cover my junk with the other while I race-walk back to my changing room and quickly get back into my regular clothes.

As soon as I'm decent, I go back into the store to find Trinity talking to Ken, who paces back and forth in front of the ladies' changing section. His jaw clenches, and I can only imagine what's going on in his perfectly coiffed head right now.

"Regina, you have to face me eventually."

"No, I don't!" she yells from the dressing room.

Would it be bad of me to laugh?

He checks his watch then steels his gaze at me. "Come on. Let's talk."

She tiptoes out of the changing area, fully dressed, face as red as the bra she was wearing. "Hi there."

Ken groans. "What were you thinking?"

Regina slams the undergarments on the counter and huffs. "I was thinking this would be a good way to get fifty thousand dollars for our wedding. Do you have a problem with that?"

Ooh, burn.

Ken rakes a hand through his hair then checks his watch. "It makes no sense, but whatever. Are we still meeting your parents for tonight?"

"Yes. Absolutely. Don't tell them about this, okay?"

Ken stares a hole through me. "It's the last thing we need right now."

I pull out my phone and check my Twitter account, trying to act nonchalant. I lost another hundred followers today. "The Jacksons were out there, so I'm sure it'll be on the blog before sunset."

"Ken, this was all his idea."

Way to throw me under the bus. "She agreed to it."

Her snake eyes burn into my soul.

"Shut up," they both say.

I check my watch and let out a sigh. "Maybe it's time for a break. I'll see you later."

As I head toward the door, I overhear Ken ask Regina, "Is something going on between you two?"

"No!" Regina yells, and I scamper out of the store before she throws the bra and panties at me.

I take my sweet time walking back to In a Jam. I can't remember the last time I lollygagged down the street, and God, I miss doing it. I relive the day's events. I haven't had this much fun in years, probably since the last time I hung out with that cute spitfire. Even doing this silly contest is tolerable with her by my side. I miss her so much it hurts. My phone chimes, and I see Regina's message with the photos from today. I especially love the devil emoji she included. It's a nice touch since it captures her current mood perfectly.

Andie greets me at the counter with a large glass of sweet tea. "How's it going?"

I throw my head back and let out a laugh. "We were doing great until we tried to combine two items on the list into one photo, and... let's just say, Regina's fiancé caught her sitting on my lap... and we were wearing only underwear."

Andie plops her head on the counter and howls with laughter. "No way. Oh my goodness. I wish I'd seen that."

"You probably will soon enough, since the Jackson sisters saw the whole thing."

I show her the pictures Regina sent me, and she giggles some more.

As she examines the photos, she scowls. "Uh, I hate to tell you this, but you don't get credit for the underwear part."

My heart beats out of my chest. Regina's going to have my hide. "What do you mean?"

"The item states 'sitting in your underwear reading a book.'" She points to the picture. "That's a catalog, not a book."

"It's got words, and it's paper."

Andie grimaces. "Sorry, bud."

My heart sinks into my shoes. When Regina finds out, she's going to skin me alive. "I think I'm going to throw up."

She hands me back my phone and asks, "So was it worth it? I mean, having her sit on your lap... practically naked."

It was fantastic. If we weren't in a storefront window, I would have snaked my hands around her waist and reminded myself of what I've been missing.

Andie clears her throat. "You're smiling."

I jerk my thumb toward the stairs leading to my apartment. "I better get ready for the football game tonight."

She giggles. "Have fun."

"Just don't tell Regina about the disqualified picture. I'd like to keep the peace for a few more hours."

Andie gives me a thumbs-up. "You got it. I'll see you at the game. I hear high school football is a big deal down here. I'm actually looking forward to it."

So am I but not because of football. I slump down on the couch and post a few benign pictures to my social media pages with the caption, "Enjoying downtime in my hometown. #memorylane."

A warm smile consumes my face as I examine all the photos Regina sent me. Money can't buy this kind of simple happiness, and I'm wondering if begging for my position is even worth it. If I leave baseball now, it will be on my terms and not from being removed from the team.

There's got to be something I can do here, and if not here, maybe in another small town nearby. I know I wanted to run and never look back, but I think small-town living is in my blood. No matter how hard I try to escape it, I will always end up right back here.

CHAPTER FIFTEEN

Regina

My grasp on Ken's hand is going to leave his fingers mangled. It's a good thing he's holding his peace offering in the other hand, or it would be a mangled mess by now. This time has to be better, or I don't know what we'll do. When I open the front door, Dad peers up from his laptop then gives his head a slow wag.

Crap.

He closes his laptop and lets out a deep sigh only a disapproving parent can pull off.

"Hi, Daddy." I hope my sugary-sweet voice will melt his frustration with me.

"Hey there, sweetie." He stares at Ken, sticks out a hand, and says, "Hello, Ken."

Ken's Adam's apple bobs up and down. He's supposed to be this big-shot executive, but around my father, he reverts into a fifteen-year-old, acting like he got caught kissing in the back seat. "Good evening, sir." He holds out a pie and adds, "I wasn't sure if you were the drinking kind, so I decided to forgo wine and bring a pie instead." He glances over at me. "Everyone likes pie, right?"

I give his hand a squeeze for encouragement. "That's very sweet of you. Daddy, don't you think it's sweet?"

Dad takes the pie. "Thank you. We'll put this pecan pie right next to the one my wife made."

Ken's shoulders slump. Poor guy. He really did try to win over my father's approval. "I love pecan pie, and it's been a long time since I've had it. I'm sure I can eat one of those pies all by myself."

Stop rambling.

Mom enters the room. "You're here." She gives me a hug and kiss, then she paints on a smile for Ken. After a lighthearted hug, she says, "We're so glad the two of you are here tonight. I made fried chicken." She sees the pie Ken brought and says, "Oh, how nice. You shouldn't have. It smells yummy."

Still holding on to Ken's hand, I drag him to the dining room table and plant him in the seat that Robert usually uses. "You sit here, and I'll help Mom set the table."

Poor Ken is like a bump on a log sitting there all by himself.

After a very audible groan, Dad sits in his usual seat at the head of the table and clears his throat. "So let's start over. I apologize if I haven't been hospitable toward you. As you can see, I'm a bit overprotective of my daughter."

For the first time, Ken sits taller in his seat, and a smile comes over his face. "I completely understand. I'm a stranger who waltzed into your home, wanting to marry your daughter. It's a lot to process at once."

As I walk around the table, placing silverware at each setting, Dad continues. "I don't doubt your feelings for Regina. It's not you. It's..." He glances up at me, pinning me in my place. "I don't know. I can't put my finger on it. Perhaps, if things weren't so rushed, I could be assured the inkling is just my imagination."

Ken bows his head. "I agree."

The forks I'm holding slip from my hand and clang to the floor. Mom comes to my rescue. "Are you all right?"

Tears prickle my eyes. After all this time, someone kind and successful has taken an interest in me, and now, with one single statement from my father, Ken wants to back off. While I agree, planning a wedding in a month will be difficult, I'm up for the challenge, especially if I win all that money.

"Ken, I thought you wanted to do this before the busy Christmas season started up."

"I do, but I've had some time to think, and I am being selfish. We can get married whenever."

Mom clasps her hands together. "This is great news. Isn't it, Roger?"

"How about in the spring?" Ken asks my father. "It will give Regina time for the purple hair to grow out."

What the heck?

"Spring sounds perfect," my mother says.

The room shrinks, and I want to scream for everyone to stop talking like I'm not even around. "I, uh..."

Dad glances over the food Mom prepared and clears his throat. "The food smells tasty. Let's eat."

After Dad says grace, we dig in. I can't get enough of my mother's fried chicken, but Ken pulls the skin off and dabs the meat with a paper napkin before each bite.

"It's good, isn't it?" I ask.

He smiles. "It's an acquired taste."

Everyone in the room gasps. Saying something like that about a Southern woman's cooking is like telling her one of her kids is ugly.

"Ken, apologize to my mother. She spent a lot of time preparing this meal for us." I add in a hushed tone, "And she's the one who likes you."

"I didn't mean it in a bad way. I'm just not used to greasy food."

Oh dear. This is not good. Even Clint knew how to get on my parents' good side. It blows my mind that Ken's fine education didn't include old-fashioned manners.

My father puts his napkin down and clears his throat. "Regina, can I see you in the kitchen for a moment?"

"Sure." I stand to leave and pat Ken on the shoulder.

Dad paces back and forth in the kitchen as I close the door for some privacy. "Dad, I'm sorry about that. It was rude, and I'll speak to Ken about his tone. He's not used to our ways."

"What do you see in him? Be honest."

I blow out a breath and try to find the right words because, after all these years, I still can't lie to my father. If he asks me a question, I answer it truthfully. That's why I stay away from him, because the truth scares the crap out of me most of the time. "He's nice to me, and... he can take care of me."

"Honey, you can take care of yourself. I hardly know him, so my opinion is obviously simplistic, but... it's a mismatched pairing, if you ask me."

I snap my head to attention. His words sting, and tears well up in my eyes. "Are you saying I'm not good enough for him?"

Daddy wraps his arms around me, and my breath hitches.

"Of course not. If anything, it's the other way around. No matter how much money he has and how financially stable you would be, I don't see a spark."

With my face buried in my father's shirt, I let out a chuckle. "Whatever, Dad." I push away from him and bounce up until I'm sitting on the counter. It was always my favorite place to be when my mother putzed around the kitchen. We solved all the world's problems while she clanged bowls and I swung my legs like a little girl at a playground.

"I'm serious. I know Clint hurt you..."

My jaw clenches.

"But, sweetie, you don't look at Ken like you did at Clint."

"And what is the *look*?"

He pats my cheek. "Like you breathe the same air."

"Pfft. Maybe so, but all that got me was a divorce before my first anniversary and a whole lot of regret."

"Does Ken know about Clint?"

I peer over at the kitchen door to make sure it's closed before I say, "All he knows is that Clint was the Pickle King."

Dad stares at the ceiling. "Honey, lying is not a good way to start a relationship."

In a sharp shrill, I reply, "I'm not lying. I'm just not being completely truthful yet, but I will. I'll tell him everything real soon." I grip the counter for support and swallow hard. "Besides, I'm grown up now and know all that stuff about breathing the same air is only a fairy tale."

He groans as he rolls up his sleeves. He begins to wash dishes as he asks, "What does Song of Solomon say about love?"

Ugh. He always pulls out the scriptures when it's convenient to make his point. "'I have found the one for whom my soul loves.'"

"Yep. It's some racy stuff in there. You should read it again sometime. What do you think it's saying to us?"

I jump down and rinse the bowl he's washed. "I guess it's saying you should love with everything you have—body, heart, and soul."

He shrugs as he gives me a pan to dry. "And do you?"

My hands tremble. I've only felt that way about one person, and I was practically naked sitting in his lap this afternoon. I don't think I have the ability to do that again. "I don't know, but I'd like to find out."

"Nothing wrong with that. All I'm saying is, what's the rush to get married? It sounds like a business transaction instead of 'till death do us part.' What do you think?"

"He's a good guy."

"But is he *the* guy?"

The guy left me a long time ago. *The* guy is waiting for me at the football game. *The* guy can't be depended on. I only know one guy like that, and he's a disappointment. Except, he's been awesome today, like he used to be before he became a big shot and forgot where he came from and forgot about me. He moved on, and so have I. And as soon as he spruces up his image, he'll sprint out of town again. If Clint is anything, it's predictable.

I fold up the dish towel and lean against the counter. "You know how much I loved Clint, but we wanted different things. He didn't love me enough, I guess."

He cups my chin in his hand and kisses the tip of my nose. "Sweet girl, Clint had a tough upbringing. While I don't condone the way he just skipped town without a backward glance, I do understand why. He's not a bad guy."

"He broke my heart."

"I know, and one day, probably too late, he'll realize it. There's someone out there for you, someone who will eat fried chicken."

I bust out laughing. "Oh, Dad. I love you." I wrap my arms around him and give him a squeeze. "We should get back out there. We're being very rude."

"Yeah."

Dad follows me out into the dining room, and we find Ken and Mom playing paper football. Mom has her thumbs together to form a goal post, and Ken flicks the paper football through, scoring a field goal.

"Woo-hoo. I think I'm getting the hang of this."

I stare at Dad. "I think he's ready to see a real football game."

"Bless his heart," Dad says.

"Ken, I have to go to the high school football game tonight to earn more points on the scavenger hunt. I was hoping you'd go with me."

Ken's face brightens into a warm smile. "I'd love to."

I kiss him on the cheek. "Wait right here. I have to find something in my old room."

As I race up the steps to my bedroom, I can't stop thinking about what Dad said. I do care for Ken, but I'm not sure if I love him with my soul. I'm not sure if I will ever love someone like that again. Having Clint in town is really messing with my emotions. Maybe after this week, when he's out of here and back to his highfalutin life, I'll be able to think more clearly. I only wish this time when he leaves, he'll take my old feelings I have with him. He makes me remember how it feels to be in love. Ken's awesome, but he's not *the* guy. I know it, but maybe he can be with time.

I open the door to my old bedroom. It's as if time stood still. My cheerleading trophies line a shelf above the closet, and my poster of Taylor Lautner still adorns the wall, but my old jewelry box is what draws me in. On instinct, I open the pink box, making the ballerina pop up and the sound of "Für Elise" fill the room. I open the tiny drawer and pull out my one-third carat diamond solitaire and matching wedding band. Like it was yesterday, I recall the moment Clint slipped those rings on my hand. I thought it was the beginning of our long life together.

I blink the tears back and return the rings to their hiding place. They're much better in the box. I close the lid and go in search of my most hideous getup for tonight's football game.

CHAPTER SIXTEEN

Clint

Thanks to Silas, I have the perfect saggy pants to wear to the game tonight. I'm glad one of us gained a little weight. My outfit wasn't hard to put together since it wasn't that long ago that I was wearing this crazy outfit. Marlo still had two pairs of shutter sunglasses, so I slide them into the pocket of my old high school letterman jacket. I top it off with my baseball cap worn backward, and it's as if I just stepped back in time to the year I graduated high school.

"You look... horrible," Silas says, snickering behind his hands.

His twin boys get a kick out of it too.

I grab one of the twins while the other one wiggles away before I can scoop him up. "Oh, you think that's funny, don't you?"

Caleb—I think—bobs his head up and down, and Silas gives his son a high five. "You're defective."

Silas belts out a laugh. "Caleb, you don't know the half of it, son."

Caleb squirms away, and he and Carson run around us, playing chase. Marlo waddles in, seeming more pregnant than the last time I saw her just two days ago. Her eyes are so droopy. I bet if she stopped for more than two minutes, she would be fast asleep. She blows out a tired breath. "You remind me of Bieber."

"That's exactly what I was going for."

She lets out a yawn as her two sons cling to her legs and raise their arms in hopes of getting picked up. Marlo brushes the hair out of Carson's eyes. "Sorry, buddy. I can't. Doctor's orders." She leans down to his level. "But I can still give the best smooches." She plasters kisses all over their faces, and they squirm out of her reach and run into their bedroom.

Silas helps her back to a standing position. She smiles at him. "Thanks. It's getting harder to move every day. This baby is giving me way more trouble than those two ever did."

"Maybe it's triplets," I say.

Marlo's face changes to an eerie shade of green. "Definitely not, but never say that again."

I give her a side hug. "Sorry. Not to make you cry or anything, but you seem beat."

Silas punches me in the arm. "Bro, stop talking. You don't say anything like that to a pregnant woman."

She shuffles to the couch and collapses on it. "You're right. I'm exhausted. The boys have amped up their activity level, and..." Marlo wipes a tear away.

Crap. Real slick, idiot.

Silas sneers at me. "The doctor has been telling her to rest more, but it's not that easy. I'm picking up double shifts with UPS to save up for the baby, and she's still working at the library. Then the boys have more energy than the Energizer Bunny." He rubs his face and leans in to whisper in my ear, "Mitch helps out as much as he can, but between being an EMT and doing handyman jobs, he's not around much. Marlo always puts us first, but I know she's at her breaking point. I'm thinking about hiring a babysitter so she can nap in the afternoons."

I nod. "That's a good idea."

"Regina was going to, but that was before this scavenger hunt stuff and..." He shakes it off. "I'll figure something out."

It appears as though Regina's been more a part of my family than I have. I should have been here helping out and getting to know my nephews, but I was doing what I do best: thinking about myself. "Would you let me hire a babysitter?"

Silas shakes his head and pats me on the back. "I got it covered. You know, I've worked my tail off to prove the deadbeat-dad gene didn't get passed down to me. I'm going to provide for my family if it's the last thing I do."

"I get it. Why do you think I left? It was my ticket to breaking the cycle. But I have money. Please let me help you. I want to." I only have a fraction of the money from my contract remaining, but what I do have left, I would give to them in a heartbeat.

We focus on Marlo, who has crashed spread out on the couch. I have to do something. It's what family does.

OTHER THAN THE DOZEN people who insisted on taking selfies with me while I stand outside the gate waiting for Regina, I've been almost ignored. Most rush right past me, carrying their black-and-gold foam fingers and pom-poms. The marching band revs up the crowd as the aroma of hot dogs and popcorn wafts through the air. I lean against the chain-link fence as a few people point and stare. I think, with my stupid shades on, they don't recognize me, which is definitely a good thing.

"Oh my gosh."

Without seeing her, I know it's Regina. Her giggly voice gives her away.

I swivel around and stop in my tracks as I see Regina dressed in a light-pink velour tracksuit and wearing fleece-lined Crocs. Only she can make something outdated look sexy, but when I see her holding Ken's hand, my gut churns.

What's he doing here?

She covers her mouth with her hand to hide the grin that's forming. "Where did you get those pants?"

I rotate in circles to show her my low-rise saggy pants revealing the waistband of my underwear. "If you can believe it, these are Silas's pants, but when he wears them, they actually stay up around his belly. You like?"

Ken snorts. "Are you supposed to be Justin Bieber?"

"That seems to be the consensus." I pull out the second pair of shutter shades and place them on Regina's face. "So thank you for the compliment."

Ken rolls his eyes.

"Aren't you a little overdressed for a football game?" *Who wears a suit to something like this?*

He peers down at his Armani suit. "I always dress like this."

"Hmm, I bet going to the beach with you is super fun."

Regina gives me a "shove it" face, so I clear my throat and wave them inside the gate. "You're in for a treat."

We climb the steps to sit at the top of the bleachers, my favorite place when we were in high school. A dad next to us yells at his son on the field, making Ken almost lose his balance. Regina grabs his arm before he topples down the steps.

"Football is like a religion in the South," Regina says to Ken.

"I live in Atlanta now."

And he doesn't love football?

Regina and I both laugh our heads off, and she says, "That's not the South anymore. That's the lower North."

The team lines up on the field, and everyone stands and yells, "Goooooo Eagles!" Then everyone except Ken, who sits like a bump on a log, flaps their hands like soaring eagles.

The cheerleaders chant, "Go! Fight! Win!"

Regina and I scream, "Beat their faces in!"

She does the motions for the cheer, just like she did back in the day. I used to get so caught up in her cheerleading that I would forget to watch the game.

She pulls Ken to a standing position. "Come on, you can do it. Go! Fight! Win!"

"Uh, beat their faces in?"

"Yeah!"

The Eagles throw an interception, and a collective groan goes through the stadium. We all sit down while the football teams line up again.

Regina gasps. "Oh my gosh! That's Kimberly Franks. I haven't seen her in years." She jumps up. "I'll be back." And before we can protest, she's gone, leaving me with her stuffy Ken doll. He seems more out of place than a whore in church.

"Uh, did you play football?" he asks me.

Staring at the field, I say, "I'm better built for baseball. I tried football, but I spent most of the time riding the pine."

Ken scrunches up his face. "I'm not sure what you mean."

I point to the sidelines at the guys sitting on the bench. "I wasn't very good, so I was a benchwarmer for the most part."

He laughs. "Ah, I get it. That would've been me if I'd tried out for the team. I went to a boarding school, and we were required to play a team sport. You probably won't believe me, but I was a beast at badminton."

Yes, I can. "Is that so?" I ask, doing my best not to grin.

"Yep." He juts his chin up high. "I handled the shuttlecock phenomenally."

"Uh-huh." I don't hear that every day of the week.

Ken's face becomes a stone. "So you and Regina...?"

"Yesterday's news."

He sighs. "Are you sure? I mean, the way she gazes at you. I just don't know. Is something going on between you two that I need to know about?"

"She was my first girlfriend. There's always a special place for your first, right?"

It's a cop-out, leaving the more important title out of my reply, but I'm not going to be the one to break the news to him.

"Yeah. Veronica Stinson. She went to the all-girls school, and we were inseparable."

"What happened?"

With absolutely no emotion on his face, he says, "I married her."

I swing my head around so fast the whiplash threatens to kink my neck forever. "Excuse me?"

He holds out his hands. "Don't tell Regina. I don't think her father would approve if he knew I'd been married before. I mean, I kind of, sort of, still am married, but it's—"

"Wait a second. You're still married?" Fire is about to explode from my ears, and if I don't breathe soon, I'm going to pass out.

"Shh."

I roll my eyes. "It's not like anyone around here knows you."

"But they all know Regina."

My blood boils. He's still married, and he proposed to my girl, my wife, and they are supposed to be getting married soon. I don't know if that makes him worse than me or on the same level. "Why do you want to get married so soon?"

"I did but can't anymore, obviously. You see, in order for me to keep my inheritance, I have to be married. Veronica wants to try separating for a while." He scoffs. "Like that's going to make a difference. Anyway, of course, I can't be married to two people, so I need to delay the wedding for a bit until Veronica gets it through her thick skull that it's over." He waves it off as if it's something like her shoe collection or who gets the dog.

My fists clench by my sides, and I want to punch this man so hard he'll land into next Wednesday, but I'm pretty sure I would go to jail plus have a huge lawsuit against me by someone who can financially outshuttlecock me any day of the week. "You have to tell Regina everything."

Hypocrite. You have to tell her too.

"I will. Eventually."

I take a deep breath to control my anger and say what I should have had the nerve to say at the beginning of this conversation. "Then if we're confessing our deepest, darkest secrets, I guess you should know that I'm still in love with her."

Through a thin-lipped smile, he stares at me. "I figured so, but you and I both know what's best for Regina."

Do we?

Regina climbs the stairs with Caleb in her arms. "See who I found?" She gives my nephew a raspberry on his cheek, sending him into a round of giggles. Behind her is Mel carrying Carson, who is more interested in stealing popcorn from the bag Mel holds.

Silas helps Marlo up the steps, but she stops and huffs. "This is as far as I can go." She rubs her bulging belly. "This kiddo isn't taking a liking to all these steps."

He frowns down at his wife. "I told you, you should stay at home."

"And miss the game? Have you lost your mind?"

She and Silas sit a few rows below us, and Mel and Regina, along with the toddlers, sit right in front of us. Regina's huge smile as she helps Caleb with the cheer warms my heart. While I was away, either living in the limelight or sitting all alone in a fancy apartment, she was here, still involved with my family, watching my nephews take their first steps, say their first words, all those memorable milestones.

"Aunt Reg, can you come over and play tomorrow?"

She steals a glance at me before she tickles his tummy. "Not tomorrow, but soon. I promise, and we'll go see *The Lego Movie*. Deal?"

Regina holds out her fist, and he bumps it.

"Deal."

Andie and Gunnar climb the stairs. Andie's decked out in black and gold and even wears a Smithville Eagles jersey. Gunnar, still in his uniform, follows behind her. She plops down beside me. "Hey! This is so much fun. Who's winning?"

"They are," we all say with no emotion.

She stands and waves her pom-poms. "Come on, Pirates! Tear the Eagles apart."

Everyone stares at Andie. Gunnar yanks her down. "*We* are the Eagles."

"Oops."

She eyes my clothes. "Nice outfit. I guess you and Regina get the extra points for dressing the part. How about I take a photo of you two at the game?"

Regina hands Caleb to his father. "Now is as good a time as ever."

I stand behind her, and with the scoreboard in the background, Regina rotates her head to gaze up at me.

Andie gives us a thumbs-up. "Got it. That's a good one."

Regina and I check out the photo. Even though we still wear our shutter shades, it's obvious we're staring at each other, enjoying the moment. I give her shoulders a squeeze before she sits back down.

I dare a glance over at Ken and catch him shaking his head slowly. Now that he knows how I feel and I know his predicament isn't much different from the one I'm in, maybe he'll back off. Then I can figure out how to win Regina back without sending her into orbit about our lack of a finalized divorce. It could backfire and send her running into the arms of a plastic rich man, but she deserves to know the truth from both of us.

Maybe tomorrow.

CHAPTER SEVENTEEN

Regina

My throat is sore from cheering so much, and it didn't even matter. We lost big-time, but it was a lot of fun. I hadn't been to a game in forever, so it was good to catch up with friends, and I got to spend time with my two favorite toddler buddies, so it wasn't all bad.

Ken and Clint walk way behind me, immersed in a conversation that I probably don't want to know about. The only thing they have in common is money, so I'm sure Ken is encouraging Clint to invest in his company. As long as they aren't trying to one-up each other, I really don't care. Much.

Andie walks arm in arm with Gunnar. Silas and Marlo hold hands as she latches on to Caleb's.

Andie scoots up next to me. "Did you get a lot of points today?"

I pull the list from my pocket and scan the items. "Almost all of them. I'm sure we're in the lead."

"Except the underwear shot doesn't count."

"What?" My voice chases away people walking around me, including Andie.

With a panicked expression, she says, "I'm sorry. I figured Clint would have told you by now."

I pivot to stare at Clint, who acts as though he got caught shopping in Victoria's Secret. "What just happened?"

My short legs won't move fast enough for me to reach him, especially since he's backpedaling to get away from me. "You knew our underwear picture wasn't going to count?"

Ken scowls, an expression he's worn a lot the last few days. "What are you? Thirteen and need to cop a feel?"

Clint holds his hands out in front of him, like he's afraid I'm going to throw a punch. With the mood I'm in, I just might.

"It wasn't like that." He points to Andie. "She disqualified the picture after we took it."

Now Andie holds up her hands in defense. "I'm a very literal person. I said you had to be reading a book. You were reading a catalog. Not the same thing."

Gunnar steps up beside Clint. "I think this calls for a do-over."

"No way," I say as I focus on the list. "We still have time to do the one thing on the list we didn't get to." I grab Clint's arm and tug him forward. "I'm sorry, Ken. I have to take care of this." We rush toward the ambulance, not waiting for Ken to respond.

"What are you doing?" Clint asks.

"If you don't hush, you're going to need resuscitation."

"You promise?"

"Ugh."

A flash goes off in front of my face, and I shield my eyes from the bright light. A man with a news camera and a person holding a microphone maneuver themselves in between us and our destination. The lady with the microphone says, "We're here from Sports Central TV and heard you were spending time in your hometown. How's it going being back here?"

The reporter, a drop-dead-gorgeous redhead with legs that go on forever, shoves the microphone in Clint's face, and like a switch, he paints on a fake smile and answers, "Hi, Laurel. It's great to be back with my friends and family." He picks up Caleb and Carson. "These are my nephews."

Carson pokes the interviewer in the face with a foam finger.

Ha!

"I forgot how much fun hanging out with these guys could be." He angles his head toward Caleb. "This one has an amazing arm." He jostles Carson. "And this one is really fast. I'm sure you'll be seeing them in about eighteen years."

Laurel. Her name is Laurel. Ugh.

"That's great. Did your most recent arrest have anything to do with your decision to spend the off-season in Smithville?"

What the heck? Off-season? I thought it was just a few days. "Arrest?"

He snaps his head toward me and hands me Carson. Maybe it's so I don't have any free hands to throw punches his way. "It's nothing. Don't worry about it."

Laurel raises a perfectly sculpted brow and asks me, "Are you a hometown fan?"

I stare up at Clint, and when his gaze meets mine, he busies himself with Caleb. I use my hand to shield my eyes from the blaring camera lights as well as to hide my hurt pride from spilling over into millions of viewers' homes.

My beauty pageant smile comes in handy. "Everyone in Smithville is a fan of Clint Sorrow. What's not to like?"

The twinkle in Laurel's eyes returns as she focuses back on Clint. I don't think I've ever seen a reporter be so obvious about fangirling.

Girl, don't be so desperate.

Ken walks up to me, and Carson holds out his arms for Ken to take him. Ken backs away and lets out a huff. "What's going on?"

"I don't know."

Clint points to his older brother. "That's my big brother, Silas. He practically raised me."

Silas waves as if he doesn't know what else he's supposed to do.

"And over there, by the ambulance, is my other brother, Mitch. He's an EMT."

Mitch salutes the reporter before he busies himself with some supplies. Laurel's eyes drink in Mitch's backside as he leans over to pick a bag up off the ground. He's the shy pretty boy of the family, and apparently, Laurel likes what she sees.

Clint snatches my arm and scoots me right next to him. "And this is Regina, my..." He stares down at me as if he doesn't know what my title is. I don't either. "She's, uh, she's my partner in crime. We're doing a scavenger hunt for charity. We've had to do some crazy things, and it's actually been a lot of fun."

He winks at me, and I want to smack the smirk off his face.

"What kinds of things?"

If he mentions the underwear pose, I'll neuter him.

He gazes down at his horrible choice of clothing. "This getup is one thing. I don't normally dress like Justin Bieber."

The interviewer giggles. I catch a glimpse of Mitch as he rolls his eyes.

"Can we tag along to see you do some of these crazy things?"

Clint stares at me, and if he says yes, I'll cause a scene. He must sense my anger, because he says, "We've already accomplished most everything on the list—except, Regina, you mentioned there was one thing left we could do. We could... do it for the camera."

I am going to pulverize him. I grit my teeth and hand him the list.

He scans it, and his eyes widen as he stares at the ambulance. "Andie, would you consider a gurney a bed?"

She shakes her head, and I am so glad, I could hug her right now. But Clint reads my mind about the item. No matter what, I will never share my explanation on how sometimes it's considered a bed.

He peers at Mitch. "Mitchy, have you ever taken a catnap on a gurney during a break?"

Crap.

Mitch stares from me to Clint. He's doomed no matter what he says. If he lies, he'll be ditching his brother, but if he tells the truth, I'll make his work life miserable. Mitch grins then says, "All the time."

Mitch will pay for this.

My shoulders slump, and when Andie says, "All righty then, I guess it's a bed," I want to cry.

Ken whispers in my ear, "This is very childish."

Clint grabs my hand and leads me to the ambulance.

Mitch pulls the gurney out from the back of the van and locks the wheels before he pats the mattress. "She's all yours."

"We are not doing this in front of national television."

"Yes, we are." He slides on to the gurney and holds his hands out to me. "Come on."

I stare back at Ken, who has a massive scowl on his face. It's not like I really have a choice, so I take Clint's hand, and he hoists me onto the gurney.

Through gritted teeth, I say, "You're going to pay for this."

"I'm sure I will." He lies back on the gurney and drags me on top of him.

I let out a yelp, causing the onlookers to wolf whistle.

He hands me his phone and says, "Say cheese."

"Cheese." The sooner I do this, the faster I can get away from this embarrassing scene.

When I try to get up, he wraps his arms tighter around me and goes in for a kiss on the cheek, but I block him with my hand. *The stuff he'll do for publicity.*

"Are we done here?"

Our noses are almost touching, and his eyes dip down to stare at my mouth before they lock on my eyes again.

In a husky voice only meant for my ears, he says, "We don't have to be."

Oh, yes, we do.

I pinch his side as I climb off of him, making sure my knee finds his groin in the process. I scamper toward Ken as Clint saunters over to Laurel to finish his interview.

"Ken, I didn't know the reporters were going to be here."

He scrubs his face. "I don't know what to believe anymore. When will you be done with this childish game?"

That's rich coming from a man who makes a living selling dolls and childish games. "We have two more days of the scavenger hunt, and then next weekend is the festival. After that, I should be finished. I promise, it'll all be worth it."

He scoffs. "I'm sure it will be." Over my shoulder, he watches the Sports Central TV reporter cozy up to Clint as she talks to him. "Which Clint is the real Clint, the one who's a hometown boy or the one who loves the spotlight and the attention from every female in a twenty-mile radius?"

I wish I could answer that question, but I don't have a clue. Seeing the switch in his personality while being interviewed reminds me of when he left for the majors. Immediately, he acted like a completely different person, and that person is standing in front of me, cozying up to Laurel, the Sports Central TV reporter.

Clint glances over to me, and we share a silent moment. If he only knew what I'm thinking. If he only knew how conflicted I am right now, he'd finish up with the interview and come whisk me away from this awkward situation, but he blinks then focuses back on Laurel as if nothing involving me matters. And that's probably the real Clint.

I stare up at Ken, who lets out an impatient huff.

"Ken, can you take me home? I'm really tired, and I have a busy day tomorrow."

He scrubs his face before he replies, "Sure. Let's go."

"Regina, wait," Clint says.

Without facing him, I throw up a hand to stop him from approaching me. As we exit, I feel Clint's eyes on me. He can't have it both ways. He chose for the both of us, and now he has to live with his decisions. I do too.

CHAPTER EIGHTEEN

Clint

Watching Regina walk away with Ken was a punch in the gut. Laurel yammered on and on about some crap. I'm not sure if it was about my stats or my contract. I don't really care. I got a bigger kick out of the teenagers photobombing us during the interview. Every time a kid shot a peace sign over my head, it made Laurel's face redder with anger.

"I think we have enough to go on." She motions for the cameraman to cut.

"Nice to see you again," I say as I take a step away from her clutches.

Her talons dig into my biceps, holding me in place. "Don't be rude. Show me around your lovely town. I'd love to see where you grew up and maybe..." She scans my body, and I feel incredibly exposed, even more naked than being in the Belk store window in my underwear. "Maybe we can catch up."

The last time we "caught up," we got caught by her boyfriend. That didn't end well.

She giggles as she tosses her hair over her shoulder. "Don't worry, Jason is on assignment in Toronto." She glances at the cameraman. "Dale, you can take the rest of the night off."

He pops his head up over the camera. "We're supposed to film Clint's life here."

"And we did," she says, shooting daggers with her eyes.

"No, we didn't," I say, and she throws the daggers in my direction. "There's lots more to Smithville than a football game." I'm hoping my dude telepathy is registering with Dale the cameraman, because I do *not* want to be alone with this wolf in sheep's clothing.

He dips his head as if to say he gets the message, and I let out a sigh of relief.

"Yeah. I'd like to see the baseball field you used to play on and the house you grew up in."

My smile widens as Laurel's fades. "Great idea. Follow me."

I take off toward my G-Wagon with Laurel and Dale on my heels. "The high school baseball team uses the football field during their off-season. Other teams were so envious because we had real stadium seats and not a tiny set of metal bleachers. Because it's a football field right now, I can show you the park where I played during summers. Follow me down this street and turn left onto Autumn Avenue."

"We'll ride with you," Laurel says.

Dale fidgets with his big camera. "All my gear is in the van. I should—"

"Then you take the van. I'll continue my interview with Clint and write down the highlights we can add later on." Laurel flashes me a grin.

Dale mouths, "Sorry," to me.

"Fine. Hop in, if you can."

I move toward the driver's-side door, and she huffs. "You aren't going to help me in?"

I know it's not very gentlemanly of me, but I don't want to get caught on camera touching her at all. "You're a sports reporter. I think you can handle getting in all by yourself."

After a few mumbled curse words, she tumbles into my wagon and adjusts the seat belt. "I can't believe you didn't lock this thing. Weren't you afraid of someone stealing it?"

I chuckle. "In this town? Who else do you think owns something like this? It's not like it blends in. Besides, most people behave. If I wanted to, I could leave the keys in the ignition."

She gasps. "You're just asking for trouble."

When I pull my wagon out onto the main road, I cut my eyes toward Laurel. "What brings you all the way down here?"

Laurel does a one-shoulder shrug. "When I get an assignment, I take it."

"Sure you do."

A hand slides up my thigh, and I almost run over Old Man Fredrick's mailbox. I shove her hand off my lap. "Don't do that."

"You didn't use to mind."

As I chew on the inside of my cheek, I try to formulate my exit plan. Too many people saw us leave together, and I'm sure it will be posted on the *Biddy's Blog* by morning. "I'm kind of tired of that kind of life."

She snorts. "Come on, give me more than that. This is the story of a lifetime for me. I need more. Is it this town? Is it your family? Is it a girl?"

I screech to a halt at the stop sign. "None of the above and all of the above. I really appreciate that you're here, but I need you to run this little story then leave. The next few days are going to be super busy for me, and I think it would be best if it wasn't shared with the world."

"Too late for that. You need as much coverage doing simple things as you can. We know all about your little pickle—pun intended."

"Phil has a big mouth."

We drive in silence as I kick myself for getting into this situation. She's very well respected in the sports community as being one of the top reporters, and most of the time, she keeps it professional. But the one time I came on to her, she fell for the line, and here we are.

I pull into the Smithville Community Park and throw my wagon into park. Dale's van slides into the spot next to us.

"This is where I played Little League all the way up until I went to high school. Not much has changed. I think they got a new scoreboard since I was last here, but other than that, it's pretty much the same."

She slides out of the wagon and motions for Dale to follow her. "Clint, switch on your headlights to illuminate the field."

If it gets this interview over with faster, I'll stand on my head. With the field lit up behind us, Dale sets up his camera as Laurel primps for the next filming. "Okay, Dale, make sure you get the baseball diamond in the background."

"I know what I'm doing."

He points to Laurel, and she smiles at the camera.

"So, Clint, this is where you got your start playing ball?"

I stare past her over to the field, and a tsunami of memories washes over me—that new-glove smell, metal cleats digging into the dirt, the aroma of popcorn and hot dogs coming from the concession stand. But one memory hits me deep down in my soul.

"My big brother would play with Mitch and me in our front yard until it was dusk and the bats came out. I'm talking about the kind that fly around and eat insects."

Laurel's smile drops for just a second before she recovers. "Go on."

"But here, on this field, are my strongest memories." I wave my arm out like a spokesmodel on *The Price is Right*. "This little girl in my grade used to come watch her big brother play ball, and she would hang out on that swing set and yell at him when he messed up." I chuckle at the memory. "She could get that swing to go so high, she almost toppled over a time or two. God, she was adorable. Still is."

"So about your playing on the Little League team..."

Laurel doesn't get it—I am talking about when I was playing.

"After a while, she started begging her brother to stick around to watch the next game, the one I played in. She and her brother would hang out on the first-base line and peer through the chain-link fence. Every now and then, I'd hear him explain the game to her, like what a double play is or when it's smart to bunt. Her big blue eyes would soak in everything he talked about." I grin as I continue. "Sometimes, when I would get to first base, I'd run past the bag in order to smile at her. The first time she waved at me, I knew I was a goner."

In a deadpan voice, Laurel says, "How nice. Now, explain what position you played first. I understand before you were shortstop, you played third base."

"The more Regina learned about the game, the more vocal she got. She'd cheer me on and bust my butt when I messed up. This went on until middle school, and by then, I had to make her my girlfriend."

Dale gives me the thumbs-up as he continues to film us.

"Okay, back to your early days playing baseball."

"I am talking baseball. In the South, it's all interconnected, and with my messed-up home life, the ball field became my home away from home. Sure, my brothers were at every game, but it was the fans that cheered me on, encouraged me to try harder and never quit." My eyes get all misty from the memory. "Those are my baseball memories, and Regina is part of that. She always was." I bow my head and adjust my ball cap. "I guess she always will be."

Laurel holds up a hand to Dale. "Let's stop for a moment." To me, she says, "Your agent wants you to show me around town, tell me about how being back here has reminded you of what the simple life is all about."

"I'm telling you that, and you aren't listening. I was just a simple kid growing up without a stable family environment, who knew how to hit a ball good enough to make it to college then got drafted to the majors. I'm not special, just lucky, really, really lucky. My older brother had to drop out of high school to get a job so he could put food on our table, and Mitch is the smart one. He's the one who should have gone to college."

She pats my arm. "That is so, so sweet. Can you say that again for the cameras?"

My trip down memory lane is squashed. "Are you kidding me? No." I walk away from them toward my SUV while I fish in my pocket for an antacid. "It was nice seeing you again. I hope you got what you came here for."

When I pull out of the parking space, I sneak a peek in my rearview mirror to see Laurel frozen in place with her hands planted on her hips. I feel sorry for Dale because she'll complain to him all the way back to Atlanta.

I have to talk to Regina and apologize for the intrusion. We were having a decent time tonight, except for the Ken conversation, then Laurel had to show up to put a damper on the evening. In her mind, I'm sure Regina thinks nothing has changed. But everything's changed.

CHAPTER NINETEEN
Regina

Clint makes me so mad, I could spit a dozen nails and frame an entire home all by myself. Ken is smart enough to avoid chitchat tonight. I'm not in the mood. He pulls up to my apartment, and we sit in silence, his knuckles white from clenching the steering wheel. This was not how I envisioned introducing Ken to small-town living.

"That was a disaster."

He harrumphs as he puts his car in park.

"I'll see you soon?" I ask, fretting over the response.

"Yeah. Sure."

Ken doesn't even give me a chance to get inside my apartment safely before he zooms off. As I fumble for my keys, footsteps approach me.

"Hi, Regina," Mel says, making me jump a foot off the ground and my heart beat erratically.

I drop my keys in the grass. "Good grief, Mel. You scared the crap out of me. Don't lurk in the dark like that."

She bends down and picks up my keyring. "Sorry about that. I figured you would need a friend after *Laurel* showed up." She rolls her eyes, and I snort.

"Don't get me started on that perfect specimen of a female." I shove the key in the lock and open the door for us.

"Ooh, somebody's jealous."

Ugh. Hearing a physician singsong is so odd, to say the least. "I'm not jealous. Clint makes me so mad. All day, the old Clint was around, but later when the cameras rolled in, it was like he flipped a switch and the cocky my-poo-don't-stink Clint came front and center."

Mel giggles as she plops down on my sofa. "I know. He sure does love the camera."

"It just reminds me of what I'm dealing with. He doesn't care. I'm so glad I'm not married to him anymore."

She scrunches up her eyebrows. "What? I mean, yeah. Good thing."

I hand her a beer. "What does that mean?"

Mel pops the top and takes a swig as I sink down on the sofa next to her. "Does Ken know?"

While I play with the label on my bottle, I reply, "Nope. It's really hard to explain. No one but me and Clint really understand why we did it."

She props her long legs on my coffee table and lets out a yawn. "Try me. I'm a good listener."

After a slight pause, I rest my beer bottle on the end table and cross my legs under me. "We loved each other. I think it was instant. I knew one day we'd get married. We were on the same page all through high school. He never glanced at another girl. When we got to college, we were inseparable." I pause, thinking back to the day our life changed. I'd never seen Clint so out of sorts before. I swallow and continue, telling her why we decided to get married so young and in such a hurry.

Mel's jaw drops when I get to the part about him not having a place to live. "Shut the front door."

"Yeah. He didn't want to do it because he was afraid people would think I was pregnant."

Mel opens her mouth to say something, but I continue with my verbal spewing. "I wasn't pregnant, but I couldn't stop what people thought of me."

"Regina..."

"I knew Clint's only chance at doing something with his life was to stay in college. He promised if he got drafted, he would defer until he graduated."

She scrubs her face. "And he went back on his word."

"Yep. Then he didn't want to be married anymore. He was afraid he would cheat, so he wanted out before he was tempted."

Mel slaps her forehead with her palm. "You've got to be kidding me."

"I wish I were." I shake my head to rid myself of those memories. "Old news now. He's out of my life, or he'll be out of my life again in a few days, and I can focus on Ken again."

Mel groans. "Seriously? He's so wrong for you."

"Speaking of so wrong, Ken announced at my parents' house tonight that he wants to postpone our wedding. He was so adamant about getting married on my dime sooner rather than later, and now he's putting on the brakes."

"Wow," Mel says as she reaches for my hand. "Do you think he knows about your previous marriage?"

All this talk about Ken and Clint makes my beer churn in my stomach, and I rush to the bathroom to expel all the contents in my gut. As I spit the gross leftovers out of my mouth, Mel appears next to me and offers me a washcloth.

"Thanks."

I flop down on the cool tile floor and lean my head back to rest it on the wall behind me, tears pooling in my eyes. "I thought Clint had changed."

"Maybe he has. It's hard. I can't imagine what life was like for him, except for what Mitch has said over the years. Money does crazy things to people. Some people can't handle the fame and the spotlight that goes with being a hotshot baseball player."

"That's no excuse."

She slides down on the floor next to me. "I know."

We sit in silence for a moment, then someone knocks on my door.

"I'll get it," she says.

Mel stands, and from my position in front of the porcelain throne, I listen to a muffled conversation. I really don't want to talk to Ken right now. He can't see me this way, because he'll think I still have feelings for Clint. I don't need any more doubts to cloud his commitment to me.

"Regina," Clint says at the bathroom door, startling me so much I bump my knee on the toilet.

"Mel, get him out of here!"

She peeks over his shoulder. "Sorry, girl. He's very pushy. I'll leave you two alone to duke it out." She points at both of us. "Don't make me stitch either of you up. Play nice."

After I hear the click of my front door, I sneer at Clint. "How's Laurel?" God, I hope my voice didn't have a tinge of jealousy in it.

He holds out his hands to help me up, but I swat them away.

"I don't need your help."

Clint has enough brain cells left to not mess with me when I'm in this mood. I push past him and stomp down the hallway to the living room. I sit in the chair, because the last thing I want him to do is sit next to me. And like the jerk he is, he sits on the coffee table, making our knees collide. I recoil from his touch and pull my knees in under my chin.

"I didn't know the reporters were going to be at the game."

"Suuure you didn't. Isn't that why you're doing this crazy scavenger hunt to begin with? So you can spruce up your image?"

"I really didn't know anyone was going to follow me here. I thought a few Instagram posts would do the trick. I'm sorry. We were having fun, and then, out of the blue, things went south."

"You got that right. Is that the kind of girl that cranks your tractor these days?" I shove him out of the way and stand, race-walking into the kitchen to get a bottle of water. "Never mind. I don't care. It's none of my business."

He follows me and towers over me as I search through the refrigerator. "You know better than that."

I jerk around and bump into his wall of chest muscles. "I don't know anything anymore. I've moved on anyway, so you can play with whomever you want, just don't make me witness it. It's disgusting."

Clint leans over the counter and groans. "Stop. Nothing happened. She was totally bored by my hometown memories."

I blow out a breath and stare at him. "Somehow, I believe that."

He reaches out to me, and my treacherous body goes to him. He rests his forehead against mine, and we breathe in sync. "She wanted to hear about how I started playing baseball, and all I could talk about... was you."

Darn you, Clint. Stop being sweet.

"You and baseball are intertwined. They're the same memories."

"Until they weren't anymore."

He gazes into my eyes and swallows, making his Adam's apple bob.

"Go home, Clint, wherever that is. I have to work this weekend. You get two whole days without me cramping your style."

Clint chews on his bottom lip then says, "You don't cramp my style, but do me a favor."

I quirk an eyebrow.

"Brush your teeth. You could wake the dead with that breath."

I cover my mouth with one hand and shove him toward the front door with the other.

He chuckles as he leaves my apartment. When I can no longer see his taillights, I head straight to the bathroom to brush my teeth. I'm thinking fifty thousand is not enough money to pay for the misery of dealing with Clint Sorrow. He needs to stop being so nice to me, because I'm forgetting why I hate him so much.

CHAPTER TWENTY

Clint

AT FIVE O'CLOCK ON Monday morning, when the rattling of keys downstairs catches my attention, I abandon all hope for sleep. On purpose, I shut the door to my upstairs apartment behind me a little on the loud side so as not to scare Mrs. Cavanaugh. The last two days have been agonizing. Regina has been busy at work, and even I am tired of watching sports. I wanted to fake an illness to visit her in the hospital, but I think that would have been a little on the lame side.

"Mornin', Mr. Clint."

"Good morning, Mrs. Cavanaugh."

She drags out pans and ingredients to start her morning baking. "Didn't get much sleep last night?"

"Not at all." I let out a yawn and run a hand through my bed head.

All I could think of for the past two days was Friday's events. I think at the end of Friday night, we were on speaking terms. In fact, I'm pretty sure she almost kissed me right before I left. I'm confident I would have let her. Now, if I could figure out a way to tell her the truth without her neutering me, that would be ideal.

"She must have been something."

"Yeah." I snap my head up, completely coherent now. "Wait. Who are you talking about?"

"Who are you talking about?"

I walk around to her side of the counter and point to the coffee machine. "Mind if I get a pot started?"

"Not at all. And hand me the milk from the fridge."

As I stare at the nectar of the gods dripping into the carafe, I say, "If you're talking about the reporter—"

"None of my business," she says as she proceeds to make a batch of biscuits while I wait on the coffee.

"How much do you know about my and Regina's story?"

Mrs. Cavanaugh rolls out the dough and uses an overturned tea glass to cut out the biscuits. "Oh, that she's a good girl, and you two decided to get married instead of live in sin during college so you could finish college with a roof over your head."

Embarrassment creeps up my neck. "Who all knows?"

She snorts. "In this town, you have to ask that question?"

I pour us both a cup of coffee, and as I gulp the scalding-hot liquid, I try to tamp down my panic attack. "What about the part where we're still married?"

She shrugs and places the circles of dough on a cookie sheet, then slides the sheet into the oven. "I suppose some might know more than they let on, but how much depends on how deep they're willing to dig."

"This is not good."

"It's been one of those hush-hush situations because Rev. Price is a good man and Regina is the town's sweetheart. Nobody wants to tarnish their reputations. You, on the other hand, you do a good enough job on your own."

I chuckle. "I guess you're right."

"Do you still love her?"

"Yes, ma'am, but she's about to marry someone else, and I'm even helping her win money for that stupid wedding."

She stares at me as if I'm the dumbest person on the planet, and it's a pretty good assessment. "You know as well as I do, she can't be married to two people. She likes chocolate chip muffins. How about I whip up a batch for you to take to her this morning?"

"Yes. That would be very nice. Thank you. Anything to get on her good side again. And as lame as it sounds, I plain forgot to file the papers."

"Freudian slip, perhaps?"

I take a deep breath then gulp down some more coffee. "I'm going to need a lot more than chocolate muffins to tamp down her rage when she finds out."

"Ha. No time like the present, right?"

"Yeah. I'm not quite sure how to say it."

As she pulls out the chocolate chips and proceeds to make a batch of muffins, she says, "Just say what we all know. Tell her you're an idiot and you forgot."

"I did forget."

"Sure you did."

If Mrs. Cavanaugh doesn't believe me, Regina never will. The longer I wait, the worse the wrath will be.

"Really, I did. I got busy, and it got buried. It was off my radar."

She stops to slurp down some coffee. "What's stopping you now? File the paperwork now. Then you can honestly say it's being processed."

I don't want to.

"I could do that."

"It would be the right thing to do. Unless, of course, you think she still loves you, too, and would forgive you for all the stuff you've pulled."

Mrs. Cavanaugh may be old, but she has a kind soul. She's grumpy as all get-out, but deep down, she's a good lady. Even though she hardly had a pot to pee in, she would always come by our house when I was young with her I-made-too-much-and-it's-going-to-go-to-waste excuse to give us food. She and the Prices kept us Sorrow boys from being skin and bones.

"Is it too late?"

"Too late to file, or too late to fix things?"

I close my eyes and mull over her words. "I'm not sure."

"It depends on how bad you want whatever it is you want." She taps me on the shoulder with the rolling pin. "Don't mess up her life until you know what you want. Don't hurt her again. This town went easy on you last time. Don't expect the same courtesy the next time you can't figure out what you want."

Leave it to Mrs. Cavanaugh to shoot straight. "Thanks, Mrs. C."

REGINA OPENS HER APARTMENT door, hair tousled. She rubs her eyes and leans against the doorframe. "What time is it?"

"Seven o'clock. Wakey, wakey. We have a busy day." I hold out the bag of muffins and the cupholder with our coffees. "These are for you."

She opens the bag and sniffs the contents. "I must be dreaming."

"Nope. Just me."

Regina motions for me to enter, and I hold my breath, terrified I'll see Ken with sex hair.

"He isn't here, if that's what you're looking for."

She's very perceptive.

"It's none of my business."

Regina slumps down at her kitchen table and pulls out a muffin, then slides the bag over to me. With a mouthful of a hot muffin, she asks, "How was your weekend?"

She's still ticked off, and I don't blame her, but in her words, I also detect a hint of jealousy. "I told you, nothing happened. Laurel left Friday night, I guess. I spent the last two days in a college and pro football stupor."

"You guess? Like you don't know?"

I sit, pull out a muffin, and peel off the wrapper. "I didn't hear from her again, thank goodness." I shiver at the thought. "There's nothing going on, if that's what you mean."

"It's none of my business." She winks at me.

Touché.

"So where's Ken?"

"He said he'd be in Macon all day today. Not sure if he's left already or not."

My eyebrows rise. "So... he's not staying here?"

"Absolutely not. I don't need that kind of rumor mill starting up."

I ball up the muffin wrapper. "Speaking of the rumor mill, how did we keep the truth about us quiet after all these years?"

She swallows, but a crumb still sits on her lip. I have to sit on my hands to keep from swiping it off with my thumb. "Because it began and ended in Athens. By the time I moved back here, it was over and done with. I perfected the fake smile that everyone loves in order to hide the pain you caused, and eventually, I even believed it myself. No one questioned why *I* left *you*. Or if they did, they kept it to themselves for once."

"Regina, I'm sorry."

She waves me off as she stands to throw away her to-go cup and muffin wrapper. "It's all in the past. You're actually more tolerable than I thought you'd be. Only every now and then do you get arrogant. Like Friday night."

"Ouch."

"It's true. When the reporter... when Laurel started interviewing you, you puffed out your chest like you were the most important person on the planet."

She struts around the room and pretends to be me, and it's a pretty good impression. I grab her around the waist and pull her down so she's sitting on my lap. At first, she keeps her hands close to her body, but then she relaxes and puts them on my shoulders. I could lean in and kiss her, but I don't.

Regina holds her wrist up and reads the time on her watch. "Whatever. You're still in the doghouse, mister, but we're going to be late if I don't get going." She runs into her bedroom and slams the door, leaving me in her kitchen all by myself.

When I hear the shower start up, I creep down the hall and open her bedroom door. It smells like her—all peaches and cinnamon. I sink onto the bed. My eyes roam the room, and I can't find a trace of a man dwelling here. Like always, Regina is telling the truth.

Knowing it's a little creepy, I slip my shoes off, lie back, and rest my head on her pillow. I close my eyes and remember the last time we slept together. Since she was so petite, she could curl up in a tiny ball right next to me and use my body as a human blanket. If I let my mind wander, I can almost feel her right next to me, like I never left.

CHAPTER TWENTY-ONE

Regina

Clint's big feet dangle off the side of my bed as he snores. My mind goes back to when he would snooze on my couch after a hard game. I used to get the biggest kick out of watching him sleep. He always seemed so innocent, like he didn't have a worry in the world, but for him to feel so much at home in my apartment after all we've been through is more than I can handle.

I let out an exasperated groan. How dare he fall asleep in my apartment, on my bed, snuggling my pillow? He has some nerve. While he's still sacked out, I slide on some shorts and a tank top and throw my hair into a high ponytail. I don't have time for makeup because if we're late, we'll lose points.

I nudge his foot with my baseball cap. "Wake up, sleeping jock."

He lets out a deep breath, then his eyes fly open. "What time is it?"

"Half past 'get the heck off my bed.'"

Clint rubs his eyes. "Yes, ma'am. Let's go."

He holds his arms out for me to help him up, and I spin around to grab my purse. "You don't need my help. I wouldn't want to cramp your style."

"Is that what you think?"

I shrug as I throw on my sneakers. "I was a boat anchor. You were on the rise, and I was going to hold you back."

Clint lets out a groan. "That's not true."

"I don't care anymore. It's old news. You're a malignant growth that I thought had been excised from my life. I need some serious chemo." Surgery, chemo, radiation therapy... I don't know if all three would make a dent. Perhaps I need to inquire about targeted therapeutics to remove him from my life once and for all.

"Maybe you need hospice care."

I pivot and bump right into his massive chest. He's got a lot of gall. He's a baseball player and should stick to sports metaphors. "You're just jealous that you're the one benched now."

Fire in his eyes makes me think I hit a nerve I didn't even know existed. "What... who...? That's not true."

I suck in a breath. "Oh my gosh. Your career is going down the tubes, isn't it? That's why you're back. You're trying to mend fences so when your world comes crashing down—and it sounds like it's about to happen—you'll have a place to land with loving people around you to catch your fall."

He snatches his shoes off the floor and stomps down the hallway with me right on his heels. "You talk too much."

"I'm right, aren't I? That's the only reason you're here. Not because of the fights. It's because you're almost a has-been, and you're not even thirty."

"No!" he yells, and I take a step back. He takes me by the shoulders and pins me to the wall of the hall. "I came back for you." His eyes pierce my soul, and I can't breathe. "You can't marry that... that... dude. You hardly know him."

With two fingers, I force a few inches of space between us, because he's starting to get to me. "I know he'd never let me down."

He mumbles something to himself then rests his forehead against mine. "Do you love him?"

"You don't get to ask me that question. Let's go."

"Did he tell you why he all of a sudden wants to hold off on getting married?"

"What does it matter to you?"

"Because you matter."

I glance down at my watch. "Oh, crap. We're already going to be late. And stay out of my business."

We tumble out of my apartment and jump into his G-Wagon. There's not time to argue about walking the four blocks to the courthouse. He slings me around in his vehicle as he takes a turn on two wheels. The way his knuckles become white, I'm afraid he's going to break the steering wheel. I bet it costs more than a week's salary for me.

Trying to break the tension, I say, "I wonder what's in store for us today."

He huffs.

"Maybe it's easy stuff like getting restaurant menus. That shouldn't take long in this town."

His Adam's apple bobs. "Yeah. Regina, I shouldn't have said any of that."

"It's already forgotten. I've gotten good at that."

When he pulls into a parking space, I take a moment to gather my thoughts. Before I know what's happening, he opens my door and holds his hand out to me. I take it and jump down onto his bare foot. He grimaces.

"I'm so sorry. Is your foot okay?"

"Maybe my favorite nurse will fix me up."

I roll my eyes. "Then again, maybe she won't."

While we rush toward the courthouse door, he asks, "Who said I was talking about you?"

He opens the front door for me as I shush him. The other teams are already there as Andie and the head of the committee scour their photos to count their points.

Andie's eyes dart up to me, and she smirks. "You're five minutes late. That's fifty points deducted from Friday's total."

"This is your fault." I punch Clint's arm.

He feigns shock. "Me? What did I do?"

"First, you fell asleep in my bed, then you got so cranky."

Andie's eyebrows rise. "I'm not listening."

Clint and I toss our phones to Andie. "According to my records, we should have three hundred fifty points."

Clint nudges me. "Don't forget, we won't get credit for the underwear—"

I clamp my hand over Clint's mouth. "Shh. Don't remind her."

Andie snorts. "Oh, I remember."

Clint sneers at me as he puts on his shoes.

Andie and the committee chair discuss the tallies and nod. She clears her throat. "Here's where we stand after the first day of the competition. In last place, with two hundred points, we have Marge and David Lane."

David throws his hands in the air. "It was a new phone. We couldn't figure out how to work it."

"Next, we have the Taylors with two hundred fifty points."

Clint rubs my shoulders, but I shimmy away from him. Now is not the time to make nice.

"In third place, we have Clint Sorrow and Regina Price with two hundred seventy-five points."

The two other teams high-five each other.

"And we have a tie for first place. Leo and Becca and Carmen and Nate both have three hundred fifty points."

Carmen does the floss dance, and I want to trip her.

Andie laughs as she passes out the list for day two's adventure. "Funny you should do that, because some of you have that on your list for today."

With Clint hovering over my shoulder, his breath tickling my neck, we scan today's list. Some of these items are easy peasy, but others are next to impossible.

Clint points to one of the items. "Where are we going to find a lime-green car?"

"Shh. I know exactly where to get that one."

The committee chair claps her hands. "This is still a very tight race, and today's items are worth one hundred points each. Every minute you're late tomorrow morning will cost you one hundred points, so I suggest you be on time. Go."

Clint grabs my hand, and we take off back to his G-Wagon. "Where to, ma'am?"

I point to the street in front of us. "Right there. Chickens."

As I run toward the crazy wild chickens that roam the streets, Clint yells, "Don't scare them! You have to sneak up on 'em."

We tiptoe out to the middle of the street, and I whisper, "Almost there." I grab my phone out of my purse to have it ready. "This is probably as close as we'll get."

Clint kneels down in front of the chickens, and I balance next to him. With the chickens in the background, I take a picture. "Got it."

Right as I take the picture, Leo and Becca run toward us. I give Clint my devious grin, and he dips his head as if he knows exactly what I'm thinking. On cue, we scream and rush around the road, scaring the chickens away.

Leo runs after them, but they're long gone. He stares at me. "You did that on purpose."

I shrug. "Maybe." I take Clint's hand, and we rush back to his G-Wagon. He helps me in, and once we get settled, we let out a round of giggles.

"Did you see Becca trying to grab that one chicken?" He leans over the steering wheel, snickering. "That thing would have pecked her eyes out if she'd touched it."

"We better go before they try to take revenge on us."

He pulls his vehicle onto the road. "Where to?"

"The high school. I'll bet you a dime to a donut we'll find a hideous lime-green car in the parking lot. Plus, the way teenagers drive, we're bound to see some roadkill close by."

He holds his palm out, and I slap it. "I love the way you multi-task."

I shrug. "I'm a nurse. That's what I do."

We drive a few blocks toward the high school in silence. Finally, he says, "Are we good?"

I blow out a breath. As much as I'd like to stay angry at him, I can't. I never could. "I guess."

"Thank God, because after all this time, I still think of you as my very best friend."

I force myself to stare out the passenger window, because if I catch his eye, I'll burst into tears. I'm not sure if that was a cheesy pickup line or the truth. It sounded honest. But after all these years, it's impossible for that to still be true. He must have tons of friends. He's got to have a bunch of guy pals on and off the field. Surely one of them would be his best friend. And if not, he's got two awesome brothers. I can't compare to either of those categories.

The only thing I can do is make light of the situation. "You should probably get a better friend group."

He chuckles as he drives into the parking lot of the high school. "Naw. Why mess with a good thing?"

I focus on the list and hope today goes by faster than Friday. If not, I'm going to fall back in love with Clint—as if I ever fell out of love in the first place.

CHAPTER TWENTY-TWO

Clint

The musty smell of Smithville High School hasn't changed a lick since I last walked these halls. Students slam lockers shut, and a few girls take photos of me while we wait in the hallway. I glance over at Regina to catch a huge eye roll from her. The sea of teens in the hallway parts when Regina's brother saunters by.

Robert and I fist-bump each other, making Regina groan. Man, I miss this guy. Even though he's two years older than I am, I've always thought of him as my third brother. And he never once threatened to beat the crap out of me when things went sour between me and his sister.

He points to a group of gawking teens and motions for them to head to class. "So what's up? Regina only stops by when she wants to run the track."

She shows him the list. "We need your help on a few items for our scavenger hunt."

Robert reads the paper and nods. "This way." He uses his fist to bang on one locker after another until one pops open. He waves his hand toward the open locker. "See if you fit."

"Pfft, my big toe won't even fit in that."

Regina snorts. "And you know that big head of his won't fit. I'm surprised it fits in the building."

Oh, it's on. I squeeze my right shoulder inside and put my right foot in, then wave for Regina to join me.

"This is crazy," she says as she tosses her phone to Robert and walks toward the locker. "Where am I supposed to fit?"

Robert points to the bottom of the locker. "Can you fit your butt right there by his size-thirteen shoe? Even for a second?"

She wraps her arm around my leg and scoots in, pushing her left shoulder behind my legs. "This is about as far as I can go."

God, her arm feels heavenly wrapped around my thigh. Robert can take as long as he needs to on this picture. I may get a cramp in my neck from my kinked-up position, but it's totally worth it.

"Got it."

Thanks, Rob.

Regina pinches my thigh, making me bang my head on the top of the locker, then she slides out onto the floor. "That's one off the list." She stands and straightens her T-shirt that slid up during the locker scene. "Got any other ideas?"

"Follow me." He leads us into the boys' locker room. "It's still homeroom, so nobody's in here, or at least, they shouldn't be."

When we round the corner, a flood of memories overcomes me. Usually, our entire team would crowd the big shower area because we were so sore from a game. There was a time or two when Regina snuck in after all the rest of the team had left, and we had our own fun in the water. Robert switches on one of the shower heads in the far back. "You're inside a shower, and you have water on in the background. Smile."

I pick up Regina, making her squeal.

"Put me down."

"Stay still, or I'll put you *in* the water."

"You wouldn't dare."

Nose to nose, we stare at each other, sizing each other up. My mouth twitches, and I can't stop myself from smiling. I jerk my body as if I'm going to run in the direction of the water, and she grabs onto me tighter and squeals.

"I'm teasing you."

I wonder if she's remembering our make-out sessions in this very locker room. Probably so, because her eyes drift to my mouth then quickly back up to meet my gaze. Before I know what's happening, she kisses me on the cheek. My foot slips on the wet tile, and I have to grab onto the wall for support. "Not that I'm complaining, but what was that for?"

She wiggles out of my grasp and straightens her ponytail before she yanks her phone away from Robert. She concurs as she checks out the photos then smiles at me. "We not only got the shower and the water shot, but I kissed a stranger."

My jaw drops.

Robert chuckles and fist-bumps Regina. "Burn. Bro, that was a good one."

"I'm not a stranger. In fact—"

Robert hugs his sister. "Nobody's stranger than you, Sorrow."

"You got that right," Regina says.

I huff and storm out of the shower. "No fair double-teaming me."

Regina catches up with me and grabs my arm. "I'm just playing with you, but hopefully, Andie won't throw that one out on a technicality. Rob, do any of the kids drive a lime-green car?"

He chews on the inside of his lip, then says, "No, but Jeffrey Clinton, the algebra teacher, drives the most amazing sled you'll ever see. Come with me."

The bell rings, and we rush out of the locker room as teenage boys file in. Robert leads us to the parking lot behind the school, and like a neon sign, there sits a nineteen seventy Plymouth Barracuda. My knees buckle. It's the most beautiful car I've ever seen.

Regina scrunches up her nose. "That is so ugly."

Robert and I both gape at Regina like she's lost her mind. "Are you kidding me? This is a classic. I can only imagine what this thing is worth."

Robert grins. "More than Jeff makes in five years. It was his pop's, and he only drives it on sunny, mild days and parks it way out in the back so no one will ding the doors."

My mouth drools as we get closer to the slick sled. "It's beautiful. I want to marry this car."

Regina snorts. "Seriously? You like that over your G-Wagon?"

Robert swings around to face me. "You have a..."

"If you can get Jeff to sell me this car, you can have mine."

Robert's face loses all its color. "I'll see what I can do."

Regina giggles. "It's definitely not a chick magnet. I bet it wouldn't be ten minutes before someone in Atlanta dented that fender."

"Shh, don't say that. I'm sure she has ears."

Regina rolls her eyes and stands next to the car. "Just take the picture."

I give a thumbs-up and smile as Robert takes the shot.

While I'm absorbed in slobbering over the beautiful 'Cuda, Regina goes, "Aww. Check this out." She points toward a corner of the parking lot where a dead squirrel lies, his poor head squished, probably by a teen late for school. "Roadkill. At this rate, we'll be done by noon."

Regina bites her lip and kneels down beside the dead critter. "Come on. You have to do this too."

When she pouts, I get on my knees on the other side of her.

She brings her palms together in front of her face and closes her eyes. "Dear Lord, please accept this creature of yours into your heavenly forest. May he always have plenty of trees to play in and more nuts than he can eat."

"Amen."

"Amen," Robert says and hands Regina her phone back. "I really have to get to work. If I leave those boys alone for too long, they start giving each other swirlies."

We do the bro hug, backslap combo, then I say, "Thanks, man."

"Have fun watching *Twilight*."

Regina pops a hand over her mouth and does her best to stifle a giggle.

My heart sinks. "No..."

She grins. "Oh, yes."

We walk back to my G-Wagon in silence. If I have to watch *Twilight* with her, I think I'll poke both of my eyes out with a fork. I practically know that movie by heart. Each time we watched it, Regina would switch from being Team Edward to Team Jacob. To me, there was no contest. Jacob in all his wolfiness beat a hundred-year-old pasty-white Edward any day of the week, but Edward did get the girl in the end, so maybe he had something going for him that I could never see.

"Uh, you were kidding about the movie, right?"

In the cutest singsong voice that I have missed so much, she replies, "I don't know. Depends on if you're a good boy."

That settles it. I'm never a good boy. I wasn't a good boy when I was a boy, and I'm sure not one now. Maybe if I'd been a good boy at one time, I wouldn't have made all the mistakes I did. I think she can hear my thoughts, because she touches my hand.

"I was only kidding. You're not a bad person. I shouldn't have said that."

I squeeze her hand as I focus on our intertwined fingers. At one point in our lives, this was a normal, everyday sight. Now, it feels odd and unexpected. Before I can stop myself, I bring her hand to my mouth and kiss each knuckle. She doesn't pull away.

"For you, I'd suffer through *Twilight* but under one condition."

She clears her throat. "And that is?"

"Please don't drool over that Edward character. It's just creepy."

She snatches her hand away from mine but falls into a fit of giggles. "Oh, hush. You've always been so jealous of Edward, the nonhulky guy that gets the girl. If you don't behave, after that movie, I'll force you to watch *27 Dresses*."

I feign shock. "You wouldn't."

With an evil grin on her face, she dips her head. "And *Prince Caspian*."

I wink. "Anything for you, darlin'."

She raises her eyebrows. I don't think that went like she hoped it would. Regina mumbles something under her breath as she stares straight ahead. "Just drive. We need to get thirty cents' worth of gas."

"Yes, ma'am."

CHAPTER TWENTY-THREE

Regina

We ride down the road toward Charlie's gas station, and suddenly the air seems stuffy between us. While I admit I'm having a tiny bit of fun with Clint, I can't let him think too much of it. His tight-lipped expression and white knuckles make me think he's deep in thought about something, and like always, I get the "can't help its."

"Cat got your tongue?"

He grins for a second, then it fades.

"If I ask you a question, will you answer honestly?"

The blood drains from his face. "Uh... maybe."

I stare out the windshield. "I'll know if you're lying, so the penalty for perjury is to let me drive this house of yours."

"How will you know?" His eyes dart toward me for a nanosecond before focusing back on the road.

"Pfft. I'm not telling."

"Whatever. Nobody drives Olivia."

My eyes bug out of their sockets. "You named your G-Wagon Olivia?"

"Yep. You like?"

"So... *fluffy* for such a dude vehicle."

As he drives into Charlie's gas station, he says, staring down his nose, "Maybe I should have named it Fredrick or Carlton."

"I like Edward."

A chuckle rumbles through his chest as he pulls up to the gas pump. We get out of his beast of an SUV, and right before I enter the store to pay for gas, Clint says, "I bet I can stop it at exactly thirty cents."

"We're wasting time. Let me just pay inside."

Clint puffs out his chest and replies, "Are you saying my hand-eye coordination is off? I can hit a fastball whizzing past me at ninety miles an hour, so I'm pretty sure I can do this."

I cock my head to the side. "What's your batting average again?"

He scowls as he jerks the nozzle out of the holder. "I can do this. Get your camera ready."

"Whatever you say." While he pumps gas into his wagon, I take a picture. "Stop!"

"What?"

"You went over thirty cents."

He groans then finishes the transaction and enters his credit card again. "Don't distract me."

Game on.

While he pumps again, I pretend to drop something on the ground. I bend down to get it and peek over my shoulder to catch him staring at my butt. I stand up and motion to the pump with my head.

"Dang it." He slams the nozzle into the pump and starts another transaction. "My credit card company is going to freeze my account with all these fifty-cent transactions."

"If you could keep your eyes off my booty long enough, this wouldn't be a problem."

He pats my butt with his hand and nudges me toward the entrance to the gas station. "Give Charlie thirty cents. We'll pay in cash like I suggested from the start."

"You're impossible."

When I return from the store front, I find Clint leaning up against his wagon, one leg crossed over the other, hands stuffed in his pockets, watching my every move with one of those I-want-you expressions.

Sorry, bud. You gave that up, remember? "Pump away. By the way, Charlie says hey."

He waves to Charlie, the big hillbilly inside the store, then proceeds to pump the gas. When the gas continues past thirty cents, he growls. "You did this on purpose, didn't you?"

I double over in giggles, then he yanks me up and throws me over his shoulder like a sack of potatoes.

"Stop, you beast. Edward would never do this."

Clint freezes then lets my body slide down his as if we're in slow motion. My nose grazes his on my descent.

Clint's grip tightens, not letting me slide any farther, my feet dangling off the ground. "Edward could never hold you with one arm."

"Actually, he probably could."

He takes his left hand and stifles a fake yawn while holding me with his right arm. "I could do this all day."

I wiggle to free myself, but he only tightens his grip.

"Let's try this one more time." He plops me down on the ground, and I pat his SUV. "Olivia, we're going to give you thirty cents' worth of gas. That should be enough fuel to get us to the first stop sign."

"She appreciates your kindness."

I hold out my hand. "Let me show you how this is done. I've bought a dollar's worth of gas too many times to count."

While I pump slowly, so as not to go over, he slides his hand in my back pocket to retrieve my cell phone.

"You could have used your phone, you know."

Right as I click off at thirty cents, he takes a picture. "But where's the fun in that?" He slides the phone back into my pocket, taking far too long in the process.

We wave to Charlie and climb back into Clint's vehicle in search of other items to check off our list.

"You never let me ask you my question."

Clint lets out a huge breath as we drive down the street in search of a full parking lot, a daunting task since there aren't enough citizens in this town to fill up any parking lot on any given day, much less on a Monday morning. If it was Sunday, maybe the church parking lot would fulfill the item.

"Fine. Ask away."

"Why did you really come back? You stay away for five years, don't keep in contact with anyone other than your brothers, then during the Pickle Festival, you decide to grace us all with your presence."

"You've been keeping tabs on me?"

I roll my eyes. "Don't flatter yourself. Mitch talks about you all the time at work, no matter how many times I try to cut him off. He's very proud of you."

"Harrumph." He mumbles words that I guess are not meant for my ears.

"I'll answer for you. It's because you found out I was getting married, and you couldn't stand to see me finally happy after all this time. You just couldn't handle someone else filling your shoes, right? Let me tell you something, Mr. Baseball, you can come back and act all folksy, but you're not fooling me."

Clint growls. The truth hurts.

"Just be honest. And remember, I'll know when you're lying." I mimic a ten-and-two-o'clock position with my hands, reminding him the penalty for lying is me taking control of the driver's seat.

He runs a hand through his hair and makes it adorably messy. I sit on my hands to keep from messing it up more.

"Maybe."

I gasp. I was hoping he would deny it. Now, I can't drive his car.

"You're horrible."

"Let me explain. I've been doing a lot of thinking, and I think our split was too hasty."

He touches my arm, and I slide out of his reach.

"Oh, so you go play the hot bachelor for five years, screwing a new girl in every town—"

"It wasn't like that. I'm not like that, and you know it."

"Pfft. While I sit at home licking my wounds, wondering why I wasn't good enough for you." Tears well up in my eyes. "I'm an idiot for asking what I don't want to know the answer to. For letting myself think we could be friends. For loving... I mean... never mind."

I squeeze my eyes shut to keep the tears from streaming down my face. He pulls into the First Bank of Smithville parking lot and yanks me over the console to sit on his lap. I let out a squeak.

"Regina, let's get something straight. I made a huge mistake. It's one I've had to live with for five long years, but there wasn't a different woman in every town. At first, there were a few women, and I'm not proud of myself for those days, but that life got old real fast. I don't have anyone in Atlanta either." He cups my face with his hands. "And no one could ever fill your size-five shoes. Ever." He rakes his teeth over his bottom lip then adds, "We are... my heart still thinks we're married. We always will be. I love you, Regina."

My lungs don't work. I don't know how to respond to that. He was all I ever wanted until he walked out on us. Then after all this time, another man cares about me, and now Clint has the nerve to waltz back into my life. It's not fair.

His lips brush across mine, and part of my frozen heart begins to melt. Right before I give in to him, the *whoop-whoop* of a siren jolts us back to reality.

"Son of a..."

My thoughts exactly.

Gunnar saunters up to us with a big grin on his face. "You two are a little old to be parking, don't you think?"

My face feels like it's on fire. If the Biddys caught us, there would be no telling what they would print. "That's not what we were doing."

Clint scrubs his face. "We were, uh, checking out the photos from this morning. Right, Regina?"

"Yeah. And speaking of, we need one with you."

Gunnar rolls his eyes. "So I heard. Come on. How do you want to do this?"

Clint and I slide out of his vehicle and mull over how the shot should turn out.

With a glint in his eyes, Clint says, "Handcuffs."

Gunnar chuckles. "First parking, then handcuffs. You two are really making up for lost time."

I swat him on the back. "I can't believe you said that."

Gunnar slaps one half of the handcuffs on me and the other on Clint.

I tug on the cuffs and say, "I guess you can't run away from me this way." I am very proud of my burn.

Clint whistles as he holds up our locked hands. "Gunnar, why don't you throw away the key?"

"You do, and I'll tell Andie all about the time you wet your pants on that camping trip to Fort Oglethorpe."

Gunnar's face drops. "You're cold."

I hold out my hand. "I'll hang on to the key. You take our picture."

He grunts and moves around to get behind us for the selfie. "Clint, you sure picked a spitfire."

"You don't know the half of it."

Clint gets the stink eye from me, but he just smiles and winks. *Ugh.* It really ticks me off that his wink still gets to me. After the selfie and removal of the handcuffs, Gunnar heads down the street but not before he lets out another *whoop-whoop* from the siren. I stare at Clint, my arms covering my chest. "I get to drive."

He laughs through his chuckle. "I don't think so."

I hold out my hand for his keys. "Whatever. I told you I can tell when you're lying."

Clint backs me up against his vehicle and gazes down at me, an arm on each side, pinning me in place. "What was my lie?"

My fuzzy brain can't think straight when his five-o'clock shadow is so close to my cheek. He used to make my face feel windburned with his scruff. "Uh... the part about us still being married."

His eyes get huge. "Regina, I can explain."

"No matter what you feel, we aren't legally married anymore. Just get used to it."

His shoulders slump. Clint reaches into his pockets and dangles the keys out for me to grab. Right before I take them, he yanks them back. "You'll be careful, right?"

"Oh, please. What could I possibly hit? Roadkill?"

He drops them into my palm. "I was thinking more along the lines of you running over me."

I snap my fingers. "Great minds think alike."

"Regina..." he says through gritted teeth.

After I settle into the driver's seat, I pat the dashboard like she's a baby. Mine doesn't feel like Italian leather. My standard-issue plastic dashboard even has a split down the middle. "Oh, hush. I'll be gentle with Olivia."

I'll be gentler with Olivia's fenders than he was with my heart. As I adjust the seat so I can reach the pedals, I take in the controls. It's like I'm in the cockpit of an airplane.

I rub my hands together. "You may never get Olivia back."

"You promised."

Yeah, so did you one time.

CHAPTER TWENTY-FOUR

Clint

It takes all my willpower to keep my hands off Regina as she drives my G-Wagon. I find nothing sexier than a pint-sized female driving a monster vehicle. Regina always loved to drive my truck back in high school and college, so this shouldn't surprise me or get to me like it does. She cranks the radio and sings along to a Jason Aldean song. If I could freeze time and spend more days with her, I would. Maybe then I could convince her to dump Ken and give me a second chance.

To get my mind back in the game, I say, "So what's next on our list?"

She wiggles in the seat and pulls the sheet from her back pocket. I could have gotten that for her, but then we may have ended up in a ditch. I can already see the insurance claim now. Reason for accident: *Grabbing wife's tushy.*

She holds the list out for me to read.

"Let's see... thanks to Robert, we got a bunch done in one setting." I stare over at her, and as if she senses my gaze, she flicks her eyes toward mine for a second.

"What?"

"I was wondering if you would do me a favor."

She holds her hands out in front of her in a defensive position. "You cannot be the best man at my wedding."

There can't be a wedding because you're already married, and he is too!

I hold my hands out in surrender. "As lovely as that sounds, I would rather eat razor blades than have a ringside seat to witness that. Thanks, but no thanks."

"Tell me about this favor."

I stare out my passenger window. "First, can I ask you a question?"

"And if I lie, I have to give up the driver's seat?" Her cheesy smile says it all.

"Exactly."

She pulls into the grocery store parking lot and puts the wagon in park. "Spill."

"Silas said you babysit for the boys sometimes."

Regina watches as the Jackson sisters wander inside the Piggly Wiggly. One of them, I never can keep them straight, takes out her cell phone and snaps a picture in our direction. I guess they're as tech savvy as I've heard.

Her grin spreads across her face. "Yes. I love those boys."

"That's obvious by the way you were with them Friday night, and they hung on your every word... and they called you 'aunt.'"

"Did that bother you? At first, I would have been their aunt." She blows her hair out of her eyes. "I helped Marlo out a lot early on, so they kind of got used to me being around." She pokes me in the side. "Just because you left your family doesn't mean I ever did. In my heart, they're still my family."

I tuck a strand of hair behind her ear. "Thank you for being honest."

She gulps and pulls back, causing my hand to drop from her face. "I guess that means I get to keep driving."

"Guess so. Now, my favor."

Regina lets out a groan. "Let's hear it."

"Marlo really needs some rest. I was wondering, since we need to watch a movie together tonight, if we could watch the boys and let their mom get a little catnap."

Without blinking an eye, she replies, "Of course. That's a wonderful idea. And so I don't have to sit through all your groans about Edward in *Twilight*, we can pick a movie from our senior year that the boys would like."

I love this woman so much. I am certifiably the biggest idiot on the planet. The only words I'm able to squeak out are, "Thank you."

"Knowing the twins like I do, they'd probably like all the werewolf and vampire stuff. It's Marlo who would never forgive me." She pulls out her phone and peruses the screen. "Hmm, how about *Bolt*? That was cute, and it qualifies because I dragged you to see that once or twice, if I recall."

"Yes, you did." However, I don't remember much of the movie, because we spent the vast majority of the time in the dark theater making out in the balcony. The way her eyes fix on mine, I think she's also remembering that glorious date. "So do you want me to talk to Marlo, or should you?"

"I think it would mean more coming from you. Uncle Clint needs some quality time with the youngest Cs of the family before you're whisked back to the big city."

I shoot up my eyebrows. "Are you trying to get rid of me?"

"Me? Pfft. I hardly even noticed you were here to begin with."

Her words say one thing, but that blush says volumes of something entirely different. I pull out my phone and text Silas to see what he thinks, and within seconds, he replies with a "thank you" in all caps.

I show her the message. "We have a busy night ahead of us."

She hits the ignition. "Let's go get them now and take them to lunch. They can help us mark some other items off our list. I think they would enjoy that."

"Regina, I don't deserve you."

"Nope. You certainly do not. Come on. Let's get our—I mean—your nephews."

She's going to beat me into next week when she finds out they really are still her family.

WITH CARSON AND CALEB safely strapped into their car seats in my back seat, we're off. Thank goodness for Regina, because she handled the car seats like a boss. *Click, click*, and we're off. With a few swipes to my satellite radio, she giggles.

"Okay, kids, here you go."

With an eardrum-piercing volume, she plays a song that starts out with a heavy, gritty guitar solo, and the twins yell, "Yay!"

The twins and Regina sing the first verse of the "Baby T. Rex" song.

I jump in my seat. "What is that?"

Regina bounces in the driver's seat as the second verse starts. "Come on, Uncle Clint, your turn."

They sing the daddy verse, the grandma and the granddad verses, and by the it's-the-end verse, I officially have an earworm that will never go away. Next season, I'll be focusing on a baseball sailing toward me at ninety miles an hour, and I'll be bobbing my head to the baby dinosaur song. That's a surefire way to lose a contract.

"Again!" Caleb yells from the back seat.

"Maybe later," Regina says. "How about some lunch?"

Thank you, darlin'.

We pull in front of In a Jam Coffee Shop, and while Regina busies herself with Caleb, I remove Carson from his seat. He jumps into my arms, and my heart swells with joy. I see why Silas is over the moon about his kids. It doesn't matter how wild or wound up they are. A moment of affection reminds even the hardest of hearts what it's all about. I sling him onto my hip, and Caleb tugs at my pants.

"Up! Up!"

"Yes, sir, little man."

Regina hoists Caleb onto my other hip then gives me a warm smile. "Do you have room for me to climb onto your back?"

"Yes, ma'am. Just say the word."

"Do it," Carson says.

Caleb joins in. "Yeah, Aunt Reg. Climb on his back."

Her eyes twinkle, and when she notices me staring, she winks. "Maybe later."

I clench my arms around the twins in order to keep my grip after her comment. *Maybe later.* I may hold her feet to the fire on that one.

"Let's get these kiddos fed so we can take some more pictures."

Before we can get two feet inside the café, Mrs. Cavanaugh peels Carson away from me. "Come here, my sweet boy." She showers him with kisses, and he giggles like only a three-year-old can. She holds out her arms to Caleb. "Did you count the kisses? You need the same amount."

"Fifty-two."

I throw my head back with laughter as I hand him over to Mrs. Cavanaugh. She stares at me. "Young-uns bring out the best in you."

Heat flames my face as I bow my head.

Regina pats my back as she walks past me to jump up on a barstool. "Can you make them peanut butter and jelly sandwiches cut at an angle with the crust off?"

"Of course. You babysitting today?"

Regina smiles, and I busy myself with getting the twins settled into a booth. "Yeah, we're trying to give Marlo some time to rest and thought the kids would like to help us on our scavenger hunt."

She pulls out bread, homemade strawberry jam, and peanut butter. "How's that going?"

Regina's mouth pulls down. "Third place so far."

From the booth, I add, "We're going to own day two because of our little assistants." I point to the two towheaded boys sitting with me, drawing on the children's menu.

"You know it," Regina says as she places two paper plates in front of the boys. "Mrs. C, this jam is mild, right?"

She snorts. "The good stuff is for special occasions only."

I scrunch my brow with confusion.

Regina leans down to me, and I get a waft of her peach shampoo. "The good stuff has Jack Daniel's in it."

My eyes get big. "So that's what it is. No wonder my mother liked it so much when I was a kid."

"Probably so." She rushes back to the counter and retrieves two small glasses of milk, then she gets our sandwiches and two glasses of sweet tea.

I dive into my PB&J and let the jam and peanut butter squish between my teeth. "Regina, how do I look?"

The twins crack up and do the same.

Regina bites her lip, but I see a grin poking out at the side of her mouth. "Now, see what you've done?"

A warm smile forms on her face, and she actually glows as she takes in the twins' antics. I rest my hand over hers, and she doesn't jerk back. The only move she makes is a tiny, almost unnoticeable swipe of her thumb across mine. She wants what's in front of her. I don't know if it's from me or Ken or even from someone she hasn't met yet, but she wants a family. She would be the best mom ever. I know it. She could have been a mom to my kids had I not gotten scared and selfish. I have to fix this pickle I'm in before it's too late and she hates me forever, and before she neuters me so I will never have a chance of offspring.

CHAPTER TWENTY-FIVE

Regina

A sandblaster would have been helpful for getting all the sticky jam and peanut butter off four grimy hands. Actually, six hands if I count the biggest kid in the booth—Clint. No one would know the twins had never met him before this week, because they took to him like ducks to water.

"I have to potty," Caleb says.

Carson bobs his head. "Me too."

"Good job telling us." I hold my hands out for them to take. "Come on. Let's see if Mrs. C will let us use her restroom."

Clint clears his throat. "They can use my bathroom. It's just upstairs."

Caleb's eyes bug out of their sockets. "You live here?"

"Yep, and it's so cool. I get to eat all the leftovers too."

"Wow," Carson says, holding his hand out to get a high five. "Can we move here?"

Clint takes Carson by the hand and leads us to the steps. "I don't think your mother would like that very much."

"But we would."

I bite back a snicker and pull a stern expression. "Caleb, that's not nice."

His lip pulls down into the most adorable pout. "Mom makes us eat green stuff."

Clint unlocks the door at the top of the steps and opens it to reveal his loft apartment. He waves his arm to motion us inside. "If you eat green stuff, you'll grow big and tall like me. Your father didn't like to eat the green stuff."

Caleb cringes. "He's fat."

I whack Clint in the stomach and give him the stink eye, a clear indication he doesn't need to egg the boys on about their father's doughboy physique.

The twins squeal as they run circles around Clint's couch. "This is so cool, Uncle C."

I catch Caleb as he makes another lap. "Let's go potty before you leave a trail to the bathroom."

"Good idea," Clint says as Carson attempts to scoot past me.

I shove the boys toward Clint. "Your apartment, your chore. Have fun. Just try to keep them from sword fighting."

Clint's face lights up. "What a great idea. Hey, guys..."

I grab Clint's arm and yank him back toward me. He snakes his other arm around my waist to pull me close. "Yes?"

His abs are calling my name, but I recite in my head the Bible verse about not being tempted beyond my ability to resist. I am at the edge of resistance, for sure. "Uh... just remember, any residue in your bathroom is your responsibility to clean up."

His face loses all humor. "Boys, one at a time." He pivots Carson and points him in my direction. "You stand right there. When Caleb's done, you'll have your chance."

Carson pouts. "Dad lets us have sword fights."

"I bet he does, hence the reason your mother needs a nap."

Carson and I walk around the room, and we stare at all the pictures in tiny frames. Most are of Miss Mary Grace, Andie's grandmother, who passed away earlier this year. She owned the building that Andie received in the will.

The bathroom door opens, and Caleb rushes out, hands still wet from what I hope was the sink. I give Carson a gentle shove toward the bathroom. "Here's number two."

"Ew. She said number two."

Ugh. Boy bathroom humor. "Do you feel better now?"

Caleb pumps his fist in the air. "Yep. Everything came out all right."

Too much information.

When Carson finishes doing his business, we climb back into Clint's vehicle to strike a few more items off our scavenger hunt list.

"So, guys, we need to pretend we are in a Disney movie. Got any suggestions?"

"*Avengers!*"

"*Spider Man.*"

Clint side-eyes me with a gleam of mischief. "Those are really, really good suggestions, but it needs to be a cartoon-type movie. You know, like *Snow White*."

"*Beauty and the Beast.*"

"Ha. That's appropriate," I say, fist-bumping Caleb.

Clint rolls his eyes. "I like *Sleeping Beauty* better. Boys, don't you think I should try to wake up Sleeping Beauty by kissing her?"

Caleb cringes, and Carson covers his ears. "Ew."

I throw my arm back for the twins to give me five. "Yeah, I was thinking the same thing."

"What about *Pocahontas*?"

They shake their head. Toddlers sure do have incredible opinions about something like this.

I snap my finger. "I've got it. What about *Lady and the Tramp*? The two dogs eating spaghetti would be cute."

Caleb faces Carson. "Food is good."

I shrug. "Okay, then which one of you wants to take the picture of Uncle Clint and me eating spaghetti?"

They both raise their hands. "Me, me."

"Okay, Carson, you get to take that picture."

He punches his fist in the air. "Yes."

"But first, Caleb, you get to take a picture of us when we stand next to some graffiti."

Caleb's mouth drops. "There's a giraffe?"

Clint ruffles Caleb's hair. "Graffiti. Like scribbles on the wall."

"Mama doesn't like 'fiti."

"I bet she doesn't, but this is on walls outside, and it's colorful and very artistic. We'll do that first then the food pic."

"Mama doesn't like 'tistic."

After we strap the boys into their car seats, Clint goes down Fulford Road. "I know just the place, or at least it used to be the perfect place." He drives toward the rough side of town, where old, rusty train cars sit in a metal graveyard.

The twins' eyes widen as they see one train after the other, all covered in brightly colored drawings.

"Wow."

"So rad."

Rad?

Clint parks, and we help the boys out of their car seats. "Which one is the best?"

They both point to a train car with a picture of ET wearing a red leather jacket, shooting a peace sign. "That one."

Clint holds out his phone and hands it to Caleb. "When we're ready, you touch—"

I stop Clint before he goes into a lecture about how to use the device. "I am pretty sure he can reset it to factory settings if you want him to. He knows how to take pictures."

He shrugs. "Okay, let's do this."

The two of us stand next to the ET-Michael Jackson hybrid and shoot peace signs. Caleb gives us a thumbs-up like he's a professional photographer. I stand on my tiptoes to see the photo, and it's darn good. "Nice job, Caleb."

"Yeah, boys, we need to beat it. Get it? Like Michael..." Clint jerks a thumb toward the artwork.

I roll my eyes. "Just stop."

Caleb whispers to Carson, "Lame."

I cover my mouth with my hand to keep from giggling. *"Out of the mouths of babes."*

Clint clears his throat. "Next up: spaghetti-eating pic. Do you think China King would help us out?"

"Yay! Chinese!"

"Oh my goodness. You just ate. Are you hungry again?"

Clint grins, and his resemblance to the twins is stunning.

Caleb agrees. "We like fortune cookies."

"Okay, let's go. One noodle and two fortune cookies coming up."

CLINT CARRIES BOTH twins as I explain to Mrs. Yu about our quest.

She scrunches up her brow and motions toward the buffet table. "All-you-can-eat for seven ninety-nine."

"No, ma'am. All we need is a plate of noodles and two fortune cookies."

Mrs. Yu motions to the buffet table. "All-you-can-eat—"

Clint steps up beside me. "We'll take two adult and two child buffets."

Mrs. Yu smiles and shows us to our table. I know for a fact that the boys will eat about twenty-five cents' worth of food, but if Clint wants to waste the money, then who am I to complain?

The first thing the boys do is tear into the fortune cookies, knowing good and well they can't read a single word on the papers. They throw the papers on the table, and I read them out to them.

"Caleb, yours says, 'You will be a rock star someday.'"

"Awesome."

"Let's see. I wonder what Carson's is going to say." I give Clint a playful wink, and he returns the gesture. "'You will be a famous baseball player.'"

Clint high-fives Carson. "It's genetic."

"What's 'netic?"

Adorable. Through my giggles, I say, "Yeah, I don't know what would happen if you had a great baseball player in the family."

"Burn," Clint says. "I deserve that, especially after this season."

I quirk an eyebrow. "That bad?"

He holds a noodle over my head, threatening to drop it in my hair. "I guess that means you haven't been keeping up with my career."

"Pfft. Why would I do that?"

He leans into me and whispers, "Because you love... your sports." His breath tickles my ear.

"Athletes are all the same. Overpaid, overvalued, unimpressive."

His eyes twinkle. "You're not going to hold back, are you?"

"Have I ever?"

Clint pulls out a chair for me to sit next to him and slides the plate of noodles over to the vacant spot. "I guess not. Okay, Carson. Are you ready for your time as the photographer?"

He grabs for the phone without answering.

"Wait until we get the noodle ready, okay?"

"Uh-huh," he says, but he's already snapping photos even before we can get the noodle in our mouths.

Clint leans in and nibbles on his side of the noodle until he's nose to nose with me. When his lips brush mine, I jerk back. That warm tingly feeling is not what I need right now.

Caleb yells, "Gross!"

"Did you get it?" Clint asks.

Carson agrees. "Yeah, and it's gross."

Clint and I examine the photos, and I point to the one right before our lips touch. "That's the best one. You can still see the noodle."

He shrugs. "I guess, but I like that one better." He points to the last picture, the one where our lips touch.

"You might want to save that pic in the cloud, because that won't be happening again anytime soon." I point at my lips. "These lips are for Ken only."

"Ew, gross."

As much as I want to agree with the twins, Clint's lips are just as soft as I remember. He has to stop touching me, because every time he gets close, he chips another chunk of ice from around my heart, and that's a terrible thing right now. The more time I spend with Clint, the more I question my feelings for Ken.

CHAPTER TWENTY-SIX

Clint

The twins run into Regina's living room like they own the place. Together, they plop down in the recliner and force it to rock back and forth.

"Okay, kiddos, before we start the movie, why don't you go wash your faces and get into your jammies?"

Carson pouts. "Are you going to wear your jammies too?"

My eyebrows shoot up as I wait for Regina's answer. Perhaps she has something skimpy in her closet. On second thought, I hope it's a fleece onesie, especially if it's the nightie Ken sees when he sleeps over.

Regina's face lights up. "If you want me to, I'll get into my jammies. What about Uncle C? Do you think he should change into some PJs too? That way, when your daddy comes to pick you up later tonight, you'll be all ready for bed."

"Yeah!" The twins rock the recliner so much, I'm afraid they're going to flip it over.

I belt out a laugh. "I don't think you want me to wear mine." I lean over Regina's shoulder and whisper, "The lack of PJs, if I am being more precise."

She sucks in a breath and swivels around to shove the boys' bag into my arms. "You go help them get ready, and I'll do the same."

"Come on, boys. The quicker we do this, the faster we can watch *Bolt*."

They race down the hallway and into the bathroom.

"I'll be back," she says as she rushes toward her bedroom.

"Make it something pink!" I yell after her.

Over her shoulder, she winks and says, "Always."

She's killing me.

After I have Carson decked out in his Ninja Turtle pajamas and Caleb in his Spider-Man set, we park our butts on the couch, waiting for Regina to return.

"What do you think she'll wear?" I ask the twins.

Carson shrugs. "Clothes."

Darn.

"Tell me about this movie."

Caleb jumps up and runs around the coffee table. "It's about a real fast dog."

"Sounds interesting." *Not really.*

"There's a little more to it than that," Regina says, entering the living room as she pulls her hair up into a messy bun. *Holy fastballs.* Only she can make pink-and-white-pinstripe pajama pants and a ratty Smithville High School T-shirt sexy. "Bolt is in an action TV show, and he thinks he really has superpowers. One day, he gets lost, and as he's trying to find his way back home, he realizes he's just a normal dog. John Travolta is the voice of Bolt, and Miley Cyrus is Penny."

While my eyes continue to rake her sexy, casual, kid-friendly getup, I say, "I take it you've seen this movie a few times."

"Duh. The boys love it."

I rub my hands together. "Okay. Kids, you ready?"

"Yes!"

Carson pulls Regina down onto the couch, almost on my lap.

Thanks, buddy.

He snuggles in on the other side of her, and Caleb scoots in on my side. Regina smells like heaven, and with the way her thigh presses up against mine, this is going to be a non-kid-friendly moment pretty soon.

Her eyes rake over my body, and my heart skips. "I see your jammies consist of you untucking your T-shirt."

"I sleep in a lot less but thought the boys wouldn't want to see all that."

She juts her chin high as she finds the movie on Netflix and gets it started. "Me either."

I chuckle. "You, on the other hand, could wear a burlap sack, and I'd think you were beautiful."

She pinches my leg. "Just watch the movie."

As soon as the movie starts, the boys are catatonic, or more like pup-atonic. And I have to admit, it's a pretty cute movie.

Regina giggles. "You seem nervous. This is a kids' movie. You know things will be okay in the end."

"Still, it's pretty stressful."

She pats my leg, and right when I think she's going to snatch it away, she leaves it on my thigh, and I don't remember anything else about the movie. Regina rests her head on my shoulder and mumbles in my ear, "Carson is already asleep."

I lean up a bit to see him snuggled into her side, his mouth slightly open while his breaths come in slow, steady succession. Caleb sighs, and his eyelids flutter closed.

"I think we're wedged between sleeping boys."

Regina yawns, and without missing a beat, I wrap my arm around her shoulders. She settles into my side, closing her eyes, and I know without a doubt in my mind I've died and gone to heaven. With the rest of the viewing group sacked out, I try to watch the movie, but I'm totally consumed by the scene I'm currently living. My mind races ahead to envision Regina sleeping on a couch surrounded by our kids. I will never be able to get that image out of my mind, even if I want to.

Knowing I should wake up Sleeping Beauty, I nuzzle her neck and plant a soft kiss behind her ear. She sighs as her eyes flutter. Our noses touch.

"Hi."

"Hello."

She swallows as she tilts her head so I can gain access to her other ear. Her soft, warm skin wakes something inside me that's been dormant for far too long.

"You probably shouldn't do that."

"Why?"

"First off, the boys."

I kiss her neck, and she lets out a faint whimper. "They're completely sacked out."

"And secondly—" She gasps as I kiss lower down her neck, near her collarbone. "I might like it a bit too much."

I work my way back up to her cheek and say with a voice so husky I don't even recognize it, "Nothing wrong with that."

She bows her head as she puts some space between us. "Yeah, there is."

Ken. As if I could ever forget the wing-tip-wearing fly in the ointment. I remove my arm and nod, staring straight at the television screen. "Sorry."

After a beat of silence, she whispers, "Thank you for helping me win the money."

"We haven't won anything yet."

"We did good again today. It was fun."

"I had a lot of fun. The twins are..."

"Amazing?" She finishes my sentence.

"Yes, and then some. I'm not letting three more years go by without spending time with them. That is real living."

She bites her lip and stares at her hands, wringing the hem of her T-shirt.

"Is something wrong?"

Regina blows out a breath and stares at the television. "Something you said a few days ago hasn't left me."

Oh dear. No telling what that is.

She brushes the hair out of Carson's eyes. "I want this. I want a whole mess of kids. I'm not sure if Ken..."

If Ken doesn't want kids with Regina, he's the biggest idiot on the planet. I take a deep breath to tamp down my anger. "You should probably have that conversation sooner rather than later."

Regina swallows as she stares at her lap. "Yeah. Ken has good qualities, but I've been doing a lot of thinking lately. I don't know if he and I are equally 'yoked,' as my father would say."

Music to my ears. Like the crack of the bat.

She scrubs her face with her hands. "I don't know why I said that to you of all people."

I can't push her any further tonight, or I'll scare her right into his arms. "Maybe at the Pickle Festival this weekend, you can find a chance to have the conversation. I won't be tying up all your spare time by then." I paint on the fake smile I use for the cameras.

She stares up at me and runs a hand through my hair, turning my stomach into a big, knotted mess. "On the field, you have incredible timing, but off the field, it's a whole different level of horrible."

I groan. "Yeah. My agent and owner say the same thing. Just between you and me, I may not get re-signed."

"I'm sorry."

I wonder if she really means that. The contract is what drove the wedge between us in the first place. It changed the trajectory of my life and led us apart.

"Can you keep a secret?"

She grins. "I think I'm pretty darn good at keeping secrets."

Yes, she is. She never told anyone about the real reason we split up, knowing full well it would only benefit me. "If I don't get a new contract, I'm not so certain I'll be upset."

Her eyes widen. "Why?"

I rest my head on the back of the couch and let out a groan. "I'm so tired, tired of everything except playing—the travel, the expectations, the people pawing all over me, the pressure of being on my A game every single day. I'm sick of chomping on antacids." I let out a breath and add, "And I'm tired of being alone."

She stares at me and doesn't add anything to my words. All she does is rest her head on my shoulder again and slip her arm through mine.

"I haven't admitted that to anyone before."

"Confession is good for the soul."

"I am so sorry for everything I've done, and there's more, so much more I need to tell you—about being married. That was the best decision I ever made, then I broke your heart by wanting the divorce. But there's something I need to confess." I take a deep breath and tell her what I've needed to say for years. "We're still married."

I exhale with relief and wait for her reply. When she doesn't say anything, I gaze down at her to notice she's completely asleep, mouth parted, and good enough to eat.

Crap. The minute I get the nerve to tell her my deep, dark secret, she doesn't hear me. Maybe in her dreams, she'll comprehend my words and ask me about them tomorrow. If not, I hope the twins didn't overhear my confession. The last thing I need is for them to spill the beans to Regina.

I rest my head on hers and close my eyes, soaking in the company, enjoying my slice of heaven. If I know Regina, when she finds out the truth, this heaven I'm in is going to become the fiery pit of hell faster than Carson Fulmer's fastball.

CHAPTER TWENTY-SEVEN

Regina

A nudge to my shoulder stirs me from the best sleep I've had in years. I come out of my fog to see Ken standing over me with the biggest scowl on his face, arms crossed over his chest. I let out a big, unattractive yawn and stretch my arms, hitting my couch-snoozing partner, Clint.

Crap.

Doing my best to sound nonchalant, I say, "What time is it?"

Clint shifts on the couch, but he's still completely sacked out.

"Ten o'clock at night," Ken says. "I was on my way out of town and thought we could have some private time to regroup." He stares from one twin to the other. Carson's sleeping with his mouth open, and Caleb's sucking his thumb. Clint's long legs stretch over the coffee table, and his T-shirt has ridden up to expose his abs.

This is way more benign than it appears. "I... this isn't what you think it is."

He scoffs. "What do *you* think I'm thinking?"

I slide off the couch and make sure the twins are asleep before I whisper to Ken, "Like a date. We had to watch a movie for the scavenger hunt, and we decided to babysit so their mother could get some rest. It was a win-win for everyone involved."

He snorts. "A win-win. Yeah. I'm starting to think this whole contest is a bad idea."

"Shh." Taking him by the arm, I lead him into the kitchen as I continue. "If you had a say in the matter, that might mean something to me."

Ken blinks then snatches his arm away from my grasp. "What do you mean?"

My cell phone buzzes on the end table, making one of the twins stir. "I mean, what I do is my business. I'm not married to you yet, so I don't have to tell you what I do. And even if we were married, I wouldn't need your permission to do someone a favor or to hang out with an old friend."

He pulls out his cell phone, and his thumbs fly over the keyboard. "Maybe we don't need to get married at all."

A week ago, I would have been devastated by his words. They would have cut me to the core, so much so I would have crawled into a fetal position for a month. But tonight, I see him not as a lifetime partner, the love of my life, but as a convenient way to not be alone anymore. If hanging out with Clint this week has reminded me of anything, it's that I deserve unconditional, take-me-as-I-am love from the person I plan to marry.

I peek over to the couch before I say in a hushed tone, "Ken, if you don't trust me—"

"I don't trust him." He points to Clint. "I see the way he gawks at you. It's not a buddy-buddy gaze, and I'm not stupid. You've been different since he waltzed back into town."

I peer over my shoulder to make sure my three sleepover buddies are still snoozing.

Again, my cell phone vibrates so much I think it's going to dance off the table.

"Different isn't always bad, Ken, and perhaps it isn't different. Maybe it's the real me."

He leans over my shoulder and points to Clint, who stirs on the couch. "What are you going to do when he leaves you again?"

My throat clogs up. When Clint left me and asked for the divorce, I didn't want to get out of bed. I was so grief-stricken I was physically ill for the longest time. It took every ounce of my energy to go to my classes.

I stare at Ken and whisper, "This isn't about him. It's about me. Answer me this one question. Do you want children?"

He blinks at me like that's the most ludicrous question in the world. "I haven't really thought about it, but if I had to give you an answer right now, it would be no. Do you?"

"Yes. It's nonnegotiable." I stare at the ceiling and let out a laugh. "I can't believe we got engaged and didn't even discuss one of the most important aspects of a marriage."

"We can work that out later."

He can't be serious right now. I stare at him like he grew a third eye. "My father's words when he met you still ring in my head like a gong. You stumbled over your reply when he asked you the most basic question—if you loved me. And then he wouldn't give me his blessing until he knew for sure you were the only one for me. This is why. We're not on the same page about something extremely important."

Ken rolls his eyes and chuckles. "Are we back in the eighteenth century? You don't need his permission."

"I don't need his permission, but I want his blessing. That's how I'm wired. One more thing that's been bugging me a lot this week. You proposed and wanted to get married so soon, then you wanted to wait, and now you don't want to get married at all. Why the paradigm shift?" God, I hate using one of Ken's business phrases, but maybe he'll understand what I'm saying.

"There isn't one."

My phone goes crazy, and I throw my hands in the air. "Hang on while I see what in the Sam Hill is so important."

While Ken scowls, I scroll through the text messages.

Have you read the blog?

OMG. Read the blog.

The blog. Read it.

Crap on a cracker. Did you know?

"Can we finish this conversation?"

I hold up a finger for Ken to wait while I pull up *Biddy's Blog*. The title, "The Big 'Dill,'" seems innocent enough. I barely get to the second sentence when I suddenly feel sick to my stomach. *Shut the front door.* This has to be idle gossip.

"Ken, do you have something you need to tell me?" I turn my phone toward him so he can read the blog. When his mouth gapes open like a fish out of water, I read the blog to him. "'We don't relish the idea of spreading gossip.'" *That's hardly true.* "'But we've been told by a reliable source that one of our Pickle Festival contestants is in a rather (cu)cumbersome situation. So, Mr. Ken Doll, let's make a dill. Come clean now about the present Mrs. Doll, or you may end up in a very "briny" situation.'"

I take a step toward him, and he backs up.

"Are you married?"

He shoves his phone in his suit pocket and fishes out his keys. "Don't act surprised. I know he told you," Ken says, pointing to Clint.

"You proposed to me while you were still married?"

He holds his hand out. "It doesn't matter anymore anyway. The ring?"

"Gladly." I slide the engagement ring off my finger and drop it into his outstretched hand.

"This would never have worked. I love it here in Smithville, playing with my nephews and working in the local hospital, having my own children someday."

"They aren't your real nephews."

He'll never understand that a divorce decree doesn't stop me from loving them like family. I swallow and wipe a tear from my eye. "They are to me. It's a Southern thing. You wouldn't understand."

Carson rolls over and snuggles with Clint. Without even knowing what he's doing, Clint wraps an arm around him like it's the most natural act in the world.

"You still love him, don't you?"

"I guess a part of me always will, but he left me. That's hard to forget. Like I said, though, this isn't about him. It's about me, and you made it so much easier to figure out."

He rotates the ring in the palm of his hand. "Do you still have the ring box? I'd like to get a full refund."

Typical.

I go in search of the ring box in my nightstand. When I find it, I rub my thumb across the velvety smooth cover, and with a peace like no other, I nod, for no other reason than to confirm for myself that I'm doing the right thing.

When I enter the living room, I catch Ken watching Clint and the boys sleeping on the couch. He huffs as if he doesn't understand what he's witnessing. He'll never get it. Even though he lives in Atlanta now, he'll never be Southern and will never understand the bond I have with the Sorrows.

I hand Ken the box, and after he places the ring safely inside, he moves toward the door and out of my life. My shoulders slump in defeat.

"Aunt Regina, I have to go potty." Carson stands next to me, rubbing his eyes.

I take him by the hand and lead him to the bathroom. "Let's get you taken care of. Your daddy will be here soon to take you home."

"I wanna stay here with you and Uncle Clint."

"You're always welcome to come back, but Uncle Clint doesn't live here, remember? He lives above the coffee shop right now, and he's a big-time baseball player, so he won't be here much longer."

"Don't be filling him with your assumptions."

Clint's words make both Carson and me jump. Carson's urine stream flies across the floor and onto Clint's socks. I stifle a giggle as I position Carson back in front of the toilet.

"I can't tell you how many times a patient has peed on me. It doesn't bother me anymore."

He peels off the sock and tosses it my way, making me squeal. "Jocks aren't any better aimers, so it doesn't faze me in the slightest."

As Carson rushes back to the living room, I take a long gander at Clint. Try as I might, I feel a pull toward him, even though I know he'll break my heart... again.

He scratches his scruffy chin. "Did I hear you talking to someone?"

I nod. "Ken stopped by."

Clint's eyebrows rise. "Sorry I crashed on you. I bet that didn't go over well, huh?"

"Not at all, but I think it was good, because I asked him something you said I should have a long time ago."

"Yeah?" His voice is barely above a whisper.

"I asked him about children. Turns out, he doesn't want kids."

Clint runs a hand down my arm, leaving a warm trail of emotions in its wake. "Are you okay with that?"

"Sure."

Clint's face becomes as stone.

"I mean, I can't change him, but he can't change me either. That's pretty much a deal breaker for me." I hold up my unadorned left hand. "The engagement's off."

His eyes grow big. "That's great. I mean, if you're happy, then I'm happy."

"Yeah. I am. He doesn't love me like I need to be loved, and I don't think I really loved him either—I liked the idea of him. That and the fact that he's married."

"I guess you can only really be married to one woman at a time." He cringes as he walks away, but I grab his arm.

"You really did know, didn't you? I thought Ken was just trying to stir up trouble."

He blows out a breath and bows his head. "At the football game, Ken told me he was married."

"What a weasel. Why would he propose to me if he's still married?"

"Because he thought he needed one in the batter's box waiting for the at-bat wife to strike out."

"I have no idea what that means."

I pop him in the stomach, and he lets out an "oof."

"That's for not telling me." A random thought pops into my mind. "This is so bizarre, but I think I dreamed that you told me about Ken still being married."

Someone knocks on the front door, and Clint jumps. "It must be Silas for the boys. As Ken would probably say, put a pin in that thought."

I roll my eyes, but the truth is, I was getting weary of the business clichés.

Silas tiptoes in and whispers, "How were they?"

"Angels, as always."

He peeks around the room. "Okay, were you babysitting someone else's twins?"

Clint kneels down in front of Caleb and brushes the hair out of his eyes. "C-One, your daddy is here."

My heart swells when he picks up a sleeping twin and wraps his big arms around the little guy. Clint's fingers spread across the sleepy boy's back, making my heart go all fluttery.

I stuff their backpacks with their belongings and hand them to Silas. "I hope Marlo got some rest."

He sighs. "You have no idea how much I appreciate you watching them. She's worn out. My goal is to get them to sleep without waking her up."

Clint rubs little circles on Caleb's back. "How about I follow you to your house and help you put them to bed?"

Silas's eyes fill with tears. "That would be awesome, little brother."

I give each twin a kiss on the cheek as Silas and Clint carry the boys out to the car.

Clint walks back to me, where I stand at my front door. "I'd say I'm sorry about you and Ken, but that would be a lie."

Trying my best not to smile, I give his chest a shove. "I'll see you in the morning. Day three should be fun."

His big hand slides down my face, sending sparks straight into my heart. "It's all been fun for me. See you in the morning, Regina."

Frozen in place, I watch until their taillights are out of sight then close the door behind me. I should be upset that I'm not engaged anymore, but I'm not. A little perspective gives me a chance to see that Ken was a stuck-up snob—and he was still married. *Who does that?*

Instead of crying into my pillow, I pull out my cell phone and text Mel and Andie. *The engagement is off.*

I immediately receive a reply from Andie saying, *Woo-hoo!!!!*

Dang. I didn't know she had such a strong dislike of Ken.

Mel doesn't hold back either. Her reply says, *What's the plan to get your real man back?*

I don't have a man, real or unreal. The only one I ever really had left me, and even though I've had more fun this week than I have in years, I know he'll leave soon, especially when spring training rolls around. I'm not going to let myself be crushed. I can't feel that pain again.

I reply to them both, *My plan is to win the money.*

Andie replies, *Day three is a doozy. I hope you're up for it.*

That doesn't sound good at all. And if I don't get some sleep, I'm going to lose points by being late to the check-in meeting again. Thoughts of men and love have to wait. I have a wad of cash to win, and even if I don't need it for a wedding in the near future, I have thoughts on how to spend it wisely.

CHAPTER TWENTY-EIGHT

Clint

While I carry a snoozing Caleb into the house, Silas cradles Carson. They both have their cute mouths open, and I have a puddle of drool on my shoulder that I wear like a badge of honor. We settle them into their race car–shaped twin beds, and it warms my heart when Silas bends down to give each of his boys a soft kiss on their foreheads.

Marlo slips into the room, letting out a big yawn. "Hey, Clint."

"Hello, Mars. Thanks for letting me hang out with these kiddos today. I needed that."

She wraps an arm around my waist and squeezes. "Thank you. They're great kids, but very energetic."

"I got christened today with pee on my sock."

Marlo stifles a giggle as she leads me out of the twins' bedroom and into the living room. "Consider yourself a real, honest-to-goodness uncle now."

We settle into the couch, and Silas joins us, slumping down into an easy chair. "At least you didn't get pee in the face, like Mitch did."

Visions of my brother getting whizzed on brighten up my day. "I wish I'd seen that."

"Me, too, bro. Change of subject. I know you're a free agent now. What's going to happen?"

I was hoping to avoid baseball talk for as long as possible, but Silas isn't the nosy type. He only cares for my well-being. "I'm up for arbitration, and I'm a liability, so there's a good chance we won't come to a compromise with the new contract. If I'm lucky, I'll be sent back down to Double-A ball, making barely above minimum wage."

"Ouch."

Marlo yawns. "What do *you* want?"

It's been a long time since someone asked me what I want. I've been like a dancing marionette doll, and anytime I've veered away from that, I've screwed up so bad, I haven't known how to fix it. The more I ran around the bases and ran from the mess I left in Smithville, the worse things got.

"These last few days, I've reexamined myself, and I don't like what I see." My throat swells, and I have to swallow hard in order to speak again. "As much as I hated Mama for leaving when things got hard, I did the exact same thing. I ran at the first chance I got. I'm very sorry."

Marlo rests her head on my shoulder. "Clint. You got drafted, and no one blamed you for taking such an awesome offer."

"I left Regina. I should have been able to have both a major-league career and her, but I didn't want to be held back. I was a selfish jerk."

Silas folds his hands and rests them behind his head. "I'm going to tell you something, baby brother, and you better listen good and hard. You are not Mom. You were young and had a great chance to make something of yourself. She was a mother with three children, and she abandoned us. Those two things are not the same."

The room fills with a thick, sober silence. I know Silas speaks from the heart, but I'm not sure I buy it.

"It doesn't matter anyway. I may be a has-been before I'm thirty." I let out a wicked laugh. "And the craziest part is that I think I'm okay with it. I'm sick of all the traveling and the stress of being perfect, and I'm so tired of the God-awful press in my face all the time just waiting for me to mess up. I want to wake up in the same bed every morning for the next fifty years and have a normal, boring life for a change."

Marlo squeezes me around the middle. "Is Smithville growing on you again? Because you just described this town."

Silas snorts as Marlo takes my hand and rests it on her bulging belly. If I'd stuck with my marriage, I might have had a few chances to feel a pregnant belly by now.

"Maybe. Not that it matters, but Regina broke off the engagement with her Ken doll. What a piece of work."

Silas chuckles.

Marlo throws a hand in the air. "Best news I've heard since I found out I was having a little girl."

Silas tumbles out of his easy chair, his face as white as a ghost. He snaps his head up from his position on the floor. "Are you serious?"

She giggles. "Yeah. I wasn't sure how you'd take it."

He crawls over to Marlo and sits at her feet. "Are you kidding me? This is... I don't have the words." He places a hand on each side of her face and kisses his wife, and I can't stop grinning.

If it's the last thing I do, I'm not going to miss out on this little Sorrow coming into the world.

"Si, that baby girl is going to have you wrapped around her little finger, and I can't wait to see it firsthand."

Silas grins from ear to ear. "She's already succeeded. I can't wait to spoil her rotten." He glows with daddy-hood.

It's easy to be a little green with envy thinking about it. "And she'll have two big brothers ready to kick any dude's butt if they mistreat her."

Marlo shrugs as she lets out another yawn. "Either that, or they'll teach her how to pee standing up."

Thinking back to my childhood, I remember Mitch, Silas, and me having sword fights as we all tried to pee in the toilet at the same time. Hardly any urine hit the toilet bowl. It might have been a contributing factor to my mother hightailing it out of Smithville and my father being a drug dealer and addict, but we were just being kids, and pee came with the territory.

"Is this still a secret, or can I tell Regina?"

"Go ahead. My parents know, and as soon as I send this text to Mitch, he'll know. Before dawn, the cat will officially be out of the bag."

I give her another hug as I get up to leave. "Thanks for letting me hang out with the twins tonight. They were a lot of fun."

"I'll remember you said that when I have a newborn in the house."

I kiss her cheek. "Can't wait."

NOT ABLE TO WAIT UNTIL tomorrow morning, I text Regina. *I've got some news. Call me.*

She FaceTimes me, her hair all over her face in a sexy bed head. "This had better be good."

"The best. Marlo and Silas are going to have a little girl."

I have to hold the phone away from my face to avoid losing my hearing.

"Oh my gosh! This is fantastic. I'm so excited. We have to go shopping. I finally get to shop the pink aisle."

The way she chatters on and on, it could be a very good segue into the bomb I need to drop on her, and there's no time like the present.

"Regina, while I have you on the phone, I need to tell you something, and it can't wait."

She frowns. "You're leaving, aren't you?"

"What? No. That's not it. I'll be at your apartment in five minutes."

She blows out a breath. "Fine. Make it fast, okay?"

"Please promise me you won't hate me."

Regina chuckles. "I can't make that promise. Come on over. Say what you need to say, and let me get some sleep."

She's going to blow a gasket, but I can't wait another second to set things straight. It's time I grew a pair.

THE WHOLE DRIVE TO her apartment, I rehearse ten different ways to tell her the truth, and every one of them includes her punching me in the nose when she hears what I have to say.

I throw my SUV in park and try to calm my breathing. This is more stressful than when I was up to bat in my first major-league game, and the stakes are way higher.

Regina opens her apartment door, saunters out onto the sidewalk, and taps her toe in an impatient manner. Like I'm walking through Jell-O, I inch closer to her.

"You have the count of three, and if you aren't talking, I'm going back to bed."

Scrubbing my face, I pace back and forth in front of her. "Give me a second."

She tugs me by the arm and leads me into her apartment, then shoves me onto the couch. "Spit it out. Now."

I lean over, elbows resting on my knees, hands on my forehead, and just let it spew. Whatever happens needs to happen. "We're still married. I forgot to file the papers, and it didn't occur to me until I heard you were engaged, and I couldn't let you get married because that would have been against the law, plus... I still love you."

I collapse back on the couch, panting like I just ran the bases. When I get the courage to glance up, Regina hasn't moved. It's almost as if she didn't hear a word I said. I hope she did, because I don't think I can say all that again.

"Regina."

"Stand up."

Not wanting to tick her off anymore, I obey. I rise and steady myself for the wrath of Regina. She blows out a breath then smiles. It's not her happy smile. It's the fake princess smile, and I'm ready to crap my pants.

"Oh, Clint, honey."

Uh-oh. I remember enough about living down here to know if a woman says "honey" or "bless your heart," they're about to explode.

"The Bible says to turn the other cheek, but right now, I want you to turn yours so I can slap both of them. How could you do this? We're still married?" If her voice rises another octave, we are going to be bombarded by all the stray dogs in town.

I'm terrified to move, so I stay frozen. "I'm sorry."

She holds out a hand to stop me from saying anything else. "Go home, Clint. We'll talk about this tomorrow."

I blink like an idiot. "You're not mad?"

Regina chuckles. "I'm not mad. I'm pissed. Go home."

"Yes, ma'am." I take a tentative step toward the door.

"I knew," she says in a quiet voice.

I freeze and rotate to watch Regina, her arms crossed, hugging her chest.

"I didn't know for certain, but that little voice inside me said things weren't completely settled with us."

"I never meant to hurt you."

"Please, go home. I need to process." She collapses into a chair and stares at the ceiling.

I nod as I scoot out of her apartment. I think that went well. She didn't kick me in the balls, and no one had to call the cops, and now the air is clear. Tomorrow is going to be interesting, to say the least.

CHAPTER TWENTY-NINE

Regina

As soon as Clint drives away with his tail tucked between his legs, I snatch up my purse, throw on some flip-flops, and stomp to my car. At first, I drive around town, not knowing where I'm going or why, but when I see the hospital up ahead, I screech into the parking lot.

I pull my car into a space at the ER entrance and dare Gunnar to give me a ticket. The emergency room doors slide open when I near them. Mitch leans over the nurses' station, his EMT belt hanging low on his hips. Mel sits at a workstation and taps on the computer in front of her while Mitch rambles on and on, like he always does when Mel's around.

When Mel sees me enter, her eyes get wide. "What happened to you?"

Mitch snickers. "Regina, are you sleepwalking? Nice outfit."

I glance down to notice I'm still wearing my pink pinstripe pajama pants and ratty T-shirt. In my fit of rage, I didn't even think to change clothes.

Mel rushes around the workstation toward me. "Are you all right?"

Without answering her, I march up to Mitch and poke him in the chest. "Did you know?"

He flinches as he tries to block me from jabbing him again. "Know what? That you're not right in the head?"

Mel steps in between us and takes me by the arm. "Let's go into the break room."

Mitch freezes in place, but when Mel gives him the stink eye, he grumbles and follows us. I pace the small room while Mel and Mitch sit at a table. They steal glances at one another, and I notice Mitch shrugs.

"I'm just going to spit it out, then I'll beat the crap out of both of you if you need it."

Mel glances at Mitch and whispers, "What in the Sam Hill is going on?"

He grimaces.

I poke him again. "Did you know Clint and I are still married?"

Mel gasps so loudly, I'm sure they heard her all the way up in the maternity ward. I think it's safe to say she didn't know.

Mitch holds up his hands in defense and says, "Regina, calm down."

Right in his face, I say, "Never tell a girl to calm down. That results in the exact opposite of calming down."

He gulps. "Noted."

I stare at the ceiling and take a deep breath. "How could you not tell me? All this time, I thought I was divorced."

Mitch stands up and rests a hand on each of my shoulders. "I did too. I promise I didn't know until the day he came back to town."

I stare into his eyes, the same eyes as all the Sorrow boys have, and know he's telling me the truth. "He told you but not me."

"It kind of slipped. I don't think he meant to say it, and I believe my brother when he says he thought you two were divorced long ago."

I let out a snort. "Yeah, sure. He 'forgot.' Who forgets to file the papers that they wanted in the first place?"

Mel stands and slides her arm around my shoulders and gives them a big squeeze. "I'm going to give you my twenty-five-cent professional opinion."

Mitch whistles. "Ooh, boy. This should be good."

Her face loses its emotion as she points to the chair and says to him, "Sit and stop talking."

In less than a second, he plants his butt in the chair and covers his mouth with his hand.

She focuses her attention back on me and says, "During my psych rotation in school, I learned that sometimes people forget important things because they block them out. Like they don't want to believe it's real. It's called motivated forgetting, and it's a defense mechanism. Maybe he really did forget because he really didn't want to dissolve the marriage."

"Mm-mm," Mitch says, beaming up at Mel. "Nothing sexier than a smart woman."

Mel's face flushes as she extends her chin higher, and I love how Mitch can lighten the mood at just the right time. Maybe Clint not filing was a mistake. I know as soon as he signed his contract, he never had more than five minutes of free time, so I can almost believe it was an honest oversight.

I chew on my lip as a tear escapes my eye. "He should have told me the day he came back."

Mitch shrugs. "I couldn't agree with you more, but he's not good with confrontation, so I'm going to give him the benefit of the doubt that he might have tried to tell you, and the situation didn't allow it."

Thinking back over the last few days, there were a couple of times when he acted like he wanted to tell me something, so maybe he did attempt to tell me. Even if he did, he didn't try hard enough.

Mel snorts. I've been around her long enough to know she's got something snarky to say. "What stopped you from going to the courthouse years ago to get a copy of the divorce papers?"

Gulp.

Mitch's grin consumes his face. "Good question, Mel." He asks me, "You got a good answer to that? If I were spitting mad at my spouse, I'd want a copy of the papers in my hot little hands to verify it was finalized."

Four beady eyes stare into mine, and I want to crawl into a hole. "I don't know."

Mitch snickers, and I smack him on the shoulder.

The phone at the nurses' station rings, and Mel says, "I've got to go, but think before you do bodily damage to him. It might have been just an honest snafu."

She leaves, and I let out a huff.

Mitch chuckles. "You have bed head. Were you and my brother rolling around in the hay when he let it slip?"

My jaw drops. "Heck no. We were taking care of your nephews, watching a movie, and I fell asleep on the couch."

"Um-hum."

I roll my eyes. "I don't have to justify my sleeping attire to you. Mitch, I trust you, but I know you're in the middle since he's your brother. What should I do? I'm so mad right now, I can't see straight."

He blows out a breath and tilts his head from side to side to get the kinks out of his neck. "This kind of puts a wrinkle in your wedding plans, doesn't it?"

"No. I broke up with Ken earlier this evening."

He grins, and I would love to smack that smirk off his face. "Then, you have to decide. Are you mad because you didn't know, or are you mad because you're still hitched to my brother?"

A ton of bricks settle into my stomach. Last week, I would have dragged Clint to the courthouse by his ear if he'd told me, but now, after he's been here a few days and I remember how good we once were together, I'm not so sure.

Mitch stands and flicks me on the nose, breaking me out of my thoughts. "That's what I figured. You're still in love with him."

I push away from him and fidget with the coffee cups on the counter. "That's impossible."

"Okay then, since you aren't getting married, you don't need all that money. So I guess you don't have to finish the scavenger hunt. Am I right?"

Dang it. I let out a growl. "Who says I don't need the money anyway?"

I feel his presence behind me. He leans over and whispers in my ear. "Keep telling yourself that. Just go easy on Clint tomorrow. Whether your feelings have changed for him, his for you have never wavered."

And with that, he saunters out of the break room.

Gah. I'll never get any sleep now.

CHAPTER THIRTY

Clint

Each step up to my apartment creaks, as if I'm being taunted by the old wood. The stairs laugh at me for being such a doofus. I close the door and switch off my phone, tossing it and my keys onto the kitchen table. Reliving the scene with Regina over and over in my mind only makes it worse. I collapse onto the couch, adjust my ball cap, and let out the loudest, most exasperated groan ever to come out of my mouth. I deserve whatever is coming to me, and more.

In the quiet dark, I think about all my hopes and dreams swirling down the toilet bowl of reality. It sucks. I no longer have any love for the sport that paid my bills. The love of my life may never forgive me, and I'll live above the coffee shop, begging Mrs. Cavanaugh for scraps, for the rest of my life. How the mighty has fallen.

Right when my brain shuts off enough for me to catch a few winks, something pops at my window. I roll over and put my pillow over my head, then I hear it again. It's probably an owl or some other nocturnal animal who's decided to make a nest against my bay window. It isn't until I hear the *whoop-whoop* of a police siren that my eyes spring wide open.

I stumble to the bay window and stare out to see Gunnar standing there, outside his police cruiser, as Mitch throws pebbles at my window. I open the window, and Mitch beans me in the face with a stone.

"Watch it, bro."

"If you would switch on your stupid phone, I wouldn't have to act like a fifteen-year-old. Open the door."

I growl. I do not want to talk to anyone, hence the reason for turning off my phone. "I'll talk to you guys in the morning."

I start to close the door when Gunnar uses his bullhorn and says, "Open up, or we'll have to break down the door."

"Shh. Jeez. This isn't the big city. People are asleep."

Mitch rears back to throw another pebble, and I say, "Okay. Give me a sec."

I jog down the steps and let the guys into the coffee shop. Mitch doesn't get one foot inside before he yanks me by the collar and hauls my butt up the steps. I may be taller than he is, but he's got me beat in muscle mass by at least twenty pounds. Plus, Gunnar is a tank, so I know I'm outnumbered.

"I'm going. Gunnar, don't you have a key to this place? You could have just let yourself in."

He chuckles. "True, but I was trying to be nice. Don't make me be not nice."

Mitch tosses me into the apartment as Gunnar closes the door behind him.

"You guys want a beer? If I knew you were coming, I would have tidied up a bit."

"Shut up, bro." Mitch's jaw clenches. It takes an awful lot for him to get to the jaw-clenching ticked-off stage, and he's there tonight. I really shouldn't mess with him right now. "I told you to tell Regina the truth. I knew it was going to be bad. The longer you waited the worse it was going to be." He pulls down the collar of his work shirt and points to his chest. "I'm going to have bruises where your girlfriend… I mean your *wife* poked me so much tonight."

Uh-oh.

"Yeah… I think she took it okay. I didn't get slapped once."

Gunnar sinks into a chair and rests his feet on the coffee table. "You're not in the doghouse. You're under the doghouse. I don't know how you'll ever crawl your way out of this one."

Mitch punches me in the arm. "At least there wasn't a camera around." He rolls his eyes for added effect. "Dude, you not only got yourself in trouble, but I was implicated in your stupidity. As soon as you blabbed it to me, you should have hightailed it over to her apartment to tell her the truth."

"I know!" My anger spews toward my brother and friend. "I know I should have. I-I'm not good at stuff like this. I love her, and I don't want to lose her, but she's so mad at me. I'll never have a chance, even if the Ken doll is out of the picture."

No one says anything for the longest time. Mitch knows I rarely raise my voice. I usually take my frustration out on a baseball, but I'm out of my league with this type of trouble. I fall onto the couch and scrub my face with my hands. Mitch sits beside me and rests his hand on my back.

Gunnar clears his throat. "Can you tell me one thing. Why did you forget to file? Or did you forget on purpose?"

Fighting back tears, I say, "I kept telling myself I'd do it tomorrow. Tomorrow morphed into next week and next month, and I got so busy with playing, I really did forget."

Mitch shoves my head. "What he's saying is that he didn't mean to forget, but like Mel explained to me, it was a defense mechanism. It even has a real medical term." He grins when he says her name. I wish they would get together and quit this little cat-and-mouse game they have going.

Gunnar yawns, then says, "That's all well and good, but what are you going to do now? You need to do something before the entire town knows."

"What do you mean?"

He throws his hands in the air like it's a no-brainer. "You either need to reconcile and admit publicly you're still married or... file papers."

Mitch stretches his arms over his head. "It was your choice last time, and you botched it. I think this time you should let Regina decide."

Now, after all this time, I don't want a divorce. Maybe this is the universe trying to tell me we're supposed to be together, but I don't deserve her, not after all the crap I've put her through. "You're right. I'll let her decide, if she'll even talk to me."

Mitch checks his watch as he stands. "She'll talk to you, but you better tread lightly, buddy. She'll eat you for lunch and spit out your bones. I have to work with her, so I'd like to still be on her good side."

I walk Gunnar and Mitch to the door, and as Gunnar trots down the steps, Mitch clasps my shoulder. "She may not like you right now, but she still loves you. You just might have to remind her of that."

Tears prickle my eyes. It's been so long since I've had a heart-to-heart with my brother, and I miss him so much. I wipe the tear away and give him a backslap and hug. "I love you, brother."

He squeezes me and replies, "Love you too. I'm glad you came home. I've missed you."

Before I can say anything else, he snatches my baseball cap off my head and slides it on his, then jogs down the stairs and out of the coffee shop. After I shut the door, I pick up my phone. I need to send Regina an apologetic text. When I power it back on, I notice I missed five calls from Mitch and one text from Regina.

Her message reads, *I don't know why you did what you did, but you better bring me chocolate chip muffins tomorrow, or I will back out of the scavenger hunt.*

My face splits with a wide grin as I text her back. *Yes, ma'am.*

CHAPTER THIRTY-ONE

Regina

If Clint's not standing outside with a large bag of chocolate chip muffins this morning, I will slam the door in his face. And after a sleepless night, I could use a bladder-buster-sized cup of coffee. I fling open the door to catch Clint on his knees, holding a brown paper bag between his teeth and a cupholder in one hand.

I groan. "Does this work for your adoring fans?"

He crawls on his knees toward me. Still holding the bag in his mouth, he mumbles, "Can I come in?"

I hold the door for him, and as he crawls past me, I snatch the bag of muffins out of his mouth. I open the bag and inhale the warm, chocolatey goodness. "You may be a doofus, but you do follow orders."

Clint climbs onto the couch and holds out a to-go coffee cup. "Thought you could use this if I caused your night to be as restless as mine was."

"Harrumph," I say as I sink down into the seat next to the couch. "I slept like a baby. A clean conscience will do that for you." I stifle a yawn as I slide one leg under my butt and take a sip of coffee.

"I don't know if you believe me, but I really didn't do this on purpose. I forgot I hadn't filed until last week."

I swallow the hot liquid and stare at him. That's the lamest excuse on the planet. "Then you proceeded to tell everyone in this town except the one person who needed to know. Did you forget about that part too?"

"Regina."

I take the first bite of my muffin, and my eyes roll back into my head. "Was it going to be in the next edition of *Biddy's Blog*? Or better yet, was I going to find out when it aired on Sports South?"

"I deserve that."

"Yes, you do."

We sit in silence for the longest time. The only sounds are the gulps we make as we slurp down our coffee and an occasional moan of satisfaction the muffins cause.

He gobbles down the last of his third muffin then asks, "What now?"

I shrug, because if I talk too much, I'll get all emotional, and things could get messy after that.

He clears his throat and trains his eyes on the ceiling. "I'll file the divorce papers today—that is, if you want me to."

What do I want? I didn't want the divorce in the first place. This could be divine intervention giving us a second chance, or it could be the universe telling me I could make him be the bad guy this time.

"Not today," I say in a quiet voice.

He snaps his head around so fast he's going to need a massage to work out all those pulled muscles. "Really?" Clint's eyes are filled with hope.

"We'll be very busy today. Perhaps tomorrow."

His shoulders slump. "Yeah. Tomorrow."

I pick up the bag and the empty coffee cups to toss them in the trash. Over my shoulder, I say, "I still want to win that money."

Clint follows me into the kitchen and leans against the doorframe, seeming very penitent. "Please, don't hate me."

I snort as I stand in front of him and crane my neck to see his face. "If I couldn't hate you for divorcing me, I don't think I can muster up the guts to hate you for *not* divorcing me."

His knees buckle. "Thank you."

"Whoa, dude. I may not hate you, *but* I don't like you very much right now."

His eyes sparkle, and I want to slap my own face for enjoying the view.

"I'll take what I can get."

Motioning with my head, I say, "Let's go. We can't afford to lose any more points."

He waves his arm toward the door. "After you, ma'am."

His Southern charm is going to be the death of me.

ANDIE HAS GOT TO BE kidding me. Day three's hunt is next to impossible. Locating a pinball machine is going to be hard enough, but there isn't a car wash within fifteen miles of Smithville. And those are nothing compared to the "doozies," as Andie calls them.

Clint lets out an "oof" when I shove day three's list against his chest. "Doozy doesn't even come close to our items for today. I don't know if we can pull all this off."

He reads the list, and a rumble of laughter bubbles up through his throat.

I pop him again.

"What's wrong with going bowling? And I'm sure finding ten different ketchup packets can't be that hard." He eyes me up and down. "Not to mention, you'll do great instructing an aerobics class."

I hold out a hand to stop him. "Oh no. That's yours." I glance around before I whisper, "But first dance, first kiss..."

"Those items are worth a lot of points. I'm sure you can put up with a little tongue wrestling from me for one moment."

Thoughts of kissing him make my stomach flip-flop. He was a phenomenal kisser back in the day, and the thought of his lips on mine again sends tingles down my spine. I catch a glimpse of Andie doing her best to conceal her giggles behind her hand, but her smiley eyes can't hide her evil mind. She did this on purpose.

I blow out a breath before I say, "Let's get this day over with."

He follows me out of the room. "You really know how to take the fun out of things."

"I learned it from the best."

Clint chuckles as we climb into his G-Wagon. "What do you want to tackle first?"

I stare out the window, trying to figure out what I should say. We could get the kiss over with, but that may make the rest of the day all awkward, so maybe that should be last. "It's too early for Ward's dress shop to be open, and they have the best storefront display, so that will have to wait until closer to lunchtime. Let's go to China King and start our way through a pile of fortune cookies until we find one with the word 'happy.'"

He puts his vehicle in drive. "You're the boss."

I gasp, causing him to swerve. "I just thought of something. The fire station has a pinball machine." I point to the street we're about to miss. "Turn there and go back to Main Street. Do it before the other teams realize it."

He swings his SUV on a dime, slinging me all over the cab. "If I get a ticket, you're bailing me out of jail."

"Considering Gunnar's fiancée is the one behind all of our shenanigans, I think we can talk ourselves out of a ticket."

Clint pulls up to the fire station, and as I slide out of the vehicle, several firemen meet us, giving Clint backslaps and bro hugs. As they catch up, I send a quick text to Andie. *Are you kidding me?*

She replies with a kissy face emoji.

Ugh. I slide the phone into my back pocket and saunter toward the firemen, most of whom I grew up with. Danny, the assistant fire chief, used to play ball with Clint, and it's like they're having a big old-fashioned bromance.

"Mitch keeps us in line when we start trash-talking you."

"Good to know someone sticks up for me."

Danny chuckles. "I'm just kidding, but Mitch is really proud of you."

"I hate to break up this little lovefest, but we're kind of on a deadline. Can we use your pinball machine for just a second?"

Danny waves us into the station. "Andie warned us we might have some visitors today, so have at it."

I clap my hands. "Chop-chop. We're burning daylight."

Behind me, I hear Danny say to Clint, "Bossy as ever, huh?"

Clint mumbles, "You can say that again."

With my hip jutted out, I reply, "I heard that, and you're still on my naughty list, so you better behave."

A round of woo-hoos fills the fire station, and I already regret my choice of words.

While Clint and I play a round of pinball, Danny takes pictures. Clint keeps bumping me out of the way with his hip and snatches my hand away to make me mess up.

"Get your hand off my flipper."

A round of laughter comes from behind us, and heat runs up my neck. "Y'all never change."

When the display announces that we scored bonus points, Clint struts around like a chicken.

I roll my eyes. "Come on, pinball wizard, we've got some ketchup packets to collect."

After a round of high-fives and fist bumps, I finally drag Clint out of the firehouse.

He says, "That was fun."

I nod. "They're good guys. I see them when they bring patients in from wrecks."

"None of them ever caught your eye?"

Jealous much? "No. I guess they were too much like brothers. They still hang out with Robert, and it's hard to tell where one of them stops and the other starts."

He smirks. "Good."

Clint has to stop marking territory that's not his anymore. Those days are over. "Stop messing in my personal life. You've done enough damage for one week."

"You know me. I won't stop until I bat over five hundred."

"No baseball metaphors, please." I roll my eyes. "Wait."

"What?"

"Go back in the fire station. If they're anything like the hospital staff, they keep every extra packet of ketchup, mayo, you name it, from every time they've ordered out."

"God, I love you," he says, swinging me around to rush back where we came from. "I mean..."

I focus on my sneakers, because if I glance at him, I might burst into tears. "I know. Just stay focused," I say as we run back into the fire station.

"Where's the fire?" Danny asks, laughing. "Sorry. A little fire station humor."

"We need to raid your stash of ketchup packets."

Danny grins and motions with his head. "You've come to the right place."

He leads us into the kitchen and opens a drawer stuffed full of salt and pepper packets, hot sauce, pepper flakes, and the biggest stash of ketchup packets in the county. Clint and I high-five each other.

"I think we hit the mother lode." He scoops up the packets and spreads them out on the counter.

Most are from McDonald's, but we find several from Krystal, Burger King, White Castle, and even one from Bud's Burgers, a burger joint that went out of business five years ago. I cringe as I hold it up, but I bet no other team will have this one.

He scoops up one and stares at it. "When did Smithville get a Burger Up?"

"Tifton has one. Ooh, here's one from Whataburger. Guys, I am so thrilled you never throw anything away."

Danny leans against the counter. "We aim to please. Just put them back when you're done. I'm on kitchen duty today, and I just cleaned this place."

"Woo-hoo. Number ten, compliments of KFC."

Clint holds all the packets in his hands, and I take a selfie with Danny in the background shooting devil horns over Clint's head.

"Thanks, Danny." Clint fist-bumps him again, and we run out of the fire station. "Did I ever tell you, you're the most think-outside-the-box person I have ever met?"

I smile. "It's called critical thinking, and that's what being a nurse is all about."

He cranks his SUV, and we travel down Main Street. "If it were up to me, we would have wasted time going to each fast-food restaurant in town searching for packets." He winks. "You're something else."

Stop doing that.

"Don't hate me, but turn around again. We're going to conduct an aerobics class with the firemen."

He swings the SUV around again, and through gritted teeth, he says, "I've made more illegal U-turns in the last hour than I have in a lifetime."

"Ready to get physical?"

His eyebrows rise, and I wish I could swallow my words.

I'm pretty sure I've already reached my target heart rate. "I didn't mean it like that. I was thinking of that Olivia Newton John song... never mind."

Clint bites his lip as he drives back toward the fire station. "Regina, I like this side of you."

I don't. Time to change the subject. I clear my throat. "So if my memory serves me correctly, you're at six years on your contract, and that means you're a free agent. Right?"

"Yep." His tight knuckles indicate he's going to break the steering wheel.

"That means you'll be in the driver's seat."

"Um, huh. Yeah. Sure." He stares straight ahead, clenching his jaw.

"That could be good for you."

He mumbles something under his breath then says, "Can we talk about something else?"

Wow. I think I hit a nerve. "Sure. Do you want to do a Zumba or a step class?"

That got a smile out of him. "Either way, you'll have to do most of the yelling. I seem to recall you used to be a pretty good cheerleader back in the day."

Sitting up tall in the passenger seat, I say, "The best. If I try, I probably can still do a few backflips."

"Promise?" He touches my face.

I swat his hand away. "I said probably. You're impossible and have a one-track mind."

"I'd like to see what my wife can still do."

I give him the stink eye. "Don't say the 'W' word. You never know who's listening."

"Oops."

As if he's the least bit sorry. "I don't believe your 'oops.' Seriously, there are eyes and ears everywhere. If my father finds out, he'll skin me alive. Please, we have to keep this under wraps."

His mouth pulls down into a frown as he turns into the fire station for the third time. "I guess you're right. Your dad has always liked me and didn't even put me on Satan's list when we supposedly ended it."

Dad is one of a kind. People sometimes think he's a hard-line pastor, but he preaches and practices forgiveness way more than he does about hell and damnation.

"That's my dad. I'd really like to keep you and me off his bad list, so work with me on this. Okay?"

"You got it."

He's going to grind his molars down to a pulp before day three is over. I think he needs a really good aerobics session.

CHAPTER THIRTY-TWO
Clint

It doesn't take Regina two minutes to round up the guys in the fire house to participate in her aerobics class. Even Chief Carl Crabtree, who could use a few cardio sessions, joins in on the fun. When she cranks "Burning Down the House," by Talking Heads, I think the roof is going to collapse with all the singing. Before the first chorus, it's more like a big jam fest than a cardio routine, but I hope it's enough to get us the much-needed points.

Watching Regina lead the burly firemen in an aerobics class is both hysterical and sexy. Her squat thrusts are legendary, and she has them eating out of her hands. When they get dispatched for a call, they sulk all the way to the fire engine, and one flips me the bird as I give him a girly wave.

Regina rocks back and forth on her heels. "So what's next? Fortune cookie or you wearing a dress?"

"I see you're skirting around the first-dance and first-kiss items."

Regina juts her chin in the air as she marches toward my G-Wagon. "More like pretending they aren't on the list. We can win without doing those two things."

"I'm not so sure about that. They're worth five hundred points each. That's bank."

She sneers, knowing I'm right. "We're not that desperate yet. Besides, I bet you don't even remember where our first kiss took place."

"No brainer. Under the bleachers in tenth grade."

Regina snorts. "Nope. That was the first mushy, gushy kiss. I'll give you that, but if you don't remember, maybe I shouldn't tell you. Then we won't be able to recreate it. Ha."

"Aw, Regina. That's harsh. Was it at your house?"

"Nope."

"My house?"

She stares at me, and if I don't answer correctly soon, she's going to make sure I never kiss anybody again.

"School?"

"Too generic, but it's still wrong. I think we should focus on who we're going to cook a meal for."

I pull into the Piggly Wiggly and park. "Was it at the Pig? Tell me it wasn't at the Pig. I'd think I was a little more romantic than that."

Regina giggles. "No, it wasn't at the Pig."

"Church."

She opens the car door. "Just stop guessing. You'll never figure it out because it didn't mean that much to you."

Across the parking lot, I yell, "Was it at In a Jam?"

She freezes in place and slowly rotates around. "Maybe." She then takes off jogging toward the grocery store entrance with me right on her heels.

"I'm right, aren't I?"

Grabbing a shopping cart, she wheels off in the direction of the produce section. "There aren't many places in town where we would have been, so you were bound to guess it eventually."

From behind her, I place my hands on the cart to cage her in then lean into her ear. "Valentine's Day. Right after the eighth-grade dance. Back booth. Mitch and Silas had wandered off with their dates and left us alone."

She pivots, and our noses brush against each other. "Lucky guess, but I'm still not doing it." Regina inspects tomatoes as if there's a single perfect one.

"We'll see. So who are we going to make dinner for?"

Without stopping her produce picking, she says, "I thought we'd stick with the Marlo theme and make dinner for your brother and sister-in-law. She needs it as much as anyone these days."

"She's your sister-in-law too."

"Shh. Don't say that so loud." Regina peeks around the bell pepper display.

"Nobody cares."

She collects the tomatoes and heads toward the fruit. "That may be true, but no one should give the grapevine any fodder to wallow in. I need you to keep your mouth shut and go find five pounds of ground beef and some ground pork too. The good stuff."

"What are we making?"

"Lasagna. I know the boys like it."

I should know this kind of stuff, too, but I don't. Regina's been an awesome aunt even when she didn't know she still was one. To me, that makes it even sweeter because it came from the heart, not from obligation.

"I'll get that and meet you in the pasta aisle."

"And try to stay out of trouble."

"Yes, ma'am, Mrs. Sorrow."

She swings around and points a banana at me. Through gritted teeth, she says, "What did I tell you?"

I wink at her. "Just trying to get a rise out of you. Is it working?"

"Yes, and if you don't watch it, I'm going to do something to get a rise out of you." I think she realizes her double entendre a second too late, because her face flushes the cutest shade of pink, and she grabs onto the shopping cart to scoot away from me.

I may have come here to stop her from making a big mistake by marrying someone while she's still married, but now, I feel like I'm making the mistake by letting her go again. This time it will be final—forever. I have to know for sure how she feels about me, and reenacting the first kiss is a good start. She may not want to do it, but I bet with Andie and Mrs. Cavanaugh's help, I can set this up without Regina even realizing it.

After one quick text message to Andie, I get a reply in a nanosecond. *Yes!* Followed by, *Mrs. Cavanaugh wants to help.*

Great. I'll have the entire county witnessing me getting slapped in the face.

I COULD GET USED TO cooking dinner alongside Regina. She rambles on and on to get me caught up to speed about how Andie and Gunnar met. She even admits how she let Gunnar's ex, Willow, put false impressions of Andie in her mind. It wasn't until she actually spent time with Andie that she realized she could be a good friend.

My arm brushes against hers as we layer the noodles, meat sauce, and cheese. I'm not sure what I'm hungry for more, the lasagna or the chef. Fortunately, she's smart enough to make two pans of lasagna, one to keep and one to share. It's a good thing, because if she hadn't done that, I would have been licking the meat sauce that got splattered on my T-shirt for the next few days.

When the oven timer dings, she gives me a big grin as she pulls the pans from the oven. I lift the aluminum foil lid, and she smacks my hand. "You'll let out all the goodness."

"Party pooper."

"We'll let this cool a bit before we take it over to Marlo. That's five hundred points for doing a good deed."

"Something tells me you would have done it even if you lost points."

Regina holds up both hands in defense. "Guilty. I love those kids like they're my own, so doing something for Marlo is a no-brainer."

"Thank you for being there for them."

"My pleasure. Mitch was the hard one to be nice to. I think I was always around him too much at work, so the last thing I wanted to do was do something nice for him in my time off. Plus, I didn't want the rumor mill to say that I'd moved on to another Sorrow brother."

Her singsongy voice makes me chuckle. "Yeah, I think I would have kicked his teeth in if he'd made the moves on you."

She rolls her eyes. "You know Mitch. He only has eyes for Mel, and Lord, I hope he can handle it if she permanently friendzones him." She gasps at her insult. "I didn't mean..."

"Yes, you did, and I deserved it. I'll never forgive myself for running away. I was selfish, and I know I hurt you."

"Yeah," she whispers.

"Please know that I've kicked myself every day for the last six years."

She points her oven-mitted hand at me. "Good to know. Let's just take the food to your brother's house before we dive in and eat it all and not feel the least bit guilty about it."

I take another whiff of the delicious food. "I haven't had a home-cooked meal in years."

Her mouth drops open as she stares at me. "We'll break your record tonight. As soon as we finish with the list, minus the kissing part, we'll come back here, watch a movie, and pig out. Deal?"

She holds her hand out, and I shake the oven mitt.

"Deal. You're not going to fall asleep on me again, are you?"

Biting her lip, she giggles. "I can't promise you that, but I'll try not to."

"Okay, ma'am. Lead the way. Let's get this food delivered. And after that, do you mind if I stop by my apartment to change shirts? I think every dog in Smithville will be sniffing me from the mess I made with this sauce."

"Sure. Then we have to get a fortune cookie with the word 'happy' in it and go back to Belk so you can try on a dress."

And the trap is set. I hope I can find a breath mint somewhere, because there's going to be some serious lip-lock happening in less than one hour.

CHAPTER THIRTY-THREE

Regina

Clint balances the lasagna pan in one hand as he knocks on his brother's front door. Silas opens it, and when the aroma of the Italian dish reaches his nose, his knees buckle.

"Oh man, did y'all do that for us?"

Clint blushes and motions with his head. "It was Regina's massive cooking skills. I only did as I was told."

Silas moves out of the way for us to enter. "Smart man. Marlo, Clint and Regina are here."

The twins barrel down the hallway and tackle us with hugs. Silas snatches the lasagna before it becomes a hood ornament on Caleb's head.

"Unc' Clint, can we watch another movie?"

Clint beams as he scarfs up Caleb in his arms to wrap him in a hug. "Not today, but soon."

Caleb's brow scrunches with a serious frown. "Promise?"

"I promise."

Clint doesn't understand he can't promise a three-year-old anything that he can't commit to. They're harder to walk out on than a spouse.

Carson tugs at the hem of my T-shirt. "Is that 'gana?"

I lean down to smother him in kisses. "Yes, sir. I made 'gana because I know it's your favorite."

"Awesome," he says, reaching for the pan in his dad's hands.

"Son, you just ate. This is for later."

"Aw. We're so hungry." Carson rubs his cute, protruding belly.

Silas rolls his eyes. "You're always hungry." He walks into the kitchen with us right behind him.

Marlo's sitting at the table, ugly crying.

Silas rubs her shoulder. "Hon, what's wrong?"

Her breath hitches. "It's... so sweet." She sniffles then buries her face in her hands to let out another round of sobs.

Silas whispers to Clint, "She's been doing this a lot lately."

Marlo wipes the tears from her face. After three attempts, she rises from her chair to wrap her arms around Clint. She motions for me to join in the hug fest. "Thank you so much. I'm having such a hard time with this pregnancy. I don't know why."

"Girls will do that to you," Clint says as I smack the back of his head. He adds, "But they're one hundred percent worth it."

Good save, Clint. Good save.

In order to lighten the mood, I say, "We needed to do something like this for our competition, and we couldn't think of anyone more deserving than you."

"The boys will love it."

"Me too," Silas says. He takes my phone and snaps a picture of us with Marlo and the boys just as Carson sticks his finger in the dish.

On our way out the door, Marlo hugs Clint again. "Please stay in town. I miss seeing you, and the boys talk about you all the time now."

He squeezes her shoulder. "I don't know what's next for me. Thank you for being the best sister-in-law ever."

Begging never worked before, so I highly doubt it will now.

After we say our goodbyes and promise another movie night in the near future, we set our course for the next item on our agenda. It's as painful as a bedsore to admit, but I've had more fun in the past few days than I have in a long time. It reminds me of how it used to be every day. It didn't matter if we were watching a baseball game, chowing down on pizza, or hanging out at the lake. Time with Clint was simple and carefree. I thought that stuff wouldn't change after we got married. It was stupid, and if I'd only waited six more months, he would've had the temptation of a major-league contract, and we would have gone our separate ways with a lot less baggage.

"Do you think we can buy a bag of fortune cookies and sift through them until we find a happy one?" he asks me.

"You have pretty good luck. It wouldn't surprise me if you found one on your first try, kind of like your draft day."

He clears his throat. "If I only knew then what I know now."

I chuckle. "You'd do the same thing all over again, and you would be a doofus to refuse it. No one ever thought bad of you for taking the contract. It was the right thing to do, even though the timing stank."

"Timing is everything. You tried to tell me to wait and finish my degree, that the pros wouldn't forget me."

"And if you had waited and gotten injured, you would have hated me forever. This way, I get to hate you forever, which is way more fun." My eyes twinkle, and I hope he knows I'm only kidding.

He throws his G-Wagon into a parking space across from In a Jam then twists to give me a smoldering gaze. "I hope we're past the 'hate' stage."

I hold my index finger and thumb an inch apart. "Just a little."

"Good. Come on. You can hang out with Andie while I change shirts, unless you want to help take it off my back."

Eye roll. "You wish."

"See? I can read your mind."

He takes my hand as we scoot across Main Street into the shop. Andie jumps to attention when we walk in the door, like she's been caught red-handed doing something illegal.

"Hey." Something's up.

"Clint went a little overboard while we were making the meal for a needy family. I hope your definition of 'needy' is subjective, because this family is at their breaking point with two little ones and a third on the way."

Andie's eyebrows rise. "Silas and Marlo? I figured you'd pick them, and they deserve it so much."

Clint takes my hand and plops me down in the back booth that already has drinks in place. "Sit there, and I'll be right back."

He rushes upstairs, and as I attempt to move to another booth, one that doesn't have so many memories attached to it, Andie shoves me back down into the seat and snaps her fingers as Mrs. Cavanaugh walks over with an iPod shuffle and switches on the music. When Lady Antebellum's song "American Honey" filters through the shop, I freeze.

This is not good.

Clint runs down the stairs, missing the last two steps, and skids to a halt right in front of me. "Gotcha."

I stand to leave and pivot on a dime, but he grabs my arm and pulls me close. "Dance with me, please."

Without waiting for my answer, he begins to sway back and forth, mumbling the lyrics in my ear, making my knees go weak.

"I love this song."

"Regina, I miss my American Honey."

"Aw," Andie says as she backs away from us.

Clint takes my face in his hands, and he gives me an Eskimo kiss. "We don't have to kiss if you don't want to."

As if.

When my lips touch his, I'm transported back to when we did this all the time. Even if I wanted to, I couldn't stop my hands from fisting in his clean T-shirt to pull him close to me. His mouth on mine makes me lose the last bit of hostility I had for him.

When we come up for air, I whisper, "I forgot to take a picture."

"I don't care."

"Me either." I pull him down for another kiss, and it's like we haven't missed a single day of being together. My arms slide up his chest and wrap around his neck. He picks me up, and we shuffle to the stairs. "Ladies, if you'll excuse us."

Andie yells after us, "That bed frame isn't for sissies!"

I'm not sure what she means, but I don't care. He holds me tight, and without even breathing hard, he carries me up the steps and kicks the door closed with his foot before he plants my feet back on the ground. As I slide down his tall body to place my feet on the ground, his hands graze my skin while he works off my blouse.

"I love you, Regina. I never want to lose you again."

"You never really lost me. You just went missing for a while. I'm glad we're still married."

He takes my face in his hands and stares at me for the longest time then kisses my cheeks. "Yeah. Me too. You're my one true love, Regina."

I'm tired of waiting for him to fling his shirt off, so I do it for him and, oh my stars, has he filled out in all the right places. Sure, his abdomen is a little softer than it used to be, but I actually like it that way. I've seen pictures on the internet, but I assumed they were Photoshopped. He is a mighty fine slice of heaven.

"You promise you won't get tired of me?"

He hugs the stuffing out of me. "Sweetie, I regretted every day away from you. I should have figured out how to have both lives, and I'll ask for your forgiveness every day for the rest of my days."

And just like that, I go from trying to hate him to not even trying to keep my clothes on. I bounce up and wrap my legs around his waist, and he waddles into the bedroom. He presses my back up against the wall while he unbuttons my shorts. I drop my legs and let the shorts fall to the floor, flinging off my flip-flops in the process.

With the force of a linebacker, I shove his body toward the bed. He trips over my shoes and lands on the bed sideways. After an eerie creak and a bang, we find out the hard way about the details of the bed's reputation. Clint's head is almost on the floor, but his feet flail in the air.

"I think you were caught off base on that one."

He grabs my hand, making me squeal as I land on top of him. "Watch it, sweetheart. You may be in for a doubleheader."

Not willing to let him get the last word in, I say, "You better not strike out, or I'll send you down to the minors."

Clint props his head up with his hand. "Are you done?"

"Nope, and you better not be either."

This may be the biggest mistake of my life, but if I don't take this chance, I'll always wonder, "What if?" After all, we're still married, and we're going to do what married people do.

CHAPTER THIRTY-FOUR

Clint

Watching Regina hog my bed while she wears my team T-shirt is the closest thing to heaven I've had in a very long time. Her blond hair falls over her face, and I twirl that incredibly sexy purple streak around my finger as she sleeps sprawled out over me.

We got reacquainted late into the night, and I hate to wake her up, because she needs her sleep. One night with her, and I want to forget about being a free agent or trying to improve my image. I'll just move back here and get a job as a personal trainer or do whatever job I can find. I'd do anything to be with her again, and after last night's romp, I would say Regina likes my image just fine. I can't believe she didn't neuter me when she found out we're still married. Somebody must have really been keeping an eye out for me when I forgot about the divorce papers. She's still my wife. God, I love how that sounds.

I slide off the mattress and tiptoe into the kitchen to start a pot of coffee. If memory serves me well, she likes it strong. My phone vibrates on the coffee table, and for one second, I consider letting it go to voice mail, but when I see the call is from my agent, I let out a breath and answer.

"Hey, Phil. How's it going?"

"How's life in the small city?" He laughs as if his words are funny.

"Good. Better than expected. We finished the scavenger hunt last night, and on Saturday, at the Pickle Festival, we'll find out who wins."

With no expression in his voice, he says, "Sounds fascinating."

And I pay for this privilege?

Focusing on the coffee dripping in the pot, I say, "Is there something you needed?"

"Actually, I need to go over several things with you. The first is everyone loved the interview you did with Laurel, and I think it struck a chord with Parkerson. I just love how you made up that story about the little girl. Very folksy, and it worked."

For the first time in days, my stomach burns, and I go in search of my stash of antacids. "I didn't see it, and it wasn't a story. It was the truth."

"So pathetic. I see why you jetted out of there so fast. Next topic. I've been in contact with Dennis Brewer from the Mariners. If you do the right PR work, they may be interested in signing you, so see? I knew a walk down memory lane with a reporter would pay off."

I move the pot so some coffee will drip directly into my waiting coffee cup. "Seattle is a long way from home."

"Home?" He cackles. "Home is where the diamond is."

Cute, and if he were talking about the kind of diamond that slips on the perfect woman's hand, I would have to agree with him, but he's talking about the one that pays the bills.

I slurp some coffee. "Can I call you back later? I need to go. I'm kind of busy."

"Wait. I wanted to make sure before I said anything to you, but about that little boat anchor..."

Suddenly, I don't need coffee to wake me up. "Excuse me?"

"Your wife, or rather ex-wife. I did some digging and found where my assistant filed the papers for you. I'm going to send you a copy of the documents."

Blood drains from my face, and I lose my grip on the coffee cup, sloshing coffee all over the counter. "What? I don't understand."

"It sounded like you thought you might still be married, and since divorce filings are part of public record, I got a copy. You wouldn't want her to get any of your money."

Through gritted teeth, I say, "You think that's what this is all about? She doesn't care about money."

Phil chuckles. "Sure... keep telling yourself that. Anyway, it was finalized years ago. Back to what's important: I need you in Seattle on Monday to have a meeting with Brewer."

"Uh..."

"I'm going to shoot straight with you. I've talked to five teams in the past week. Five. Nobody wants you. You're already washed up. Having the Mariners even consider you is something you can't pass up. My assistant will set you up with the flight details."

"But—"

"No buts."

He hangs up, and I want to crush the phone. This is the worst timing ever. An arm slides around my waist, and I yelp.

Regina giggles. "Did you forget I was here?"

I count to three before I swing around, a smile painted on my face. "Hardly. I thought you were still dead to the world." I scoot past her toward the coffee pot. "You might need this today."

A blush sweeps across her neck as she takes the cup from me. "Totally worth it."

I'm mesmerized by her lips as she sips her coffee. "You can say that again."

"Totally worth it."

Since we're starting over, I need to be completely up front with her about my career. She's not going to like it, but I have to be truthful with her. "Regina, that was my agent on the phone."

Her gaze drops to the floor while she nibbles on her bottom lip. "Fun time in Smithville is over, right?" She hustles into the bedroom and places her coffee cup on the dresser as she collects her clothes strewn across the room.

"It appears as though only one team wants me."

She slings on her shorts and pulls her hair into a messy ponytail. "That's good, I guess. Can you take me to my apartment? I need to change before the pickle meeting, and I'm not sure I'll see you afterward. I have to work tonight."

I block her from leaving the bedroom and tip up her chin with my finger, forcing her to look me in the eyes. "I know what you're thinking. Same as last time, right?"

She throws up her hands in frustration. "Isn't it? You got what you wanted. The reporter came down here to make you appear wholesome, and it worked."

"I'm not the same this time. It will be different. I promise, and I don't care about my image anymore, except for how you see me." I slide my hands down her arms and pull her close. With her chest pinned up against mine, I feel her heart racing out of control. "But we do need to talk about things."

"What team?"

"Uh... the Mariners."

Her eyes bug out of their sockets. "Seattle?"

"First off, they haven't signed me, and secondly, I haven't said I would agree to the contract."

"But you will. I mean, you should, and when that contract is up, you'll have teams all over the country kicking their collective butts for not signing you."

"I love you, Regina."

She bows her head "I know you do. I believe you, but you have to do what you think is best. We've been down this road before. Neither of us wanted a long-distance relationship then, and I certainly don't want one now. But..." Her lip quivers. "I don't want to lose you again."

Her breath hitches, and I grab her into a big hug, stroking her ponytail. "You aren't going to lose me. I need to go to Seattle for a meeting on Monday and see what they have to say." I tip her chin up with my hand. "This is how things work. You get one team interested, and word gets out, and others feel like they need to see what all the fuss is about. I'm hoping Atlanta will want me."

I kiss her lips, and she wraps her arms around my neck, deepening the kiss. Breathless, we break away.

"We better leave. Can't afford to be late again."

My phone pings, and I notice the message with the divorce papers attached. I shove my phone in my pocket and proceed to get dressed for the day. I'm not sure how to tell her we aren't married anymore. After what we did last night, and we were thinking it was completely appropriate because of our marriage bond, I need to tell her. But after the news about the potential new major-league contract, I don't know if she can handle too many fastballs thrown her way at one bat. I'm still trying to wrap my head around the bombshell.

We tiptoe down the stairs in hopes of sneaking out of the shop before anyone sees us.

"Morning," Mrs. Cavanaugh says, and Regina screams. "Regina, nice outfit."

Regina's eyes bug out of her beet-red face.

I point to the door. "We gotta go."

I grab Regina's hand, and we race outside. The last thing I hear is Mrs. Cavanaugh's knowing chuckle.

After a quick wardrobe change, we drive to the courthouse. "I've had fun this week," Regina says as she laces her fingers with mine. "You know, I tried to hate you, but I never could, so I directed my disdain toward myself. I wasn't a very good girl these last few years, and to think I was technically cheating on you..." She lets out a sigh as she stares out the window.

"Shh. We didn't know. I don't hold it against you, and I wasn't a saint either. Can we talk about something else?"

We're definitely not going to talk about the fact that we aren't really still married.

She bobs her head so much I think it's going to come loose. "Yes. Do you think we're going to win?"

"Of course. Who else had such an awesome multitasker for a partner? We were able to check so many off the list with one stop."

Regina pulls out the list and gasps. "Oh no. We didn't do the mannequin or the dress items."

I scratch the back of my head. "Yeah, I think we got a little distracted."

She pokes me in the side. "You tricked me into stopping by In a Jam, didn't you?"

"In baseball, we would call that a slider."

In a fit of giggles, she covers her mouth. "I could take that so many ways, but if we lose because of those missed points, you will never hear the end of it."

"Duly noted. Totally worth it, don't ya think?"

She gives me a one-shoulder shrug. "I don't know. You were a little rusty. You need more batting practice."

"Yes, ma'am. I take my skills seriously."

Regina fans her face. "Is it just me, or is it hot in here?"

She's hot, and her temper is going to be hotter than blue blazes when I get up the nerve to tell her about our divorce. I get myself out of one pickle and jump feetfirst into another. After the festival, I'll clear the air. Maybe after winning the competition, she'll be so excited, she'll think this little mishap is actually funny.

Keep dreaming.

CHAPTER THIRTY-FIVE

Regina

Andie's smug smile tells me everything I need to know. She knows what we were up to, or more like it, she heard what we were up to. One day, I'll thank her for the help in getting me and Clint back together—but not today.

"Happy Wednesday, everyone!" Andie smiles. "I want to thank everyone for participating. It was fun seeing all your photos. The Taylors had to drop out due to other commitments, and Carmen and Nate spent more time fighting than taking photos, so it's down to you three groups."

I gaze up at Clint, and he winks.

"Clint and Regina get thirty points removed from their day's points for being late." Andie tsks us.

I punch Clint on the arm. "This is your fault."

He rubs his arm as if it really hurt. "Me? You kept me awake well into the wee hours of the morning."

Marge and David Lane's mouths drop open.

Becca cringes and says, "Gross."

Andie gathers all our phones. "So between now and Saturday, we'll evaluate your photos to make sure they're time-stamped and fit the categories, and we'll tally the results. Make sure you're at the Pickle Festival at one o'clock sharp for the announcements."

After Andie downloads our photos to her file system, I hear Leo say to Becca, "We got this."

Clint wraps an arm around my shoulders. "Don't listen to them. They may have youth, but we have each other."

I hip bump him but couldn't agree more. Trying to hold it in, I let out a yawn as we leave the courthouse. "As much fun as this has been, I need to go home and take a nap before my shift. What are you going to do?"

"I think I'll get a workout in at Big Ash Fitness Center then see if Mitch wants to hang out."

"He's probably exhausted from working three straight days for me."

"When I was out on the road, playing ball, I'd call him for company. Every time I'd talk to him, I'd ask him about you, or the conversation would somehow find its way around to talking about you. He'd tell me how good you were at your job and how much he learned from you. Every conversation revolved around you."

My heart warms knowing even if he wasn't here with me, he was still thinking about me. Many miles may have separated us, but I wasn't too far from his thoughts. Mitch was a good listener. He let me ramble on sometimes, especially when it first went south, all without judgment. It would have been easy for Mitch to play the brother card and place all the blame on me. He could have made my life miserable, but he didn't. He was going through his own personal trials, so he never judged others.

"And Gunnar..." Clint grins. "He sent me messages of encouragement when I had lackluster games, which was happening more and more often lately."

"Seems like Gunnar and Andie will be getting married soon. Word on the street is it may be as soon as Thanksgiving."

He belts out a laugh. "Never in a million years did I think he would settle down after his failed attempt down the aisle. Sounds like this one might actually happen, and I wouldn't miss it for anything in the world."

"You just want to see me in a sexy bridesmaid's dress."

He scrunches up his nose and says, "Naw. I'd rather see you *out* of the bridesmaid's dress."

I roll my eyes. "You are such a dude."

He drives up to my apartment, and my butt won't move out of his car. We both stare out the windshield. Tension fills the air, and I don't know why he scratches the back of his neck and asks, "I'll see you later?"

"I have to pull a double shift to make up for taking off this week, so you go do some dude stuff."

His eyebrows pull together. "Three days without you? I'm not sure I like the sound of that."

"You'll survive. I'll see you on Saturday at the festival."

He salutes me. "Got it. I'll be on time, and you better come hungry and ready to enter the pickle-eating contest."

Bile rises in my throat. "You're on your own with that one." I lean over and kiss Clint on the cheek. "Bye, Clint."

"Bye, Regina."

His eyes seem sad for some reason. I hope he's not already regretting us getting back together. I'm overjoyed about having him in my life again, but something tells me he doesn't feel the same.

"Everything okay?"

Clint nods but stares off. "Yeah. Like you, I'm tired. I better hit the gym before I fall asleep in my car."

He's a terrible liar, but I don't have the energy to push it. "See ya."

He sits in his car until I unlock my apartment and am safely inside. I was hoping he would ask if he could come inside and get a little more tired, but it's probably a good thing he didn't. If I don't get some sleep, I'll be like a walking zombie at the hospital this afternoon.

As much as I want to, there's no way I'll be able to rest. My brain won't shut off after one glorious night with Clint. He's always had that effect on me, and that's why no other guy has ever done it for me. I was so stunned Ken wanted to marry me, but now that I've had a few days to let it sink in, I know I would never have been truly happy with him. He never had my heart anyway. It was already taken by someone else.

AS SOON AS MY HEAD hits the pillow, I hear a knock on my door. I stumble down the hallway. Right before I open it, I perk up. Maybe it's Clint wanting to cuddle. I fling open the door, and my shoulders slump when I see Andie and Mel standing there.

"Hey, girl," Mel says, making herself at home in my apartment. "We're doing some wedding shopping today for the bride-to-be and wanted you to come along then go to lunch with us."

I yawn. "I'd love to, but I'm so tired. Plus, I have to be at work at three o'clock."

Mel gives me a motherly expression. "You know as well as I do, if you take a nap now, you'll never wake up in time for work. Go get a shower, and we'll keep you awake for your shift."

Andie wiggles her eyebrows. "Unless you have a midday sleepover planned."

Heat runs up my neck. She may not have grown up here, but she already knows me like yesterday's news. "Oh, hush. We'll talk about that later."

Andie holds her hand out to Mel. "Told ya. You owe me lunch."

I gasp. "You guys were betting on me?"

Mel squeezes my shoulders. "Just a friendly little wager."

I sneer at them. "I'll be out of the shower in two shakes. Make yourself at home." As if Mel hasn't done that already.

Andie snickers as I leave them. No telling what they're going to talk about while I'm in the shower. All I think about as the water drizzles over my tired, sore body is how Clint's hands felt as he held me last night. I could kick myself for missing out on that feeling all these years, especially since we were still married. Thank goodness we get a second chance to get this right.

I sling my hair up in a ponytail and feel like a new woman. When I walk into the living room, I find Andie and Mel in a huddle. When I clear my throat, they jump apart.

"Let's go. I need coffee."

Andie claps. "Yes, coffee, then we go finalize flowers and cake choices."

When Clint and I got married, it was a very small wedding, just family and a few friends at my father's church. We didn't have a reception or anything. In fact, we went to Shoney's to eat afterward, and I was okay with it. None of that mattered as long as we were together.

With the strongest coffee available in Smithville, we head over to Becca's Bakery. They have the cutest designs, and I love how Mel and Andie *ooh* and *aah* over every one. It's precious. I think Mel is taking mental notes of what she likes in hopes she'll be in Andie's shoes someday.

"Which one do you like?" Andie asks.

I tap my finger to my chin as I mull over each cake design. "The three-tier design is pretty and traditional, but the one with the extra layer of cupcakes is really different and cute."

Andie agrees. "I love it."

Mel giggles. "You're so easy to please. I was thinking I'd have bridezilla on my hands."

Andie rolls her eyes. "Oh, please. This is fun. I never thought I'd walk down the aisle, so I'm not going to get all discombobulated over a cake. So you and Clint...?"

I hold up a hand to stop Andie's train of thought. "We're good. Getting reacquainted, you know." Heat flames my neck, and I'm sure it doesn't go unnoticed.

With a singsongy voice, Mel says, "Someone's blushing."

Andie chuckles. "I like that color on her."

Mel gives my shoulders a quick squeeze, then says, "Next stop: lunch. My treat."

Lunch sounds good, but in my mind, I can't keep my thoughts from running back to the last conversation Clint and I had. I don't know what I'm going to do if Clint leaves again. I need a husband who is present every day, not just in the off-season. I'm definitely putting the cart before the horse, or as Clint would say, I'm already mentally striking out before I even step up to the plate. We both deserve a second chance to get it right.

CHAPTER THIRTY-SIX
Clint

Slinging iron is the best way to work through my guilty conscience. I pump out a set of alternate dumbbell curls as I stare at my ugly mug in the mirror. Slamming the dumbbells back onto the rack, I get the evil eye from Mr. Pippenger as he chugs along on a treadmill at less than one mile per hour.

"Dang, you're going to break something." Gunnar plops his gym bag down on the bench and removes his T-shirt. "What did those weights ever do to you?"

"They should have known better than to get near me today."

Gunnar whistles as he does a light warm-up set of shoulder shrugs. "I thought you were having fun with... you know who."

I glance around to see who's listening. The only person near us is Mr. Pippenger, and he's got his entire attention on a *Seinfeld* episode on the treadmill display.

"I have been. I am. I mean..."

Heat flames my neck, making Gunnar chuckle. "Let me guess, you figured out the curse of the bed."

"Yes. Totally worth it, but I think it's time to invest in a new bed frame."

"Yeah, I think it's charmed, so you better watch out."

Even a magical bed can't fix the pickle I'm in. "If I tell you something, can you promise not to tell anyone?"

He fist-bumps me. "Absolutely."

"You know the part about the little mix-up, about still being married?"

Gunnar grimaces. "I take it she knows now."

"Yeah. After she got over the initial ticked-off phase, and with a little help from Andie..."

He whimpers. "She loves to meddle. I swear she was meant to live in this town."

"True, but she helped Regina forgive me. And last night, we, uh... you know, did what married people do."

"Exhibit A is the bed."

He almost makes me grin. I guzzle from my water bottle. "Yeah. And this morning, I went from riding high to striking out."

Gunnar sits on the bench, and I take a deep breath while I make sure Pippenger is still more interested in George Costanza than my pathetic life.

"My agent called. He did some investigating and found out his assistant filed the divorce papers for me years ago." I stare up at the ceiling and groan. "We aren't married after all, and Regina isn't going to believe me. She's going to think this was all a publicity stunt."

I lift the bar off the rack and wait for Gunnar to nod then take my hands away. He pumps out ten reps with no problem then slams the bar back in its place. He sits up and stretches his arms over his head. "Now it's more?"

"I want her back."

As he slings another forty-five-pound plate on each side of the bar, he says, "Just tell her, then marry her again."

"You make it sound so easy."

Mitch stumbles in, still wearing his EMT uniform. He lets out a yawn. "They've pulled me in from the road to work the ER because of this pickle competition. I've had to work double shifts. You owe me big time." He leans up against the squat rack as he stretches out his quads one leg at a time.

"Sorry, bro. I appreciate it. I really do."

"So what's so easy?"

Gunnar holds up his hands. "I've been sworn to secrecy."

Mitch stares at me, and his pretty-boy face gets stern. "Spill it, bud."

"I finally get the nerve to tell Regina about still being married, then this morning, I found out we aren't, and I don't know how to tell her, especially since we..."

Mitch side-eyes me then focuses on Gunnar. "The glitchy bed got him, didn't it?"

Gunnar guffaws. "Works every time."

I grimace and ask Mitch, "Did you break the bed too?"

"Nooo. I've just heard about it." He slides plates onto the squat rack. "I don't see what the problem is. If you still love her, then just marry her again."

Gunnar holds out his arms. "Exactly. That's what I said."

"That's what I'd do," Mr. Pippenger says as he walks past us toward the locker room. He runs his thumb and finger across his mouth. "My lips are sealed."

That's all I need. He'll tell his silver singles group, and word will get back to Regina's father. It might be better if I go ahead and castrate myself. At least that way, I can be in charge of the anesthesia.

"She's been mad at me for six years. I finally got her to handle breathing the same air as me. She even broke up with her rich Ken doll..."

Mitch rests his shoulders on the bar and cranks out a set of squats. When he sets the bar back on the rack, he says, "What do you have against being rich? I mean, you're rich too."

If we weren't around a cop, I would punch my brother.

"That's different. His is old money that never goes away. Mine, well, I worked my tail off to get it, and it can be snatched away from me at any moment."

Mitch's eyebrows rise. "You're a free agent this year, aren't you?"

I nod. "My hothead reputation coupled with my sucky average last year… let's just say Seattle is the only team that's offered me a contract. Regina isn't happy about that either."

"Can you blame her? It's like déjà vu all over again." Mitch grins at his allusion.

"Now is not the time to be quoting Yogi Berra, but I know. And I'm just going to spit it out right now. I don't think I want to sign with them, or anyone, for that matter."

Gunnar's grip loosens on his dumbbell, sending it crashing to the floor. He has to do a little jig to keep from crushing his toes. "Are you insane?"

I chuckle. "Apparently. I don't know what I want until I have something else, then I want what I don't have anymore."

Mitch stares at the ceiling. "Sounds like Mom, except she never wanted what she didn't have anymore."

I guess the apple doesn't fall far from the tree, but I'm going to break this chain in the cycle. "What do I do?"

Mitch and Gunnar glance at each other, then Mitch pats me on the back. "Come clean to her. Tell her you didn't hide anything from her and you want another chance. Trust me, I've caught her too many times in the break room at work over the years sniffling over something she was gawking at on her phone. One time for sure, I saw her watching one of your games, so no matter how much of a happy face she puts on and no matter how many men she's dated over the years, it's a smokescreen to cover up the fact that she's never gotten over you."

Now, I feel like an even bigger heel than ever. I've kicked myself every day for hurting her. If she thinks I'm hiding something again, she'll never give me another chance. "She's got to work tonight, but the Pickle Festival is this weekend. I'll pick her up and come clean with her then."

"I'd do it today," Gunnar says, sliding on his shirt. "Why wait? The gossip train is pretty fast in this town."

Mitch shakes his head. "If you make her mad at work, I'll have to come in and cover for her. Then, you'll have two people angry at you. If I were you, I'd wait until after you win a pile of money. She'll be so happy about that, she might even laugh about this little snafu."

They're both right, but Mitch knows Regina better, so I'll take his advice this time.

"I think I'll spend tonight watching ball and figuring out how to keep my balls intact."

On instinct, Mitch and Gunnar both cover up their family jewels. I know exactly how they feel.

CHAPTER THIRTY-SEVEN

Regina

If I yawn one more time, I am going to scream. Working on only a few hours' sleep is something I haven't done since my early nursing days. In order to stay awake, I force myself to stand or keep walking. Even on my break, I lean against the wall and scarf down my food. If I sit, I'll be snoring at the break room table.

Mel giggles as she reviews a chart. "This is what happens when you don't get much sleep at night."

"Thanks, Dr. Obvious. Just remember, I wanted to take a nap, but some tall whacko doctor said I shouldn't."

She signs an order for Vanessa Pilot to be discharged and slides it toward me. "It wasn't too long ago when I was the one barely hanging in there on a long shift. There were months at a time during my residency when I had to check my ID to remind myself what my name was."

"I appreciate Mitch for filling in for me this week. I bet you enjoyed that, huh?" I ask with a cheesy grin. Anything to get the spotlight off me.

"Don't go there." She huffs. "Mitch and I are just friends and coworkers."

I clutch my chest. "Ouch. You friendzoned him. Harsh, Mel."

"Pfft," she says as she focuses on the next chart. "If it were meant to be, it would have happened already."

I throw my head back and chuckle. "Yeah, if it weren't for you cockblocking him every step of the way."

Mel grimaces. "I'm not a cockblocker."

I raise an eyebrow. "Mel, do I have to give you specific examples? How about the time he asked you to prom, and you said no because your dog was dying? By the way, Mr. Scribbles lived three more years."

Mel covers her mouth, but I see a smile forming. "I thought he was on his last leg."

Drumming my fingers on the counter, I continue. "Okay, there was the time when he punched Preston Miller in the face for getting handsy with you after you repeatedly told him to back off. He made this grand gesture, and you had the nerve to leave with Preston anyway."

She holds up a hand to stop me. "I had it all under control. Mitch didn't need to step in."

"Mm-hmm. What about the time—"

She snaps her head toward me. "Are we going to do this all night?"

I back away from her. "Sorry. I just thought it would be fun to have you as a sister-in-law."

Mel throws a pen toward me. "Speaking of the nuptials, have you told your parents yet?"

Good deflection, Mel.

My parents loved Clint like their own. In fact, I think they were more upset about losing him as a son-in-law than dealing with my heartbreak, but this is different. "They're going to flip when they find out we're still..."

"Married?"

"Yeah. Kind of weird, and I feel so guilty for the things I've done."

She waves off my concern. "Don't worry about it. I'm sure the good Lord won't hold it against you. You thought it was finalized."

"But it's all so strange. I never thought all these feelings would come crashing back, but I think he's really sorry for wanting to bail on our commitment."

"Y'all were too young to get married. You should have just shacked up for a while."

I give her a knowing glance. "You know my daddy would never have approved of that." But she's right. If we had just lived together, then Clint could have left, and our relationship would have fizzled with no hard feelings and certainly no legal issues to deal with.

Mel hands me a chart to review. "You're probably right, but things turned out okay for you. You get a second chance. That's rare. I'd say take it."

I bow my head as I nod.

"But?"

"He's got a contract offer with the Mariners."

Her face loses all emotion. "That's a long way from here, isn't it?" After a beat, she smiles. "But you can make it work. You have a multistate nursing license. You could go with him."

The thought of leaving Smithville makes me all twitchy. Being away from my hometown during college about did me in. Thank goodness for Clint being at the same school, because I wouldn't have made it by myself. And when he left before we graduated, I almost didn't survive. If it weren't for my nursing school buddies, I would have flunked out.

"I don't know if I can do that. I'd be swallowed up in a place like Seattle."

"It's amazing what we're able to do when we want something bad enough. The question is, what do you want and how bad do you want it?"

I want Clint. I never stopped wanting Clint. "I never stopped loving Clint. There may have been a time in my life where I didn't like him very much, but I couldn't stop loving him. Does that make sense?"

She nods. "It makes perfect sense."

Mel reviews another chart and clears her throat. "To keep you awake, I'll let you take Mrs. Kleinfeld in room two. She claims she hasn't had a bowel movement in seven days."

My shoulders slump. "You're horrible."

"I'll still do all the crappy stuff—pun intended."

"That doesn't make me feel any better."

"It'll be all worth it on Saturday when you're at the Pickle Festival. I hope you win the money."

I feel like I've already won something bigger and better than a pot of money, unless the pot takes off again.

My phone dings, and it's a text from Clint. My face breaks out in a grin.

This is your Wednesday evening wake-up call. Are you still awake? he asks.

Surprisingly, yes.

Want an encore performance tonight? He adds a heart face emoji and a smiley face emoji blowing a kiss.

Biting my lip to keep from saying yes, I write back. *Sorry, bud. I told you I would be working for the next few days. Besides, I'll be lucky if I make it through my shift. I'll see you Saturday AM.*

He sends me a frowning face emoji, making me giggle. Another text follows from Clint. *Love you.*

I take a deep breath then type, *I've been thinking about Seattle. If you go, would you mind if your wife tagged along?*

It's a huge step for me to even consider moving out of town, and if it were for anyone else, I don't think I would even have the courage to consider it. Figuring he would send me a text immediately, I stand there, but nothing comes through.

Mel clears her throat. "Mrs. Kleinfeld needs to be cleaned out."

"Yeah. Sorry. I'm on it." I slide my phone back into my pocket and go in search of a bedside commode. This is going to be one poop-filled evening.

An hour later, after Mrs. Kleinfeld's bowels are free and clear and she's sleeping peacefully, I check my messages. One from Clint came in not long after I texted him. His said, *Okay. Let's discuss it tomorrow.*

Okay? I was expecting some dude comment or a baseball metaphor about stealing home. But all I got was an okay. I'm too tired to worry about it right now. In the past, I was always good at reading Clint like a book, but he's been all over the place this week. Maybe this is the new and not-so-improved Clint. After I let out another wide, ugly yawn, I force myself to focus on my job.

CHAPTER THIRTY-EIGHT
Clint

Saturday could not get here fast enough. No amount of babysitting the boys and lifting weights made time move faster. As much as I wanted to, I didn't bother Regina these past two days so she could work and be good and rested for the festival today. All I've done at night since Wednesday is toss and turn, trying to find the right words to tell her the news. Part of me doesn't want to tell her, because I really like how she's warmed up to me again. She'll probably go back to hating me after I spill the beans, so I want to enjoy this for as long as I can.

At ten o'clock sharp, I knock on Regina's apartment door. The door swings open, and Regina stands there, wearing a loosely tied robe, showing enough of her sweet body to make me fully awake. She motions with her finger for me to follow her back inside, which only a fool would resist.

She slams the door shut and pins me against it. She jumps up and wraps her legs around my waist. Yep, the robe is the only item of clothing she has on. I may be dumb, but I'm not that stupid.

"I missed you." Regina closes the gap between our lips and kisses me hard, clinking our teeth in the process.

"I missed you too. Nice surprise."

She slides down my body, and when her feet hit the floor, she takes my hand. As she leads me down the hallway, she says, "I'm just getting started."

Have mercy.

"What about the festival?" I've really lost my mind if I'm more interested in a stupid celebration than what's before me.

"We have plenty of time."

I swing her around and plant faint kisses down her neck as she hums in satisfaction. "In fact, I don't even remember anything about a festival." I slide the robe off her shoulders, and it slips to the floor. While she tackles my pants, I fling my T-shirt over my head then back her up to the edge of her bed. "Does this bed have any issues?"

She giggles. "It's practically new and certainly hasn't seen as much action as the one over the shop."

"It better not have."

As she crawls onto the bed, she quirks an eyebrow. "Jealous?"

I flop on top of her, making the mattress bounce. She sucks in a breath, and we both lie still in anticipation of the mattress falling to the floor.

"I take my marriage vows seriously."

A pang of guilt rushes through my stomach, but it's quickly extinguished when she slides her hands up and down my back. I can't help myself. I don't care if she's not really my wife anymore. In my heart, she always will be.

She pushes me back and tilts her head to the side. "What is this?" She holds my arm up to expose the tiny tattoo close to my armpit. "A stethoscope with the tubing in the shape of a heart?" She squints to see the tat more clearly. "Are those initials R and P inside the heart?"

I pin her back to the bed. "Maybe."

"Are those special initials, or do you have some fantasy about a nurse that I don't know about?"

I groan and stare at her. "Both. You know there is only one nurse for me, Regina Price."

Regina casts her eyes on it again, then runs her fingers across the ink. "When? Why? Why there?"

Tilting her chin back to kiss her neck, I say, "So many questions. When? Right after we split. Why? Because I needed a reminder of you every time I raised the bat. Why there? Your sweet noggin' always fit right under my arm. That's where I remember you being. It just felt like a logical place. That's all."

She squeezes me tight. "I'm not a tat fan, but that's the sweetest thing I've ever heard."

"You want a baseball on your boob?"

Regina belts out a laugh as she flops me onto my back. "No thanks. Now, where were we?"

For the next hour, I remind her of where we were before we got distracted by my tat. As she lies sprawled out on her bed with one leg splayed over mine, I play with her hair. I never want this feeling to end, and I certainly don't want to move and go to some festival celebrating stupid frickin' pickles.

She pops me on the stomach and rises. Her hair sticks out in a dozen different directions, the purple streak falling across her forehead. "We better get ready for the festival. I may not need the money for a wedding anymore, but I don't want the Lanes to win it on a technicality."

Even my puppy-dog face doesn't convince her to stay put, so I drag myself out of bed, throw on my clothes, and pretend I'm not too disappointed. While she showers and dresses, I mentally practice several different scenarios for how to tell her we're not married anymore.

Honey, guess what? We're not married. Isn't that hilarious?

Babe. Want to get married, because we aren't married anymore?

A funny thing happened the other day. We're single after all.

All of those are lame and will result in me getting a slap to the face and a kick in the rear.

"You ready?"

Her words make me jump two feet off the ground. "Yes," I reply, my voice about two octaves higher than normal.

Regina cocks her head to the side, and I'm afraid she's reading my mind. "Are you okay?"

Not really. "Sure. Let's go."

GUNNAR'S FACE FALLS when he sees me winding up to throw a baseball at the dunking-booth target. He knows he's going to get wet. He waves his arms in the air. "No fair. He's a professional."

"It's for charity," I say as I let the ball fly right at the target, making the bell ring and causing Gunnar's seat to collapse. He splashes into the dunk tank, and everyone roars with cheers.

When he resurfaces, he points at me. "Dude, I will remember this. If you drive one mile over the speed limit, you'll be spending the night in the pokey." Gunnar climbs the stairs and repositions himself on the bench, wringing out his shirt.

Andie stands behind her booth, selling her famous special jam. She cups her hands to her mouth and yells, "Take it off!"

A few catcalls issue from the crowd, and Gunnar's face turns a hilarious beet red.

Regina giggles into her hands. "I love it when he gets embarrassed. Ooh. Come on." She grabs me by the arm. "Mitch and Robert are doing the pickle-eating contest."

Mitch and Robert shove pickle after pickle in their mouths, juice dripping off their chins. Mitch squeezes his eyes closed. He's not a dill pickle person, so I'm guessing this isn't as fun as he thought it would be. By the way Mel cheers him on, I can only assume that's why he got roped into participating. But Mitch and Robert don't hold a candle to Stanley Culpepper. He takes two bites, and each pickle is devoured. If I were keeping count, I would say he eats three pickles to Mitch's one. He has definitely mastered the art of scarfing down food.

When the buzzer blows, Stanley is the clear winner. Mitch spits out the remaining pickle in his mouth, and Robert slumps back into his chair, panting.

"Good try, Robert!" Regina yells to her brother.

He salutes her then laughs with Mitch.

The band plays a country tune, and Regina pulls me toward the dance floor. "Come on. Let's see if you still have two left feet."

I wrap my arms around her waist. "My feet are made for running around bases, not doing some fancy two-step dance."

"I bet you can do both. You don't have to be one thing or the other." She grins. "Or we could sign you up at the pie toss booth. I'd even volunteer to eat whatever whipped cream lands on your face."

I let out a chuckle. "As tempting as that is, let's stick to dancing."

Her smile fades. "I've been thinking. About the contract offer..."

I put a finger to her mouth to stop her from saying anything else. "I don't want to talk about that right now."

Out of the corner of my eye, I see familiar movement. Several TV crews huddle, and my stomach acid threatens to spew up my throat. *What are they doing here?*

Over the intercom, the mayor announces, "It's time to reveal the winner of the Pickle Festival Scavenger Hunt." The crowd claps. "If I could have all the participating couples up on the stage, we'll get this started."

With the brightest smile on her face, Regina says, "Let's go, partner in crime."

I follow her onto the stage, and as we stand there, waiting to find out who the winning couple is, I can't stop thinking that I've already won my prize. Too bad I may have it ripped from my hands and my heart before I can completely enjoy it.

CHAPTER THIRTY-NINE

Regina

My knees knock together as we climb the steps to the stage. Marge and David Lane follow behind us as Leo and Becca bring up the rear. The mayor hands Andie the microphone as the crowd gathers around the stage.

Andie waves to the crowd. "Thanks, everyone, for coming out to this year's Pickle Festival. This is my first time, and I've had so much fun already."

The crowd claps for their newest member of Smithville.

"As you may know, this year, we decided to shake things up a bit. Past winners of the Pickle King and Queen competed in a three-day photographic scavenger hunt. They had to do some really silly stuff. I'm sure you saw them running around town, trying to gain points. We had two teams that had to back out of the competition, so in the end, we had three teams complete all three days' events. After the committee verified all photos for accuracy, it was a very close call." She pauses for dramatic effect.

Clint clasps my hand, and I give it a squeeze.

"And the winners by only fifty points are... Marge and David Lane."

David does a jig on the stage, and Marge fans her face like she has the vapors. Becca crosses her arms over her chest and huffs off the stage.

I give Marge a side hug. "Congrats. It was a lot of fun."

Right before we leave the stage, Andie reaches out to snag my arm. "One more thing. Since it was so close, I'm giving the other two couples five thousand dollars each."

My mouth drops open. "You are the most generous person I've ever known."

"Aw. I can never repay this town for adopting me."

My heart swells. I know if we had grown up together, we would have been friends from the start.

Clint grins at me. "What are you going to do with the money?"

I shrug. "Not sure. Maybe put it toward a down payment on a house."

The crowd parts as Laurel, the perfect reporter, sashays toward us with her cameraman hustling to keep up.

She shoves the microphone under Clint's face. "We're here for a follow-up interview. How do you feel about not winning? You aren't used to coming in second place."

Behind her, five other cameras appear, big sports networks that I only hear about on television. The Jackson sisters take selfies with some of the journalists while I stand there like a bump on a log.

Clint shows off his pearly whites as he switches from sexy, fun Clint to I-love-the-spotlight hotshot athlete.

"That may be true, but I think I won something more than money." He glances down at me and winks, causing the crowd to ooh and ah. "Coming home was just what I needed."

Andie puts two fingers in her mouth and lets out a wolf whistle. Mitch and Robert, fresh off the pickle-eating competition, lean against the stage while Gunnar slides up to Andie. The Jackson sisters document the event by recording the scene, as I expected they would.

"Coming home," Laurel says in a dry tone. "What does home mean to you?"

He slips an arm around my shoulders to pull me close, so close, I'm sure I'm in the camera shot too. "This little cutie is home to me. This is Regina, my wife."

A collective gasp gushes through the crowd. One of the Jacksons says to the other, "I knew it. Pay up, sister."

The other Jackson sister curses under her breath and harrumphs.

Clint chuckles while I search the crowd for my parents. I need to know how they reacted to his bombshell. The cat is out of the bag now. I might as well embrace it.

Laurel cocks her head to the side and, with a Cheshire cat grin, asks, "Are you sure about that?"

How rude. I stare at Clint, who has gone ghastly white, and he squeezes his eyes closed. Under his breath, he says, "Laurel, stow it."

I take a step away from Clint to read the situation. "What's going on?"

Laurel motions for the cameraman to cut then says, "Oh, honey, he's been playing you like a fiddle. Isn't that how you say it down here?" The other camera crews keep filming as this little showdown continues.

Clint scrubs his face with his hands before he says, "Regina, let's talk somewhere private."

He takes my hand, but I yank it from him. "No, you don't get to drag me all over Smithville for a week, sprucing up your image in public, for you to now 'talk in private.' You like a camera in your face, so you're going to have it that way. What's going on?"

He glares at Laurel, but she seems unfazed by his anger. "You had to stir up trouble, didn't you?"

She holds out her hands in surrender. "I just report the facts."

Crossing my arms over my chest, I ask, "And what are the facts?"

Robert appears by my side, and Laurel undresses him with her eyes.

Ick.

"Are you okay, sis?"

"I don't know. Clint?"

Clint goes from squeezing his eyes shut to staring at the sky. In a quiet voice, he says, "We aren't married."

I suck in all the air in the town and stumble backward. "Are you kidding me?"

"He filed the paperwork." Laurel pulls out a folded sheet of paper. "Clarke County Courthouse had the proof."

I snatch the paper out of her hand in hopes of giving her a massive paper cut and read the document. Sure enough, the divorce was final years ago. My hands tremble so much, the paper falls to the stage floor. "I don't understand."

Clint takes my shaking hands in his. "Let me explain."

I yank my hands out of his grasp and snarl at him, "You lied to me. I can't believe you would do this."

I storm off the stage and walk away from the completely silent crowd watching my very public meltdown. Right on my heels, my lying, traitorous, sorry excuse for an ex-husband follows me away from the stage. No matter how fast I march, he and the media keep up, which ticks me off even more.

Clint reaches for my arm, but I swat his hand away.

"Don't touch me."

"Let me explain."

I swing around to stare at him. Poking him in the chest, I say, "You played me like a fiddle, didn't you?" Using the phrase Laurel did gets my goat, but it's what spewed from my mouth.

He clenches his jaw and spits out, "You've got it all wrong."

"Oh, yes, you did. You did this for a publicity stunt so you could get more contract offers. Hometown boy cozying up with his high school sweetheart." I fling my arms in the air for added flair. "Oh, it makes for great reality television, but it didn't work. You're a slimeball. How dare you use me like that?"

"I didn't, and this probably cost me the only deal I had going."

The reporter from America Sports says, "Actually, you now have five offers on the table. Your agent sent out a press release this morning."

Clint's eyes widen. "Five? Really?" He retrieves his phone from his pocket and reads a text message. Nodding, he says, "You're correct. New York, Chicago, Tampa, Baltimore, and Atlanta."

I storm away from him, but he catches up to me. "I swear I didn't know."

"You didn't know we weren't married anymore?"

"No, I knew that part, but I didn't know about the offers."

"Ugh. You're despicable. Go away, Clint."

Tears stream down my face. I should have known it was too good to be true. Clint's a liar who puts himself first always.

"Let me take you home," Clint says barely above a whisper.

I stick my finger in his face. "I would throw up in that fancy G-Wagon, and we can't have that. It wouldn't be good publicity. I'd rather walk home."

I take off in a sprint, hoping he won't follow. If he knows what's good for him, he'll steer clear of me for about a decade.

I race down the street, not caring where I'm headed, when out of the blue, a hand snags my arm. I swing around and slap the face of the person trying to keep me from running.

"Dang, girl. I didn't do anything wrong." My brother rubs the red splotch on his face where my hand connected with his cheek.

"Oh, Robert. I'm sorry."

He grabs me in his arms and hustles me toward his truck. "Come on. Let's get you home."

Through my ugly tears, I say, "I'm such a fool."

"Shh. We'll talk about your foolery later. Right now, you need to cry it out then possibly get a big stiff drink."

He helps me into his truck, and I bury my face in my hands and weep like I did years ago when Clint told me we should never have gotten married. It's like ripping open that old wound again and pouring rubbing alcohol straight into it.

I can't believe I let Clint use me. I can't believe I slept with him twice, and he knew we weren't married anymore. That's a new low for him.

Robert drives while I stare straight ahead. He knows better than to interject his two cents right now. I'm not in the mood. I keep falling for the wrong man, and I will never learn from my mistakes.

CHAPTER FORTY

Clint

Running like I'm trying to make an infield home run, I rush back to my car in time to see Robert peel out with Regina. I make a U-turn onto Main Street and hope Gunnar's still busy with festival tasks. This is not the time to get stopped for disobeying traffic rules.

Robert takes the street leading to Regina's apartment, and I breathe a sigh of relief. Maybe I can get her to listen to me at her apartment. If she was going to her parents' house, it would be very awkward to relive this painful scene. His truck stops, and he scoots around to help Regina out of the truck. I come to a screeching halt next to them, making Regina scamper backward.

She plants her hands on her hips. "Haven't you done enough damage for one day? I guess not, so you have to attempt to kill me too." She marches toward her door with me right behind her.

Robert tugs on my shoulder. "Man, you might want to let her cool down first."

I shake my head. "I can't do that. I have to tell her the truth."

Robert backs away and lets me keep going. "You're digging your own grave, not mine."

Regina slams the door in my face, but I force it open before she has a chance to lock it.

"Go away."

From behind me, Robert says, "Sis, take a breath. What's the harm in hearing him out?"

Her eyes shoot daggers at her brother. "Whose side are you on?"

"I'm not on any side. Now sit down. Give him five minutes. If you still feel like filleting him, then I'll find the knife and the seasoning."

Regina rolls her eyes and huffs as she plants herself on the couch. "Speak. Your five minutes have started. Ticktock."

I sit on the coffee table and reach out for her hands, but she yanks them from my grasp and sits on them.

"I am sorry I didn't tell you, but I wanted to."

She snorts. "If wishes and dreams were candy and nuts, we'd all have a merry Christmas."

I glance over at Robert. He motions with his head to continue. At least he's not ready to skewer me—yet.

"Can I back up and say that everything I said, every 'I love you,' every 'I missed you' was completely sincere?" I beg with my eyes, but she won't make eye contact.

Regina chews on her lip as it trembles. "It doesn't matter. You led me to believe we were still married." Her voice cracks.

"Let me explain."

"And you even went so far as to sleep with me... twice. Sorry, Robert." Tears stream down her face, but she swipes them away so hard, she's going to leave bruises. "Is your reputation so trashed that you would use me to get more contract offers?"

"No. What I feel for you is real."

She stands and pushes me out of the way to pace back and forth. "The last time you hurt me, I had to endure this all by myself, all the snickering behind my back, the snide comments from the old biddies. You were gone living the dream, and I was here taking the brunt of your decisions." She flings her hands in the air in wild, exaggerated movements.

"Regina, if I could go back in time, I would do things so differently. I'm not that same person anymore."

She chuckles a wicked, evil laugh. "Oh, buddy, you're not the only one. I should have listened to my mother and not gotten married in the first place. We were too young and stupid."

Robert presses himself against the wall as if he would like nothing more than to sink into it to keep from hearing this conversation.

She flicks her hair over her shoulder and stands as tall as a five-foot-two-inch person can. "But I'm a forgiving person. I got over the hurt and made something of myself. Eventually, I was even able to endure hearing the locals talk about how proud they were of you for being some big-shot baseball player. I got so numb, I didn't care who I was with."

My eyes grow big.

She scoffs. "Yeah. Because of you, I became a very promiscuous person. Then Ken came around, and he acted like he liked me. But that's over, and I'm sure you're thrilled about that."

I roll my eyes, and it's probably not the best thing to do, but it was a knee-jerk reaction. "Oh, come on. You know full well you didn't love him. Plus, he's married."

Robert cringes and tries to wave me off, but it's too late.

"I'm serious, Regina. You can't blame me when you wanted to marry someone you barely knew. You should actually thank me."

Robert bangs his head on the wall. "Not helping, dude."

"Shut up, Robert." She focuses her anger back on me. "As if marrying someone I've known my entire life was any better." With a slim finger, she points at me. "You don't get to lecture me, Mr. Screw-Every-Supermodel-on-the-East-Coast."

"Not true. Can we get back to—"

"I don't care. Go away. Sign whatever contract you want, especially if it takes you far, far away from here, and make sure you never come back this time."

Robert groans. "You don't mean that. You're not letting him finish."

"Oh, hush." Her laser gaze turns back to me. "I was right about you all along."

Regina starts to walk into the kitchen, but I stop her, forcing her to look at me.

"What's that supposed to mean?"

She takes a step closer to me, hands on her hips and fire in her eyes. "You're just like your mother. Go. Get out of here before I call the police."

My heart can't beat from the sucker punch she delivered. The silence is deafening, and I couldn't form words right now if my life depended on it. I glance toward Robert, and he leads me to the door.

"We'll talk later. Okay?"

I think I nod, but I'm not quite sure. I stumble to my G-Wagon, and right as I pull away, Regina's parents drive up. It's best I leave, but I feel so lost, I don't know what to do.

I meander down the street, past my apartment at In a Jam. Memories of our night together are too painful. I don't know if I can ever spend the night in that room again. Not knowing what else to do or where to go, I drive aimlessly down Highway 26 for God knows how long. In my mind, I replay her words. *You're just like your mother.* If there weren't a hint of truth to those words, I would be spitting mad, but she's right. My mother was a rolling stone, and I guess I inherited the rambling gene from her.

But I don't want to be that way, and Regina didn't give me a chance to explain—not that it matters anyway. Her accusations about me must be pent-up feelings that would have bubbled to the surface eventually.

My phone buzzes for the tenth time, but I ignore it again. The only person I want to talk to is the last person who would be calling me right now. I wipe my face and swing my G-Wagon back around down Belkover Road toward town and speed to Silas's home. Mitch's truck sits in the driveway. Before I reach Silas's door, Mitch opens it, and I fall into his arms.

"I've lost her for good this time." I crumble into a defeated heap on the front porch and cry more tears than I did the day my mother left without a backward glance.

CHAPTER FORTY-ONE

Regina

If I weren't as mad as a wet hen, I would be in a heap on the floor bawling my eyes out. Robert is smart enough not to get in my way as I pace back and forth in my living room. He stands in the corner, and if he knew what was best for him, he would run for the hills.

"I'm sorry you had to witness that, but actually, I'm glad. This time, people won't think I'm just a hysterical ex-wife causing small-town drama."

"Clint isn't the type of person to trick anyone."

I give him the death stare, and it's enough for him to sink into a nearby chair. "Now is not the time to be taking sides with the enemy."

He chuckles, but my sneer causes him to swallow the laughter. "He's not the enemy, and you know it."

"Sweetie," Mom says from the front door. I swing around and find her and Dad standing there, appearing as frazzled as I feel.

My shoulders sag. "Guys, please go home. I'm sorry if I embarrassed you. I should have known this was going to happen." I plop down on the couch, and Mom sits next to me.

"Honey, I have never been embarrassed by you."

"Neither have I," Dad says, sitting on the other side of me. "I'm worried about you."

I sink into the couch cushion, hoping it will swallow me whole. The anger starts to subside, but sadness takes its place, and the tears trickle down my cheeks.

Dad embraces me. "Oh, honey, everything is going to be all right."

"Daddy, Clint lied to me. He made me think we were still married."

Robert scrolls through something on his phone as he says, "Uh, sis. Something doesn't smell right. This doesn't seem like the Clint I remember."

Mom takes my hand. "Baby girl, I don't know the details, but why would he say you were still married if it wasn't true? What would he have to gain?"

"Everything. He's a free agent, and he needed to mend his hothead reputation. What better way than to show everyone he's married to his small-brained hometown girlfriend? He's a jerk."

"Stop!" Daddy yells.

The only time I've ever heard my father raise his voice is when he would get emotional during one of his sermons. He never raised his voice in anger, ever.

He closes his eyes for a second then says, "Don't ever call yourself that. I'm going to tell you something, and you're going to listen without interrupting. Clint came to me all those years ago and asked for my permission to marry you. Jerks don't do that. He loved you, and I may not have thought you two getting married at such a young age was the wisest decision, but I knew his feelings were true. I don't know what happened to make him want to bail on you, and I've always supported you, but he came back and did the right thing. Once he realized he messed up, he didn't want you to make a mistake by marrying someone you didn't love. Now, I don't know if he was telling the truth about you being married still or not, but I'm grateful that he stepped in and made you second-guess marrying that corporate suit you barely even knew." Dad finally stops and takes a deep breath.

Mom smiles at him. "Exactly. Do you remember when we met Ken, and your father asked him if he loved you? He hemmed and hawed around and couldn't answer the most basic question. When your father asked Clint that, he didn't miss a beat with his reply. He said, 'With my whole heart and for as long as I live.' Don't settle for someone who's just going to keep you from being lonely, because if you do, I won't dance at your wedding."

Robert chuckles. "That may not be a terrible threat."

I sniff away my tears. "Yeah. Mom, you're a terrible dancer."

She feigns shock. "Anyway. You know what I mean."

"I do. It's over. I don't think I will ever date again. I might as well adopt a bunch of cats and let the rumors begin. Regina the spinster cat lady of Smithville. I think it has a nice ring to it. I should call up the Jackson sisters to see if they have an opening on their blog."

Mom and Dad hug me, and even though I feel horrible and heartbroken, I do feel a tiny bit better about myself. None of this is my fault, and like the last time when Clint left me, I'm going to hold my head high and pretend I don't hear the gossip train whizzing by that will be all over town by tomorrow morning. I need to focus on my work, and I have five thousand dollars to add to my bank account. That's a nice cushion for emergencies. It's the only good thing that came out of this ordeal. I wish I had won the big money, but even more so, I wish I had won the guy.

CHAPTER FORTY-TWO

Clint

The twins curl up next to me on the couch. God love them. They're so adorable with their slobbery hands and infectious giggles. They take so much of the pain away. I stare at the cartoons on the television, not sure what show we're watching. Mitch, Silas, and Marlo sit at the kitchen table and converse in hushed tones. It doesn't matter what they're talking about. I ruined any chance of getting Regina back. I've lost everything that meant anything to me, and the worst part is, I deserve every bit of it. It's like my pea brain couldn't figure out how to have both a loving wife and a multimillion-dollar offer to play major-league baseball.

The front door opens, and Gunnar and Robert enter. I whimper. Now Gunnar is going to read me the riot act, and Robert is going to kick my butt. That's all I need. Maybe it's a good thing the twins are sitting next to me, because no one would dare lay a hand on me if they are close by.

Gunnar sits in the lounge chair, and Caleb abandons me to crawl into Gunnar's lap. *Traitor.*

"Hi, buddy. What are you watching?"

"*Scooby Doo.*"

Gunnar's eyes light up. "I love *Scooby Doo*. Do you like Scooby Snacks?"

Caleb giggles. "Yep."

"Why don't you and Carson go in search of some Scooby Snacks for your Uncle Clint?"

The twins run off, almost slamming into Mitch and Robert as they rush from the living room.

"Okay, let me have it. I know you want to."

Mitch plops onto the couch next to me and rests his feet on the coffee table. "Where's the fun in that if you give us permission?"

"So," Robert says as he picks at a fingernail, "are you married or not?"

"We're not married, but I thought we were, up until Wednesday. I promise."

Robert peers over at me. His sneer makes me think he's unconvinced. "What does that mean?"

"It means, I didn't file the divorce papers. I meant to, but life got busy, and I forgot."

Mitch sits up and glances over at me. "So who did file?"

"Apparently, my agent's assistant did. I swear, I thought we were still married, and when my agent called Wednesday to tell me he checked into it, he found out we were indeed legally divorced."

Gunnar clicks through the television channels until he gets to ESPN. "When were you going to tell the wife—or ex-wife?"

"I wanted to." I stare at Robert. I squeeze my eyes shut before I admit the rest. "I promise I still thought we were married when we had sex the first time."

Mitch shushes me. "Little ears, dude. You have to spell words around them, and that's not going to work for much longer. Caleb is a master of sounding out words."

"The first time?" Gunnar chuckles.

"TMI," Mitch says, and I punch his shoulder.

"I was ready to tell her this morning when she practically attacked me, and things got a little crazy. I admit, I missed a perfect opportunity, and I messed up."

Robert sits up straight. "Wait a second. Are you telling me you thought you were still married right up until Wednesday?"

I nod. "I promise. You've known me my entire life. You're like another brother to me. I wouldn't lie to you."

Robert mulls over my words. "We're only talking about a few days. I'll talk to her."

Mitch clears his throat then tugs on the baseball cap he stole from me earlier this week. "I have to take some blame for this. He told me Wednesday, and I talked him into waiting until after the festival."

Gunnar holds out his hands, palms up. "I tried to tell you."

Robert smacks the baseball cap off Mitch's head. "Bro, you are not qualified to give out romantic advice."

Mitch snatches the hat off the floor and places it back on his head. "You have a point."

"She hates me," I mutter.

Gunnar pats me on the back. "That's up for debate, but my question for you is, what do you want?"

I take a deep breath. "I'm a free agent, and I now have six offers on the table. It's a great and horrible situation to be in."

"You didn't answer my question."

Leave it to the policeman to catch my attempt to slide around the answer. "I want Regina." I take a few calming breaths and say what I've known to be true for some time. "And I don't want to play ball anymore."

Silas pipes in from the kitchen, "Are you crazy?"

Marlo huffs at her husband.

It's the first time I've wanted to smile all day. "It appears so."

Mitch slaps me on the back. "Okay, we know who you want, and what you don't want. Do you have an idea of what you're going to do now that you're a washed-up, has-been major-league player?"

My brother likes to call the ball like he sees it. I peer over at Robert. "I have an idea, but it may be the biggest strikeout in the history of baseball."

He holds his hands out. "Let's hear it."

I take in my friends and family. I'm crazy to have left them in the first place. I don't want to be like my mother. I want to fight for what's important and not run away after the first shiny thing that gets tossed my way. I want my family back. I want Smithville. Most importantly, I want my wife back.

"I have to leave for a meeting, and I'm sure I'll be flying coach back home after I refuse the offer and become an unemployed, washed-up, has-been baseball player."

They all get a chuckle out of it. It's nice to know they don't think I'm crazy for walking away from a potential million-dollar deal, except for Silas. But I know he's only kidding. I want what he has—a wife, kids, and the comforts only Smithville can provide. That's pure heaven, and it's priceless.

"When I get back, I'll have a better plan laid out. Just don't let Regina run away and get engaged again before I return."

Each one of them points to another person in the room. At the same time, they all say, "You're it."

Now, all I have to do is work up the courage to decline a great offer, fire my agent, then discuss my finances with my accountant. I've got a lot of work to do before I find the courage to face the love of my life again.

CHAPTER FORTY-THREE

Regina

Word on the street is that Clint hightailed it out of town Saturday night. It's just as well. I would rather lick my wounds without his peering eyes. After two days, a half gallon of mint chip ice cream, two romantic comedies, and a sleepover with Mel and Andie, I think I've cried my tears out enough to actually work today without sobbing while I start an IV.

I hover at the break room door while Mitch wolfs down his food.

With a full mouth, he asks, "Have you heard from Clint?"

I snort. "How can you ask me something like that? No, I haven't heard from him, and I won't anytime soon. We're over."

He shrugs. "Things aren't always what they seem."

Of course he's going to stand up for his little brother. I should know better. "He lied to me."

Mitch groans and puts down his fork. "For all that is good and decent in this world, he found out you two were divorced on Wednesday. That was *after* y'all did the nasty the first time. Yeah, he probably should have told you before you did the horizontal bop the second time. I'll give you that, but he didn't lie to you. In fact, I was the one who told him to wait until after the Pickle Festival to tell you. So if you want to be mad at anyone, throw your anger my way."

I can't form words. *Clint really thought we were still married?* He didn't lie to me. Sometimes, I could just kick myself. "Doesn't matter. He's probably already signed with that team in Seattle or Tampa or whoever was tempting him with the biggest offer."

He shoos me away. "Go. You're bugging me. I'm so glad I didn't have any sisters growing up. I would have wanted to pinch their little heads off."

"You love me, and you know it."

He growls, just as the radio at the nurses' station announces a call coming in from an ambulance. I scoot up to the nurses' station to hear, "Ambulance B3 calling Smithville Regional. We have a female in her early thirties, pregnant and in labor."

I hit the call button. "Roger that. I'll call maternity."

Mel rushes into the hospital, her hair in a messy clump on top of her head. "Where's Mitch?"

"He's back in the break room eating his dinner. Are you okay?"

She shakes her head frantically. "No. Silas called me. It's Marlo. She's in the ambulance, and the baby's early."

"Oh my God!" I yell. "Mitch! Get out here!"

A chair crashes to the floor, and Mitch stumbles out to the nurses' station. "What's going on?"

Mel takes his hands in hers. "It's Marlo."

All color leaves his face. "This can't be happening."

Mel glances my way. "Get a room ready, and prepare to transfer to L and D."

I prep the room as the driver enters with Marlo on the gurney.

Silas runs next to her. "Is she going to be okay?" He begs with his eyes.

Mel puts on her confident doctor face. "Marlo has been down this road before. She's a pro."

"But it's a bit early." His voice trembles. "I can't lose..."

I squeeze his hand. "Shh. Think positive thoughts."

The phone rings, and Mel answers it. She talks in her doctor voice then hangs up. "They're ready for her in room 315. Go."

The EMT scoots past us right into the elevator. Mel and Mitch stare as the elevator doors close.

I say to them, "You guys, go. Dr. Crandfell and I can handle the ER. Go be with her."

"I'll keep you posted," Mel says as she wraps an arm around Mitch's shoulders and leads him to the elevator.

The next hour is the most excruciating for me. I don't hear any updates about Marlo, and we don't have any urgent patients to keep my brain occupied. With limited personnel, I can't even take a break to visit Marlo. I'm pacing back and forth at the station, wringing my hands, when the ER door swings open, and Clint jogs in. He's the last person I expect to come barreling through the doors.

We stare at each other for the longest time. A tentative grin slides across his face. "Hi."

I gulp. I never thought I would see him again, and after what Mitch just told me, this is a miracle. "Hello."

"Marlo?"

Pointing down the hallway in the direction of the elevator, I say, "Third floor, room 315."

He cheeses as he runs for the elevator. "Thanks." He skids to a halt, pivots on a dime, and runs back to me. "I forgot one thing." He swoops me up into his arms and kisses the life out of me.

I wrap my arms around him and kiss him back before my brain can tell me to punch him.

"I love you. Please forgive me for the misunderstanding, and I'll be right back."

All I can do is nod. He kisses me one more time and runs to the elevator before the doors close again.

When my shift is over and I'm relieved by another nurse, I slip up to Marlo's room, praying the entire way that everything is fine. No one has called to give me any updates, and it would have been unprofessional to pull up her electronic medical record. I walk down the hallway to the labor and delivery ward and hear all sorts of chatter coming out of room 315. It all sounds upbeat.

I peek in and see everyone surrounding Marlo, who sits up in her bed, hair plastered to her face, holding the sweetest, most precious little baby girl ever born.

When Marlo sees me, she waves me over. "Come meet Chloe Sorrow."

Mel's eyes bug out. "I tried calling you a dozen times. What happened?"

I check my phone and notice my battery had died. "Sorry."

"Want to hold her?" Marlo asks.

"Absolutely. There is nothing better than holding a new baby."

She places Chloe in my arms, and I'm in love at first sight. The baby smells so fresh. I pepper her little cheeks with kisses. "Hello, Chloe. Welcome to this world. You have two big brothers, but if you ever want to go shop the pink aisle, I'm your girl."

Silas chuckles as he wipes a tear away. He's the proud papa times three.

Behind me, a deep voice says, "She's beautiful, isn't she?"

I peer over my shoulder to see Clint standing behind me, tears in his eyes. "She's perfect in every way."

I hand him the little bundle, and he doesn't even hesitate to take her from me. I figured he would be squeamish about holding such a tiny human, but he knows exactly what to do. At the sight of him holding a baby, oh my stars, my ovaries pound in my gut.

"You're a natural."

He plants a soft kiss on Chloe's forehead, and she lets out the most adorable yawn. "I hope so. She needs a bunch of cousins."

Mitch pales. "Don't look at me."

Mel pokes him in the ribs.

We need to clear the air, and there's no time like the present. "Can we talk?"

Clint blows out a sigh of relief, and we walk toward the door leading to the hall. As soon as he crosses the threshold, an alarm blares through the hallway. "What did I do?"

Silas says, "You can't take the baby out of the room."

Clint gives the baby back to her daddy. "What, do they have LoJack on the infants?"

"Something like that."

We walk down the hallway in silence.

I'm not sure what to say to him. I don't even know where to begin. "How did your meeting go?"

He grins. "Real good. I had them clamoring all over me. My agent was as giddy as a kid on Christmas morning."

My heart sinks. No matter the fact that he just told me he loved me, he loves baseball more. It shouldn't surprise me, but it's still painful to hear. "That's good, I guess. You have options."

When I start to walk away, he says, "I turned them all down."

Freezing in my tracks, I glance over my shoulder. "Come again?"

He takes me by the shoulders and rotates me to face him. "I declined the offers. I don't want it anymore. I know you mentioned you would move for me, but we'd both be miserable."

"You can't give up your dream. You're so good."

His grin is contagious. "I'm nothing without you."

I shake my head as I backpedal. "You can't do that. I won't let you. You would hate me later."

Throwing his shoulders back, he says, "I'm the new baseball coach at Smithville High School."

My mouth drops. "Why are you doing this?"

"Because I want to renew my contract with you with no expiration date—if you'll have me. I'm nothing but a washed-up former-pro-baseball-player-turned-high-school-coach in double knit shorts and knee socks. It's not very sexy."

I cover my mouth to keep from laughing. Clint can make even the tackiest uniforms seductive. Tears form in my eyes as I process the news. "Are you sure?"

He nods as he closes the space between us. "I want babies. I want this town, and I want you. Forever. What do you say? Marry me again?"

I nod and jump into his arms. Life is full of ups and downs, and I don't know what the future holds for us, but I know at every step of the way, I want Clint. I'll even conduct another aerobics class, collect more ketchup packets, or buy another thirty cents' worth of gas if it means I'll have Clint by my side. There's no pickle we can't get out of together.

Acknowledgments

Erica Lucke Dean – the best mentor and writing buddy I could ever ask for.

Maddie and Mark – You mean everything to me.

Mary Dunbar, Kelly Hopkins, and Jymie Smith – you are awesome critique partners.

Jessica Anderegg and Amanda Kruse for your patience during edits.

Also by Cindy Dorminy

Left Hanging
In a Jam
Right for Me
In a Pickle

Watch for more at www.cindydwrites.com.

About the Author

After several decades of writing medical research documents, Cindy Dorminy decided to switch gears and become an author. She wanted to write stories where the chances of happy endings are 100% and the side effects include satisfied sighs, permanent smiles, and a chuckle or two.

Cindy was born in Texas and raised in Georgia. She enjoys gardening, reading, and bodybuilding. She can often be overheard quoting lines from her favorite movies. But her favorite pastime is spending time with Mark, her bass-playing husband, and Maddie Rose, the coolest girl on the planet. She also loves her fur child, Daisy Mae. She currently resides in Nashville, TN, where live music can be heard everywhere, even at the grocery store.

Read more at www.cindydwrites.com.

About the Publisher

Dear Reader,

We hope you enjoyed this book. Please consider leaving a review on your favorite book site.

Visit https://RedAdeptPublishing.com to see our entire catalogue.

Don't forget to subscribe to our monthly newsletter to be notified of future releases and special sales.

Made in the USA
Coppell, TX
21 July 2020

31259479R00163